Feeding Time

Sartak knelt beside the homeless derelict and bit him in the neck. Zane thought he heard a tiny pop as the fangs broke through the skin. He wanted to look away, but couldn't.

After a while, Sartak lifted his head; his lips were dark with blood. "This is what I am and what I do," he said. "I am not a human being. I belong to the Kindred, the race your kind call vampires, and to me your breed is nothing more than food. Now, do you still want me for an ally?"

Zane remembered Rose alive, laughing, sketching him, kissing him. And he remembered her dead, skull broken, brain scooped out. He hesitated for only a moment before he answered:

"Yes."

Netherworld

Richard Lee Byers

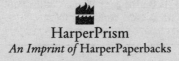

HarperPrism
An Imprint of HarperPaperbacks

This is a work of fiction. The characters, incidents, and dialogues are products of the author's imagination and are not to be construed as real. Any resemblance to actual events or persons, living or dead, is entirely coincidental.

HarperPaperbacks *A Division of* HarperCollins*Publishers*
10 East 53rd Street, New York, N.Y. 10022

Cover illustration by Larry MacDougall

First printing: June 1995

Printed in the United States of America

HarperPrism is an imprint of HarperPaperbacks.
HarperPaperbacks, HarperPrism, and colophon are trademarks of HarperCollins*Publishers.*

❖ 10 9 8 7 6 5 4 3 2 1

For Martin

1

Zane Tyler knew it was time to quit fighting. He was outnumbered three to one and his hands were cuffed behind him. Further resistance would only give the cops an excuse to finish beating the crap out of him.

But he was too angry to quit. He hadn't done anything wrong. He'd merely had the bad luck to wander into a bad part of town just as the police were sweeping the homeless and any other undesirable-looking characters off the streets. If there were any justice, the damn cops would be *helping* him. He thrashed, trying to shake their grips off his arms, and kicked backward.

His shoe glanced off a cop's shin. The man cursed. Then pain ripped through Zane's kidney. His knees turned to jelly, dumping him on the concrete floor.

He tried to curl into a ball, tried to protect his face and groin. Without the use of his hands, it wasn't easy. Nightsticks thudded on his arms and back, and steel-toed shoes slammed into his ribs. The world turned gray and distant, but the pain didn't fade. That didn't seem fair, either.

Finally the punishment stopped. One cop took the cuffs off, then opened the holding cell. The other two picked Zane up and shoved him forward. Too weak and sore to catch his balance, he sprawled back onto the floor. The door crashed shut behind him.

For a while, all he could do was lie and listen to the jail's unending din. Voices screaming, singing, and pleading. Steel doors clashing. The ancient elevators grinding up and down. A blend of stinks—BO, puke, cigarette smoke, industrial-strength cleansers—stung his nose. At last he managed to lift his head.

Obscene graffiti scarred the cell walls. Holes and a paler, slightly cleaner rectangle marked the spot where a pay phone had once hung. Looking as sullen and indifferent as abused animals, his fellow prisoners stared back at him.

Then a squat, bowlegged man stepped out of the crowd. He wore thongs, ragged jeans, and a high school kid's letter sweater with no shirt underneath. Grime and soot encrusted him from his callused feet to his jet black, matted hair. He'd been beaten too. His forehead was cut. He looked Asian, though the layers of filth and blood made it hard to be sure.

Zane wondered if the bum meant to help him up or rummage through his pockets. So far, the cops hadn't even bothered to ask his name, let alone confiscate any of his belongings, so he still had his wallet. Hoping that a show of strength would prevent any attempt at molestation, he tried to stand. His body throbbed, wringing a groan out of him.

To his surprise, the little man walked right past him to the bars. "Wait," he said.

The three cops had started back down the hall. The lanky black one glanced around. "You'll get your phone call when we're ready to give it to you," he said.

"I don't need one," said the Asian. "I just thought you might want to be here when I did this." He gripped a bar in either hand and pulled. The metal squealed and bent.

Zane gaped in astonishment. How could the small man be so strong? Maybe he was on drugs, but he seemed too calm, too rational.

In a moment, the space between the bars was large enough to squirm through. Which the Asian proceeded to do.

"Shit!" yelped the black cop. He ran forward, club raised. His partners turned, jerked in surprise, then followed.

The black cop's nightstick whizzed at the Asian's head. The prisoner brushed it aside to clang against the bars. His fist streaked up at the tall man's jaw. Bone cracked, and the cop fell.

The other two cops, a chunky woman with straw-colored hair and a bozo wearing mirror shades indoors, at night, plunged in, nightsticks flailing.

Dodging faster than Zane had ever seen anyone, even the sergeant who'd taught him unarmed combat, move, the Asian ducked or sidestepped every blow. In fact, the way he was smiling, Zane almost suspected him of playing with his attackers. Maybe he was reluctant to strike back because that could end the dance.

Finally, though, he grabbed the male cop and slammed him face first into the wall. The sunglasses shattered. The policeman slumped to the floor, leaving a sunburst of blood where he'd hit.

At the same time, blue eyes wide and face white as

paper, the blond cop backpedaled, dropped her club, and fumbled for her revolver.

Still smiling, the Asian stood and waited till the gun cleared the holster. Then he pounced, covering the three yards that separated him from the cop so quickly that Zane nearly missed it. He grabbed her shooting arm with one hand and her throat with the other. Lifting her off her feet, he strangled her till she stopped thrashing.

She was the one with the key ring. The Asian yanked it off her belt, dropped her, then turned toward his former cellmates. "As you've probably guessed," he said, "I'm leaving. Would anyone like to come along?"

Everyone just stared. Perhaps the others were too scared of the cops to try to escape. Or maybe, like Zane, they were afraid of the Asian. Suddenly his small stature, grubbiness, and clownish clothes didn't matter anymore. With his victims at his feet, he seemed uncanny, and as deadly as a tiger.

The little man smiled contemptuously. "Then I'll say good-night." He turned away.

And abruptly, to his own surprise, Zane said, "Wait! I'm coming." His bruises aching, he wormed through the gap in the bars.

The Asian waved at the unconscious cops. "Help yourself to a weapon if you like." He sauntered on down the corridor.

Zane hesitated. Mad as he was at the Tampa Police Department, he certainly didn't want to shoot anyone. But on the other hand, he had a nasty feeling he was going to have to fight. He snatched a club, then trotted to catch up with his companion.

"Where are we going?" Zane whispered. Even so, his voice seemed to echo down the cellblock.

"Back to the elevators," the Asian replied. Inside the cage to their right, an old man mumbled and rolled over in his bunk. The springs squeaked. "There must be stairs somewhere, but it might take time to find them. And if we don't have the right key, we could make a lot of noise breaking down the door that leads to them."

Zane frowned. "But the elevators are right beside that glassed-in guard shack."

"Yes, they are. Try to be inconspicuous."

The next bend in the corridor brought them in sight of their goal. To Zane's relief, neither of the guards in the station was paying attention to anything outside. One was on the phone, and the other was reading a stripped paperback. But unfortunately, no elevator was waiting on this floor.

Zane and the Asian strolled into the open. The short man pushed the call button and the elevator mechanism grumbled to life. Then he flipped through the keys on the ring, found a heavy brown iron one, and stuck it in the lock beside the door.

Zane's mouth was dry. His heart pounded. He tried to hide the nightstick behind his leg. At last a green bulb flickered, signaling that the car had arrived. The Asian twisted the key, and the outer doors slid apart. The inner grillwork ones opened vertically, like jaws.

The two prisoners stepped in, and the Asian inserted the key in the interior lock. He pressed the button for the ground floor. Zane slumped with relief.

Then a voice yelled, "Hey!" He spun around. The one guard jabbered into the phone, and the other scrambled from the office. The Asian gave him a mocking wave. The doors slammed and the elevator juddered downward.

The Asian said, "Get behind me. Crouch."

Zane said, "You want me to use you as a shield? Why? What good—"

"There's no time to explain. Just do it. Or don't. It's up to you."

Feeling a little cowardly, a little ashamed, Zane got behind him.

The car bumped to a stop. The doors began to slide apart, without the Asian turning the key. Someone was controlling them from the other side.

Zane peeked around the tramp. Four cops stood outside the door. Thank God, they had clubs in their fists, not guns. Evidently no one had found the three guards the Asian had taken out, so nobody realized how dangerous he was.

"Okay, boys," said the grinning cop in the middle. "Game's over. Turn around, spread 'em, and grab some wall." The sections of grille began to rattle apart.

The Asian turned, then spun back around and dived through the narrow gap. He hurtled into the leering cop and slammed him against the wall. Two of the other policemen stumbled around and started clubbing. The bum evaded all but one of the blows and rolled to his feet, punching and kicking.

The grille doors stood completely open now. Zane rushed the one cop who still had his eye on him.

The guard's nightstick flew at his head. He blocked with his own. The impact stung his fingers and jarred his arm. Then he rammed the end of his club into the cop's gut. The man fell down and retched.

Zane looked wildly about. The other cops were down, too. The bum grabbed his arm. "Come on! This way!"

They ran into a sort of bull pen, where operators in headsets monitored phones and radios. A camera, probably used for taking mug shots, stood on a tripod in the corner. Rows of battered desks lined the dingy linoleum floor.

A half dozen cops edged forward. Four had already drawn revolvers, and the others were reaching for theirs.

Zane started to raise his hands, fully expecting his partner in mayhem to do the same. Instead, the bum grabbed a desk, swung it over his head, and threw it. Before it could even crash down, he seized another. A blizzard of papers and file folders filled the air.

Guns banged. Clerks and dispatchers threw themselves flat and screamed. None of the bullets hit Zane, probably because all the cops were firing at the Asian. Once the bum staggered, but didn't fall, so evidently they hadn't hit him either. Maybe the flying furniture spoiled their aim.

The shooting faltered. Maybe everybody had run out of ammo. The Asian pivoted and rammed his shoulder against a door, tearing it off its hinges.

The fugitives dashed through it, across a waiting room, and out into the parking lot. The cool April air felt warm after the chill in the cellblock. A white Camaro pulled into a space and a willowy woman in a long skirt got out.

The Asian charged her. Her mouth fell open. She whirled, trying to scramble back into the car, but the bowlegged man caught her before she could.

"Keys," he said. Whimpering, she handed them over. He dug his fingers into the side of her neck, cutting off the flow of blood to her brain. When she passed out, he tossed her across the nose of a Honda.

He and Zane jumped in the car. The bum cranked the engine, then pulled out, tires screeching. In moments, the jail was far behind.

Zane listened for sirens. He didn't hear any. Evidently the Asian had wreaked enough havoc to prevent immediate pursuit.

Zane took deep breaths, trying to calm down. He felt the way he had after skirmishes with the bandits in Somalia. Half-exhilarated because he was alive and free. Half-scared because, after all, the bastards could have killed him.

Gradually those emotions gave way to the familiar hollow ache. That and worry. "You didn't kill that woman, did you?" he asked.

"The one in the parking lot?" replied the Asian. Inside the Camaro, his BO was almost unbearable. The pine-scented air freshener dangling from the rearview mirror was no match for it. "I was in too much of a hurry to be gentle, but I don't think so. I wasn't trying to."

"How about the cops?"

The Asian shrugged. "Again, I doubt it, but who

knows? You'd have to go back, pick up the desks, and see what is or isn't breathing underneath, and I'm nowhere near curious enough to do that. Feeling guilty?"

Zane thought about it. "I guess not. They had it coming. Besides—please, don't take this the wrong way—I know *I* didn't kill anybody."

The Asian snorted. "How comforting for you." He turned up a narrow alley and pulled into the cramped space behind a pair of Dumpsters. "Of course, you would be an accessory, but unless the police booked you in, I doubt they'll be able to find you. If they did, leave town at once. You can keep the car, but I don't advise it. When our benefactor wakes up, she'll report it stolen. Good-night." He opened his door and slipped out.

Banging his door against a Dumpster, Zane scrambled out, too. "Wait!"

The little man kept walking. Though he'd only taken a few strides, it was already hard to see him, almost as if the shadows were embracing him. Gravel littered the cracked and pitted asphalt, but none of it crunched beneath his feet. Farther down the alley, a cat yowled.

Zane ran after the Asian. The bum pivoted. "Perhaps you didn't understand," he said. "I'm parting company with you. Since I've done you nothing but good, it would be ungrateful for you to try to stop me. Ungrateful and unsafe."

"Please," said Zane. "I didn't have to break out of jail. I'm sure the cops were only going to charge me with vagrancy or something just as petty, and my brother is a lawyer. He would have gotten me out in the morning. I risked getting charged with real crimes, hell, getting shot, because I need *you*."

"That's absurd," said the Asian. The scabby gash above his eye now looked like a shiny ridge of scar tissue. Zane guessed it must be a trick of the dark. "You don't even know who I am."

"No," Zane admitted. "But—" He faltered, groping for words. It was difficult to explain his actions when they didn't even seem rational to him. "A few days ago, something terrible happened to me. Something nobody knows how to fix or even explain. At least, nobody has so far. But when I saw you bend the bars and take out those first three cops, I thought, that guy only looks like a bum. Really, he's . . . I don't know, *magic*! He can do things other people can't. And maybe he's the one man who can help me.

"I know it doesn't make sense. It shouldn't matter that you can do strong-man tricks and kung fu. As near as I can figure, what I need is Sherlock Holmes. But nothing in my *life* makes sense anymore. I'm taking this hunch seriously because hunches and instinct are all I've got." A tear slid down his cheek.

The Asian said, "But I don't care about you, and I don't want to get involved in your affairs. I hope that's blunt enough to be clear."

"I'll pay you."

"I don't need money." He turned.

Zane scrambled around him and blocked his path. "Then what do you want? Everybody wants something."

The bum stared him in the eye. Zane thought, *I pushed him too far. He's going to hit me.* But after a moment, the other man sighed. "Tell me something I haven't heard before."

Surprised, Zane blinked. "What?"

"Tell me your story. If it bores me, you'll stop bothering me, agreed? If your problem intrigues me, I'll consider helping you if I think I can. But don't get your hopes up. I haven't heard anything that's unusual to me in a long time."

Zane's smiled bitterly. "No?" he said. "Well, listen to this . . ."

3

Zane awoke to the scent of coconut tanning oil and the aftertaste of piña colada. The air was cooler, the beach quieter, no boom boxes blaring or kids yelling anywhere nearby. He guessed he'd been napping for a while. He opened his eyes and, sure enough, the sun was a red ball, drowning itself in the Gulf of Mexico.

Smiling, he rolled over. If Rose was asleep, he'd wake her with a kiss. If she was already awake, he'd kiss her anyway. But her side of the blanket was empty.

He wondered if she'd gone back to the open-air bar without him. It didn't seem likely. Probably she was just stretching her legs. But when he sat up, he saw the writing in the sand:

I'M SORRY I LOVE YOU GOOD-BYE. Beneath the words she'd sketched a rose, signing the message the way she did her drawings.

Zane had to look at it for several seconds before the meaning sank in. She was leaving him.

But that was impossible. They'd been too happy these past two months. Hell, the note *said* she loved him. It must be some kind of joke. He looked around, expecting to catch her watching and laughing at him.

Fifty feet away, a chubby, sunburnt tourist couple packed up their belongings. Beyond them, near the vacant lifeguard chair, two teenagers sailed a Frisbee back and forth. Overhead, gulls hovered and swooped.

No sign of a slim, auburn-haired girl in a daisy yellow one-piece bathing suit. And now a chill oozed up Zane's spine.

He unzipped his black leather fanny pack. His keys were still inside, so she hadn't taken the car. Unless she'd brought her own keys, hidden in her towel or somewhere like that.

Stupid thought. It was his car, and she wouldn't steal. Still, he jumped up and jogged to the parking lot. In the twilight, the rows of meters reared like cobras.

The red Mustang was still where he'd left it.

Maybe someone had picked Rose up, but who? All their friends were mainly *his* friends, people he'd introduced her to. It didn't make sense that one of them would help her sneak away from him.

And why would she slip away at the beach anyway? Why not leave from the apartment while he was at work, so she could take her stuff? For that matter, why sneak away at all? He'd never given her any reason to be afraid of him. If she'd told him she wanted to go, it would have killed him, but he wouldn't have hurt her or forced her to stay.

So what in God's name was going on? He ran back to the blanket, sand crunching and shifting under his feet. Maybe he'd find her waiting.

He didn't. But now he noticed the footprints. Mostly the tracks of the two of them walking together. But also the ones where she'd slunk away alone.

He followed the trail, hoping that was exactly what she'd wanted. Maybe this was all a joke after all. Maybe she and his buddies would pop up out of nowhere and yell, "Surprise!"

The dainty footprints led straight into the hissing surf. A wheeling gull laughed.

Rose had done just what she'd needed to do to make sure he *couldn't* follow. Or had she simply wanted to swim out so far that she couldn't swim back?

Zane shook his head. He had to get hold of himself. Stop thinking crazy. Once in a while, Rose got sad and moody, but she'd never even mentioned suicide. She was still alive, still on the beach, most likely. He just had to find her, and then they'd straighten out whatever was wrong.

So he strode up and down through the gathering gloom. Distant figures blurred into shadows. He squinted to make out their features. One by one, the stars came out, and a breeze began to blow. A black ship crept along the horizon.

Until finally it was night. And he admitted she was really gone.

Maybe he should find a phone and call home. She might be there. Call his brother and friends, in case she was with one of them. He didn't believe it for a second, but he didn't know what else to try.

Head bowed, he trudged away from the water. Then something caught his eye. The tracks of a pair of small, bare feet, closely spaced, as if they'd been running. They were almost invisible in the dark. If he'd walked by five minutes later, he probably wouldn't have seen them. His heart beat faster.

He told himself not to be an idiot. Plenty of people with little feet had come here today. Still, he'd learned some basic tracking in the army, and these prints looked *exactly* like Rose's, even when he knelt to examine them closely. And some irrational part of him was certain they were.

So why not follow them? What did he have to lose? He jumped up and paced along, eyes fixed on the trail, afraid that if he lost it, he might not be able to find it again.

Soon he realized it led under a fishing pier. The red tips of cigarettes glowed above the water. Occasionally a flashlight winked on or off.

Suddenly Zane froze. The hairs on the back of his neck stood on end.

Because he felt eyes watching him from the black cave under the pier. The unseen gaze was cold and cruel.

He told himself it was just his imagination. Goaded himself on. After a few more steps, the feeling faded.

But as he ducked under the edge of the splintery boardwalk, he caught the coppery scent of blood. And a second later, he saw what was left of Rose.

She lay in a pool of gore with her head in the water. The foaming waves whispered as they played with her hair. Everything was shredded, her bathing suit, her Salvador Dali Museum T-shirt, and the flesh beneath. Chunks of her were missing, bitten away, and a shiny loop of intestine bulged through one of the slashes in her stomach.

Zane screamed her name and scrambled to her. For a moment, he *knew* she was still alive. But when he reached her side, he saw the jagged hole in the top of her head and the emptiness inside.

He felt dazed, numb, as if this weren't real. But he also felt a pressure building. In a little while, it would crush his disbelief.

Eventually—everything, including his thoughts, seemed to be creeping along in slow motion—it occurred to him that somebody *had* been watching him. The killer. He looked around, but no one was there now.

Sometime after that he thought of the police. He should get them fast, before the murderer ran any farther away. He scuttled out from under the pier and sprinted back to the parking lot.

Fortunately, the Clearwater cops patrolled the area all the time, mostly to keep kids from drinking, fighting, vandalizing, or doing drugs. Though it felt like forever, it only took a minute to flag down one of their Jeeps.

A paunchy, middle-aged cop with a deep tan climbed out of it. His heavy jaw ground away at a blob of gum. "What's the trouble?" he asked.

"My girlfriend's been murdered," Zane said. The feeling of unreality had begun to crumble, but the words still sounded silly, like a line in a bad movie.

The cop cocked his head. "Here on the beach?"

"Yes." Zane pointed. "Under the pier."

The policeman reached into the Jeep and brought out a flashlight. "Okay, show me."

They walked past a rusty litter barrel and a decaying sand castle. The cop's stolid pace made Zane crazy. Why couldn't the son of a bitch hurry up?

When they finally reached the pier, Zane suddenly felt that he couldn't bear to look at Rose again. If he did, grief and rage would overwhelm him. "Go on," he said. "She's right at the edge of the water."

The cop disappeared around one of the concrete

support columns. The flashlight beam flicked back and forth. After a while, he said, "I need you in here."

Zane's fists clenched. He took a breath to steady himself. "Okay." Stooping, he edged under the platform. And then gasped.

"Where's the body?" said the beach cop. "Point it out."

Zane couldn't. Rose was gone. Her tattered swimsuit and shirt were still there, but they weren't blood-soaked anymore. In fact, there was no blood anywhere. The sand shone pale and stainless in the dark.

Everything in the interrogation room was gray. The metal folding chairs. The ashes in the ashtray. The long mirror, which Zane suspected was one-way glass. And Lieutenant Morris. His rumpled wash-and-wear suit, narrow eyes, crew cut, and five o'clock shadow. Even, under the harsh fluorescent light, his skin. He sipped coffee from his mug and said, "Let's go over it again."

"Come on," said Zane, shifting his weight. He'd been sitting so long that the hard seat was hurting his butt. "I've told you everything at least three times. Why don't you try to catch the killer and question *him*?"

"I'd like to," Morris said. "But first I have to know there's one to catch. Which means I need a victim."

Zane fought the urge to jump up, grab him by the lapels, and shake him. "The victim is Rose Cooper."

"Who you met in January, right? Where, exactly?"

Zane sighed. "On the Franklin Street Mall in downtown Tampa. She was drawing caricatures of people.

That's what she does for a living. I was on my lunch break. We started talking—"

"And you found out she didn't have a place to stay, so you told her she could spend the night at your place. I remember. Fast worker, aren't you? Don't you ever worry about getting ripped off, or catching a disease?"

"This was the only time I've ever done anything like that. And I didn't plan it, it just happened. Rose was special." He noticed he was talking about her in the past tense, and had to swallow before he could go on. "Sweet. Gentle. Full of life. I felt something for her right away, something I'd never felt for anyone else. And she felt it for me."

"Very touching. So she came to your apartment and just stayed on and on." The cop opened his jacket, exposing the gun clipped to his belt, and took a pack of Camels out of the inner pocket. "But for some reason, during the two months you were shacked up, she never told you anything about her past."

"I found out she didn't like to talk about it, so I stopped asking. But she told me a little. Her parents were divorced. She grew up with her mom in Tallahassee."

Morris pulled out a cigarette. "Excuse me. I should have said, she never told you anything *real*. I made what calls I could in the middle of the night. Tallahassee never heard of a Rose Lillian Cooper, not a twenty-odd-year-old redhead, anyway."

Zane said, "That has to be a mistake." Morris snorted. "Look, if there's really no record, then maybe Rose lied to me. And I have no idea why. But she was a real person! If you don't believe me, call my family and friends. Everybody met her."

The detective blew a streamer of smoke. Zane's

eyes stung. "Okay, say she was real. I still need proof that she got killed."

"You've got her clothes," Zane said. "She wouldn't tear them up and walk away naked."

"People do all kinds of crazy things. You'd be surprised. Let's look at the whole picture. You found the body, you went away, and you came back with Officer Buchart in about what? Five or ten minutes?"

"No more than that," Zane admitted.

"And during that window, the killer, or somebody, came by, picked up the corpse, and carried it off, apparently without attracting any attention. How likely does that sound to you?"

Zane felt as if he were being backed into a corner. "It was dark. Maybe he put her in a bag."

Morris said. "Far-fetched, but maybe he did. But how did he clean up the crime scene? How did he pick up every speck of flesh? Wash every drop of blood out of the clothes and the sand? We know the waves didn't do it. You said only her head was in the water."

"I don't know. But I do know what I saw."

"What *only* you saw," said Morris. "After you got drunk and passed out."

Zane glared. "Do you think I drank so much I was completely crazy? That I still am?"

The policeman grimaced. "Not really. The blood alcohol level we drew wasn't all that high, and the drug screen didn't pick up anything either. You don't *look* nuts, just upset. So I don't know what I think, and maybe that's just as well. If I was sure this was a prank, I'd have to arrest you."

Zane stood up. Morris flinched back a step. "I told you the truth. Rose is dead. You tell me what you're going to do about it."

"Make some more phone calls in the morning," said the detective. "Go back and look things over in the light. Maybe talk to some of the guys that hang around out there, see if anybody saw anything. But I have to be honest. Beyond that, if we don't turn up more than we have so far, I don't see that there's anything more we *can* do. I'll have somebody drive you back to your car."

5

The Asian said, "Amazing." Partway through the story, he'd jumped up to sit on the rim of one of the Dumpsters. His filthy feet dangled, and a crescent moon leered over his shoulder. "I *am* interested. I like a puzzle with a lot of pieces. Who was Rose? How did she know danger was on its way? And on a crowded beach, in broad daylight, what threat was so terrible that she ran off alone so her beloved wouldn't have to face it? And what did happen to the corpse and blood?" He cocked his head. "You never told me your name, did you?"

"Zane Tyler."

"Mine is Sartak. Before you ask, it's Mongol. What happened then?"

"I flipped out," Zane said ruefully. Somewhere in the night, the cat he'd heard before ran into a rival. The two animals spat and hissed. "Nuts as I probably seem now, I'm not as bad off as I was before. I guess getting arrested and roughed up shocked some sense back into me. Anyway, I blew off work. Didn't even call in, just didn't go. Prowled around the beach for a while, then started walking around Tampa. First the parts where Rose spent time, then others. The last couple days I didn't go home, didn't eat, wash, or sleep."

"Why?" Sartak asked. "What were you looking for?"

"Answers," Zane said. "Revenge. I guess I knew I wouldn't find them just wandering around, but I couldn't think of anything better to try." He hesitated. "There's more, but it sounds even crazier."

Sartak smiled. Zane noticed his teeth were white, a startling contrast to his general dirtiness. "Stop saying that. I have some experience with madness, and in my opinion you have a mild case at worst. Tell me."

"Okay. When I went back to the pier, there was no body. So what if, in a way, Lieutenant Morris was right? What if, somehow, Rose *isn't* dead?" A spasm of grief shot through him. It sounded so pathetic when he said it out loud.

"If what you found was a mannequin—"

Zane shook his head. "I touched her. She was still warm. I smelled her. And I saw fresh . . . freshly killed bodies in the service."

"Then most people would say your hope is impossible," the Mongol said. "I don't, but I will say this. If Rose could, in any sense, survive the wounds you described, you might be better off never finding what's she's become."

Bewildered, Zane stared at him. "What are you talking about?"

"Almost certainly nothing. With the brain gone, it probably *is* impossible. So let's accept that vengeance is the best result we can reasonably expect."

Zane's pulse quickened. "Are you saying you're going to help me?"

The little man shrugged. "You have a mystery, and

I have a need for entertainment. That's why I let them throw me in prison, for the sport of breaking out. If I believed in fate, I might think it had brought us together. Still, when you learn more about me, you may not want my help."

"No!" said Zane. "Whatever—"

"Don't say that," Sartak snapped. "Don't choose blindly. Don't you know any legends? Any folktales?" He sighed. "No, of course you don't." He slid off the Dumpster. "Come with me."

"Where?" asked Zane.

"I'm going to show you something, which means I have to create the opportunity. It will help if you keep quiet."

They walked down the alley. Sartak didn't appear to move with any particular care, but his tread was as silent as before. Periodically he sniffed, his nostrils flaring.

Before long, Zane's curiosity got the better of him. "What do you smell?" he asked.

"You," said Sartak. "Garbage. The piss of a sick, drunken man and a large dog." He smiled. "And, most pungently, myself. Nothing useful. We'll probably have better luck on the street."

They turned at the next corner. At first glance, the narrow street looked as deserted as the alley. Steel gates sealed the store entrances, and burglar bars sliced their windows into sections. The handwritten signs behind the glass were bilingual, in English and Spanish. Spray-painted gang names and a jumble of what looked like hieroglyphics covered walls, a mailbox, and two parked cars. Sartak paused to study them, sniffed, then ambled down the sidewalk.

Without warning he pivoted, reached into a recessed doorway, and yanked a skinny Hispanic guy out. A joint tumbled from the man's mouth and bounced down his shirtfront, showering sparks. He started to speak, but before he could get any words out, Sartak smashed his head against the wall.

Zane froze in horror and amazement. It was one thing to fight cops who'd beaten them and locked them up. It was something else to attack an inoffensive stranger. He had to stop this. He lunged forward.

A second man, dressed in a tank top, scrambled out of the doorway. A gold chain glittered on his neck. Strewing dark liquid, he swung a bottle in a brown paper bag. Sartak ducked and kicked him in the chin, snapping his head back. The bottle spun out of his hand and shattered.

Zane grabbed the Mongol's shoulder and tried to drag him back. "Stop it! Stop—" Sartak's elbow stabbed into his solar plexus. He reeled back and fell, landing half on the sidewalk and half in the litter-choked gutter. He tried to jump back up, but he couldn't. He couldn't gasp in enough air.

Sartak glanced at his victims, evidently making sure they were unconscious, then turned to Zane and opened his mouth. His canine teeth were now impossibly long, and looked as sharp as needles.

He knelt beside the thin man and bit him in the neck. Zane thought he heard a tiny pop as the fangs broke through the skin. Sartak's Adam's apple bobbed. Zane wanted to look away, but he couldn't.

After a while, the Mongol lifted his head. His canines had shortened again, but his lips were dark with blood. "This is what I am and what I do," he said. "I'm not a human being. I belong to the Kindred, the race you kine call vampires, and to me your breed is nothing more than food. Now, do you still want me for an ally?"

Zane felt dizzy, as if he were standing on the edge of a long drop. He remembered Rose alive, laughing, frowning intently as she sketched, kissing him. And Rose dead, flesh torn, skull broken, brain scooped out. He finally managed to suck in a deep breath, drawing in red wine and marijuana fumes along with it, and said, "Yes."

Sartak smiled. "Good. Then here's to our partnership, and here's to the Masquerade." He bent to drink again.

Zane paced restlessly around the apartment. Past the water skis, scuba gear, and spear gun that, to Rose's annoyance, he'd left sitting in the corner of the living room. And the stereo, TV, and VCR. All the toys he'd cared so much about that didn't mean a damn anymore.

Beyond the sliding glass door and the wrought-iron balcony railing, the sky was black. Where was Sartak? Maybe he'd decided not to come. A part of Zane almost hoped that that was true.

Or maybe the vampire wasn't even real. How could he be? Maybe all the events of the last few days were just a dream.

For a moment, Zane almost believed it. Then his gaze fell on a framed photo of him and Rose at Busch Gardens. She'd been real, her absence was real, so everything else, all the pain and craziness, was, too. Something twisted in his chest.

The doorbell rang. Zane jumped.

He found it took an act of will to cross the room and answer it. That was dumb, since even if there was a homicidal monster waiting outside, he had nothing to fear. The worst disaster in the world had already happened to him.

Sartak looked—and smelled—like he had last night, except that the mark on his forehead had disappeared completely. "Hello," he said.

"Come in," Zane said. "That's right, I *have* to invite you in, don't I?"

Sartak snorted. "Don't believe everything you read or see in the movies. The Kindred have gone to a lot of trouble to make sure the stories about us are laced with misinformation. Did you buy me new clothes?" Last night he'd said it would be easier to search for Rose's killer if he upgraded his image.

"Yeah."

Sartak started unbuttoning the letter sweater. "Then you might want to get rid of these quickly. I'm reasonably sure they have insects or insect eggs in them somewhere."

Zane got a trash bag from the kitchen. The vampire stood in the middle of the living-room carpet and stripped, stuffing his rags into the plastic sack. The skin underneath was just as grimy. When he was naked, he went into the bathroom. The shower hissed.

It took him a long time to wash. But when he finally emerged, toweling his hair, the mask of dirt was completely gone, and Zane saw him clearly for the first time.

The vampire's face was broad and flat, the dark eyes lustrous and hard, like shiny stones. His skin was a dusky yellow, but with a grayness underneath. He was lean, almost gaunt, but muscular, and scars striped and spotted his torso and arms.

"Don't just gawk at me," he said.

Zane quickly lowered his eyes. "Sorry."

"I'm not complaining about your manners," Sartak said, "abysmal though they are. But you were staring as if I was some sort of fabulous, murderous beast. I am, of course, but that's not the point. If we're going to hunt together, bring down your enemy together, you have to get at least a little comfortable with me. So try to relax. I'm not your friend, but I don't mean to hurt you, either. And if you wonder about something, ask. I don't promise to answer, but I won't take offense."

"All right. If the cut on your forehead healed completely in less than a day, why do you have all those other scars?"

"Because I got them when I was still breathing." He pivoted and tossed the towel through the bathroom door. "Chingis and Subedei often put my *tumen*—division—in the *mangudai*. The suicide corps. It was our job to engage the foe, pretend to break, and lead him into a trap. And it was dangerous."

"Chingis? You mean Chingis Khan?"

"Yes." He smiled. "And now your mouth is hanging open again. Theoretically, the Kindred can live forever. That part of the legends is true. My clothing?"

"In the bedroom." Sartak turned and went to get it.

Zane followed. "If you're eight hundred years old, why were you living in the street? Why aren't you rich?"

The vampire tore open the pack of Jockey shorts. The plastic rustled. "You mean, through the miracle of compound interest? Actually, I understand the concept, and I have funds salted away here and there in case I ever need them. But I got tired of wealth. In time, you get tired of anything. I thought it would be interesting to be a hobo, always on the move, with no possessions but the clothes on my back, scrabbling every morning to find shelter from the sun. And for a while, it was."

Zane tried to imagine himself voluntarily going homeless, just for a change of pace. He couldn't.

Sartak zipped his slacks, then shrugged into his sport coat. "Good," he said. "Everything fits."

"Is it okay?" asked Zane. "I didn't know what you'd like."

"I notice you chose black," said the vampire drily. "I suppose I'm lucky it's not a cape and tuxedo." He smiled. "This is fine. As my last outfit probably demonstrated, I don't much care about fashions anymore. I've worn too many, each more peculiar than the last." He picked up one of Rose's drawings, a picture of an owl, off the dresser. The silver frame gleamed. "She did have some talent."

A wave of anguish rolled over Zane. It had been like that all day. Sometimes the grief receded, but not even the distraction of a walking, talking dead man could hold it back for long. "Yeah. Yeah, she did. Do you really think you can help me find out what happened? I know you must have powers—"

"Over the years, I've gotten good at solving riddles. Better than most kine, simply because I've had longer to hone my wits. But I don't want to mislead you. Most of my specifically vampiric talents lie in the realm of the physical. They make me strong and fast. I might be able to unravel your mystery telepathically if I were highly psychic, but I'm not. I have just enough of that power to sharpen my eyes and ears. But that's good. If I could simply pluck the answer out of the ether, it wouldn't be any fun. Did Rose leave a wallet or a purse?"

Zane had begun to get used to the little man's sudden changes of subject. "A purse, but I've been through it. There's nothing there."

Sartak drifted back into the living room. Zane followed. "Did she ever get mail?"

"No. Except for my friends, nobody knew she was here."

"Did she keep a journal?"

"No," Zane said glumly. "She didn't leave anything we could use to trace her."

"Don't be so sure." Sartak pointed at the sketches, one a realistic picture of a horse and carriage, the other a cartoon of Zane in mask, snorkel, and fins, hanging behind the TV. "She left these, and in one of them she may have provided a clue to where she came from, or what she was afraid of. It's worth a look."

"My God," said Zane. "Why didn't I think of that?"

"Because you're distraught. Collect them, will you? Every scrawl and doodle you can find."

Zane strode to the bedroom closet and threw open the sliding door. It bumped against the frame. He grabbed a cardboard accordion folder and carried it back into the living room. "We should start with these."

"Fine," said Sartak. "Why?"

"When Rose got sad, she drew pictures that were different than her usual stuff. Morbid. Gruesome. If she'd been a Stephen King fan, or had just enjoyed doing them, I might not have thought anything of it. But I could tell she didn't. It was more like a compulsion. Almost like she was in a trance. Once or twice I tried to get her to talk about it, but she never wanted to. And since she didn't get depressed very often, and it never lasted long, I let it go." His jaw tightened. "God, what a jerk I am. I should have seen she was in trouble. Would have seen, if I'd only opened my eyes."

Sartak shrugged. "Everyone keeps secrets, and most people prize them more than love. If you'd pried, you might only have driven her away. In any case, it's too late to worry about it now." He held out his hand. "Give me a stack."

When Zane opened the folder, he was surprised at how full it was. Rose must have gotten depressed more often than he'd realized, sat sketching scenes of death and suffering for hours while he was at work. Another pang of grief and guilt lanced through him.

As he flopped down on the couch, his bruises twinged, despite the double dose of Tylenol he'd taken. He started examining pictures, laying each on the oval glass-topped coffee table when he finished. Beside him, Sartak did the same.

Most of the sketches were charcoal, a few pastel. All were just as creepy as Zane remembered. In each, it was night, and the architecture was as somber and ornate as that of a haunted mansion. Gargoyles leered from rooftops, and black figures scuttled down colonnades. Narrow staircases twisted into darkness. Rooms were either immense vaults or cramped as closets, with pockets of inky shadow in every corner.

In one picture, a happy little girl in a ruffled dress scampered into a dark parlor. For some reason, Zane got the impression that she was hiding in a game of hide-and-seek. A horde of tiny creatures lay in wait for her, crouched under chairs, on top of the door-frame, and on the mantel, behind the clock, a vase of wilted roses, and framed miniatures. Zane couldn't tell exactly what the vague forms were. Only the glittering fangs and eyes stood out clearly.

Another drawing showed a man asleep in bed. Leering maniacally, his reflection oozed from a full-length mirror.

In a third, a naked man with eyes all over his body blew a whistle, and a woman shattered like a piece of glass.

And so on, each scene more disturbing than the last. A teacher dismembering a bound, screaming child and serving the pieces to a line of her eager classmates. An old woman clipping off her own fingers with a pair of scissors. A doorway, which, when examined closely, was really a gaping set of jaws. A groom carried his bride across the threshold.

"A lot of the female characters, the victim characters, look like Rose," said Sartak.

"I know." Zane cringed at the thought of her torturing herself again and again on paper. Had she hated herself this much?

"Do you recognize anyone else?"

"No."

"How about the settings?"

Zane shook his head. "I guess Tampa's like any other big city. It has its share of old, fancy, kind of spooky-looking buildings. Some of the churches and hotels downtown are covered with gargoyles. So are a few of the houses in Hyde Park. But I can't match what's here to any specific place. Maybe there is nothing here, nothing we can use. She didn't draw anything *real*."

"I'm not certain of that," Sartak said. "But I admit, you're probably right. They're *sur*real. But that just means they're speaking to us in symbols. Let's look for recurring images. My drawings have a lot of storms."

Zane flipped through his pile. Any time they showed the night sky, through a barred casement or above a field of twisted, leafless trees, it was full of mountainous clouds. Often jagged forks of lightning split the page. "Mine too."

"Was she afraid of thunder, or electricity?"

Zane shrugged. "Storms made her a little edgy. If lightning struck close by, she jumped. But she didn't have a phobia about it. She could use electrical appliances with no problem."

"I also notice a lot of fangs, and people being eaten."

"Yeah," said Zane. "Even when the evil characters are human, they have big toothy grins. I—God!" He scrambled off the couch.

Sartak sprang to his feet. Looked around. "What?"

Zane dived for the corner. The spear gun wasn't loaded, so he snatched the lance and spun around. "You," he said, edging forward. "Teeth. It's you, isn't it? You killed her, and now you're playing some kind of sick game with me."

Sartak didn't back up. Didn't look worried, either. "Not a completely stupid theory. It must seem like a huge coincidence that you met someone like me just days after she died."

Zane lunged. Supposedly vampires died if you speared them through the heart.

Sartak grabbed the dart and jerked it out of his hands. The move slung Zane staggering sideways. He bumped into the coffee table and almost fell across it.

Certain Sartak would counterattack, he flailed his arms to recover his balance. But the vampire just kept talking.

"But coincidences do happen. And the theory doesn't explain how I arranged for the two of us to wind up in the same jail cell. Or how I knew you'd escape with me, then try to persuade me to play detective for you. Or why I played hard to get when you did."

Zane's anger dissolved, leaving shame and fear behind. "You're right. It doesn't. I'm sorry."

"Don't worry about it," said Sartak. "I *am* the enemy, in the sense that every cat is the enemy of every mouse, and you feel it in your bones. I expect you to suspect the worst about me from time to time.

That's one of the reasons I haven't asked to sleep here." He sat back down and laid the spear across the drawings on the table. "So. Storms; gloomy, ponderous architecture; and teeth. Adding up to what?"

"I don't know." Zane sat back down, a little warily. It was hard to grasp that he'd just attempted to *kill* the vampire and apparently it hadn't even annoyed him.

"Neither do I. Let's look at some more."

Zane flipped to the next drawing in his stack. A moment later, he leaned forward.

Sartak turned. "What have you found?"

Zane passed him the charcoal sketch. It showed two pit bulls with gashed bodies and foaming jaws, tearing at each other in the center of a ring. A crowd of spectators yelled and waved fists full of money. Each looked as savage as the animals. Behind them, lightning snaked across the sky.

"It's just as ugly as the other pictures," said Zane. "But it's not . . . weird."

"No," said Sartak. "It's a fairly realistic picture of a dogfight. Do they have them around here?"

Zane frowned, thinking. "I guess. They aren't legal, but every year or so, you hear about one getting raided. But Rose would never have gone to anything like that. She loved animals, and she hated to see anything get hurt."

"Maybe at one point she had to spend time around the sport whether she liked it or not. And perhaps, if we seek out people who are still involved, we'll find one who can tell us about her past. If you could spend tomorrow talking to some dog breeders . . ."

"All right."

"Until tomorrow night then." Sartak rose and headed for the door.

7

The narrow dirt lane wound a long way back through the oaks, pine, and scrub. The bumps bounced the Mustang up and down. Finally, just as Zane was beginning to think the kennel owner had given him bad directions, a final turn revealed a number of parked cars. Quite a few were mud-spattered pickup trucks, some with cages in the back.

He pulled off the road at the end of the line. Tall grass scraped and rattled under the car.

He and Sartak climbed out. This far out of town, the sky was blacker, the stars more numerous. Mosquitoes surrounded him at once, whining past his ears. One landed on his arm. When he swatted it, it burst, leaving a splash of somebody else's blood behind.

Sartak pointed at a path that snaked away through the palmettos. A torch on a pole stood at its mouth. "That way, I imagine."

Once they passed the burning marker, the way was dark. Zane realized he didn't like it that Sartak was

behind him. He tried not to picture the vampire suddenly pouncing on him, tearing his throat, dragging
him down.

Ahead, sound murmured. Grew louder. Yellow firelight wavered.

The trail opened into a freshly mown clearing
ringed by a circle of torches. In the center stood a
wooden pavilion with low bleachers inside. People
jammed the seats, or clung to the columns like mon-
keys, with kerosene lanterns hanging beside their
heads. Others were on the grass, tending their pit
bulls or just loitering. And at the far end of the open
space leaned a shack on the verge of collapse. Amber
light shone through the broken window.

"Let's get to it," said Zane, slipping a snapshot of
Rose out of his pocket. Sartak nodded and sauntered
away. The crowd in the pavilion fell silent for a few
seconds, then gradually started to babble and shout.

At first Zane was leery of approaching anyone with
a pit bull. But though some of the stocky-legged terriers growled at him, their owners quieted them easily
enough. And many wagged their stubby tails. Maybe
they were saving their aggression for the ring.

Not that it would have mattered if they had kept
him away. Nobody admitted to knowing Rose.

Zane looked around for somebody else on his side
of the clearing—Sartak was presumably working the
other—someone he had yet to question. Finally he
noticed two hunched shadows, sitting or kneeling on
the ground.

He started toward them, and heard sobbing.
Moving closer still, he saw that the smaller was a
towheaded little boy crying over a dead dog. His
father mumbled to him and patted him awkwardly on
the shoulder.

The kid had loved the dog and his dad had let it be killed. Zane's fists clenched. He wanted to yank the man to his feet and beat him.

Wanted to, but wouldn't. But he didn't want to intrude on the boy's sorrow, either, couldn't have talked calmly to the father if he did. He turned away.

Palmetto leaves rattled. Two people and a pair of dogs emerged from the end of the trail. Zane hurried forward to buttonhole them before they could enter the arena.

Torchlight glinted on auburn hair. An upturned nose and high cheekbones. He yelled and started running.

The black-and-white pit bulls lunged and snarled. Rose leaned back, pulling on their leashes. "No!" she said. "Easy! God, are you crazy? You don't just run up on dogs like these. They'll tear you apart."

Zane stumbled to a halt. "Rose! It's me!"

"And isn't that a thrill," said the slender redhead, "Now get out of the way, okay?"

Zane stared at her. Every time he thought the nightmare might be about to end, it just changed. Found a new way to baffle and hurt him. "You're acting like you don't know me. It's *Zane*. Are you mad at me? My God, what for?" Despite himself, he stepped forward. The pit bulls surged to meet him.

"No, Gyp!" said the woman. "Rebel, stay!" The terriers stopped pulling. "I *don't* know you, asshole. And here's another news flash. I don't want to."

"You do know me," Zane insisted. Was her memory really gone? Well, they'd torn her brain out—no, that was ridiculous. He was thinking crazy again.

"I believe this is a case of mistaken identity," said the woman's companion in a husky cracker drawl. It startled Zane. He'd forgotten all about the guy, a stooped, bald old man with blotched, leathery skin. He smelled like liniment. "She may look like she's your Rose, but she ain't. Her name is Meg Irons and she works for me, taking care of the dogs and the rest of the animals. And now, if you don't mind, we want to go win us some money. Gyp has one of the *special* matches tonight."

Zane shook his head. She *was* Rose. Except, now that he saw her up close, he wasn't sure. Rose's skin had been fair and Meg's was deeply tanned. Old scars pocked her right hand, as if a dog had once bitten her badly. And there was nothing of Rose in the twist of her lip and her wide, mannish stance.

But on the other hand, the resemblance had to mean *something*. "Please," he said. "I don't mean to bother you. But if you aren't Rose, you must know her. You're related to her, a sister or cousin or something. Her full name is Rose Cooper."

"Never heard of her," said Meg. "I don't have any relatives. Now move it, or as far as I'm concerned, the dogs can have a piece of you." Zane reluctantly stepped aside.

"Good evening to you," said the old man. "Whatever the trouble is, I hope things work out."

Zane looked around for Sartak. He was supposed to be the master puzzle solver. Maybe he'd know what to make of this. But the vampire was nowhere in sight.

So Zane followed Meg. It hurt to look at her, yet he couldn't bear to let her out of his sight.

She and the old man waited outside the arena for two more fights. Then he led in one dog while she held the other.

He took the pit bull to the center of the ring, then clasped him between his legs. Another man and dog came through the opening in the opposite wall to face them. The referee raised his arm, then dropped it. The men released the dogs and they hurtled together.

The terrier that Meg had kept spun around and snarled. Zane realized he'd drifted closer to her without realizing it. She turned and scowled.

"I'm sorry," said Zane. "But you really are just like her. Are you sure—"

"Yes," said Meg. He got the feeling that she was trying to avoid feeling sorry for him, but not quite succeeding. "Man, you've got it bad, don't you? Does this have something to do with how you got those bruises?"

"More or less."

She snorted. "Just goes to show, people are better off if they don't give a shit about anybody else."

"Last week, I wouldn't have agreed with you. Tonight I have to say, maybe so." He moved closer. The pit bull bared yellow fangs.

"No, Gyp," said Meg. The dog growled. "No, I said! Sit!" The animal slowly obeyed. "What's your problem tonight?"

"Maybe being this close to the fight is making him nervous."

"No, he's used to that. I guess he just doesn't like you." She smiled crookedly. "I always said he was a good judge of character." She turned to watch the action in the ring. "Get him, Rebel! Get him! Get him!"

Zane felt a need to keep her talking. She might say something that would throw some light on what was happening. But more than that, it was an excruciating joy to hear her. Her voice wasn't *quite* Rose's—it had a faint country twang—but it was as close a match as her looks. "Have you been doing this long?" he asked.

"Yeah. I mean, I've only been working for old man Partridge a couple months, but I've been taking care of animals all my life. It's what I'm good at." She scratched Gyp behind the ear. Perhaps the dog hadn't forgiven her for reining him in, because he didn't wag his tail, or show any other sign of pleasure.

In the ring, the pit bulls had locked together. Evidently that signaled the end of a round, because the referee and another man beat them with clubs till they broke apart. The owners grabbed them, hauled them to opposite sides of the ring, and faced them away from each other.

Somewhere in the night, somebody else's dog growled. Gyp quivered.

"If you love them," said Zane, "doesn't it bother you to see them hurt?"

Meg grimaced. "I didn't say I loved them. I said I was good with them. Look, they're bred for this. If we didn't have the sport, they wouldn't even be alive."

The owners brought the pit bulls forward. "Who do you think is going to win?" asked Zane.

"My money's on Rebel," said Meg. She swiped stray strands of hair out of her eyes. "He's cut pretty good on the shoulder and under the eye. But he's bigger, and look how the other dog is limping." The men let the terriers go. "Get him, boy! Kill him!"

The pit bulls plunged together. But after a few moments, they broke apart. Heads low, blood dripping from their wounds and drool from their muzzles, they circled the ring.

"What the hell is this?" said Meg.

In the clearing, a dog snarled. Someone said, "No!" A hand or a stick smacked flesh. More animals growled. Zane felt something building in the air, as if lightning was about to strike.

Partridge stepped in front of Rebel and stooped, stiffly, hands extended. Evidently he meant to grab the pit bull and haul it back to its starting position. Rebel shied, then sprang. Caught the old man by the throat and wrenched him to the floor. Blood sprayed.

"God!" cried Meg, striding forward. Gyp bit her leg and yanked it out from under her.

Sartak moved through the clearing, asking questions. He wasn't surprised to find that nearly as many city people as—what was the current term?—rednecks had come to the games. In every age and place, people of every station relished blood sports.

His belly felt hollow, his throat, dry. It shouldn't be that way. Wouldn't be, if he were younger. He'd drunk deeply from the man in the doorway two nights ago, and from a woman he'd surprised at an ATM last night. In fact, he'd nearly lost control with the latter, almost guzzled till she died. Not that that would have bothered him, but on the other hand, there wouldn't have been any point. It wouldn't have cured what ailed him.

He knew what would, but the timing was bad, now that he'd promised to solve Zane's mystery.

So what, old man? he thought sardonically. *You're supposed to enjoy challenges and complications.*

Zane shouted.

Sartak whirled and sprinted toward the sound. When he spotted the mortal, the idiot was racing toward two hostile pit bulls, but he floundered to a stop just out of their reach.

Since the kine didn't need rescuing, Sartak sharpened his senses to see what had made him so reckless. An instant later, he grunted in surprise.

Was it Rose or not? The sun-damaged skin was different than the fair complexion in the photos, and her every move conveyed a pugnacity at odds with the gentle nature Zane had described. Still, if she'd died, become some form of Kindred, zombie, or something stranger, aspects of her form and demeanor could change.

He sifted the scents in the air—urine, excrement, blood, insect repellent—till he caught the aroma of her skin. Felt the warmth of her flesh and listened to the thump of her heart. As far as he could tell, she was an ordinary living human being.

One of Rose's relations, then. But why was she denying it? Perhaps he should join the conversation and question her himself. But he doubted that she'd be any more forthcoming with him. Probably he and Zane would have to follow her away from here, conceivably abduct, threaten, or torture her, to learn the truth.

In which case he might as well hang back and watch the confrontation from afar. Sometimes an observer noticed things a participant missed.

He could tell it was agony for Zane to find Rose, yet not find her at all. He wondered if he'd ever loved a woman that much. If so, he couldn't remember what it felt like. The reflection brought a twinge of melancholy.

Of course, such nostalgia was absurd. Like most of the elders he'd known, he'd learned the hard truth that your dear one always betrayed you in the end, if only by changing, becoming tedious, or dying. It was a blessing to lose the ability to love. The trick was finding something besides madness to fill the void it left behind.

Behind him, someone jabbered.

Sartak turned. Several yards away slouched a heavyset man in a black Jack Daniels T-shirt and a baseball cap. Pimples mottled his homely, beady-eyed face. He was talking into a cellular phone. "Yeah, I'm sure it's her! What? Why? Okay, sure, whatever you say." He hung up.

Sartak started toward him. This man was kine, too. His heart thudded and his guts gurgled. But the tang of his sweat differed subtly and enticingly from the norm.

Suddenly the man straightened up, squared his shoulders, blinked, and looked around. His head bobbed forward in Zane and Meg's direction, then jerked around toward Sartak. The Kindred was surprised. Though he couldn't become invisible like certain others of his kind, he was naturally, instinctively stealthy. People rarely sensed him approaching in the dark.

"Hello," he said.

"Good evening," said the big man. Despite his loutish appearance, he sounded better educated now than he had while babbling on the phone, and a cool intelligence informed his pimply features. "I don't know you, do I? My mistress is part owner of this enterprise. She'd want me to ask your name and clan, and what business brings you here."

Sartak was surprised again. The ghoul recognized him for what he was. Otherwise, he wouldn't have spoken so. Though the Kindred's Blood-Bound servants almost inevitably possessed at least a little special knowledge, this man must have a keen eye to discern his nature instantly, in the dark, when his coloring was less distinctive than the ivory pallor of Caucasian Cainites.

"My name is Sartak. I don't have a clan. To the best of my knowledge, my bloodline is extinct except for me. I'm here because I enjoy animal fights. I was told the public is welcome, even if the law isn't."

"That's true. But you've entered the Prince of Tampa Bay's territory. Have you called on him?"

Sartak cocked his head. "He claims his rule runs this far into the countryside? What do the Lupines have to say about it?"

The ghoul smiled. "The few that survive know better than to say anything."

"Really? My congratulations to everyone involved. As it happens, I'm heading back to Daytona right after the fights. But if I pass the way again, I'll certainly visit your Prince and pay my respects." Across the clearing, Meg, the old man, and their dogs walked on. The ghoul's head twisted, tracking their progress. "You seem interested—"

The big man's knees buckled, and his upper body flopped forward. Afraid he was about to fall, Sartak caught him by the arm. "Are you all right?" he asked.

The ghoul jerked upright and yanked his arm out of his grasp. "Let go of me!"

Sartak was annoyed, but he tried not to show it. "I was trying to help you," he said.

"Why?"

"Call it a courtesy to your mistress. Are you sick? Epileptic?"

"How do you—I mean, I don't *have* a mistress! You're crazy! Get away from me!" He whirled and shambled toward the shack.

Sartak watched him cross the sagging porch and force the warped door open. The bottom grated on the floor. The Cainite wondered what to do next, and smiled at his own uncertainty. It had been a long time since existence had been this interesting, at least at moments when he wasn't fighting for survival.

Since Meg was a key to the mystery, should he stand guard over her? Perhaps the person the ghoul had phoned was coming to hurt her.

But Zane would watch her. It looked as if the poor fool couldn't tear himself away. What's more, there were other people around, and surely it would take anyone a while to reach this isolated spot. She ought to be all right for the time being.

So why not pursue the ghoul? Since the subtle approach had failed, and he'd been kind enough to remove himself from public view, why not *wring* some answers out of him? Answers and something equally desirable. His belly aching, Sartak skulked forward.

He managed to slip across the porch without making any of the soft boards groan, but the squeal of the misshapen door gave him away. The ghoul's head snapped around.

The interior of the shack was as ruinous as the outside. Termite wings and piles of sawdust littered the floor. The big man stood at the far end of the front room, beside a heating stove with a broken pipe, his phone in one hand and a half-empty pint of bourbon in the other. The odor of the liquor mingled with the musky reek issuing from a pile of cloth-covered boxes. The latter smell differed from any Sartak had smelled before. All he was sure of was that the animals were sizable mammals, diseased, and, judging by their shallow breathing, asleep.

A kerosene lamp atop the stove provided the only

light. After the darkness outside, it was unpleasantly bright. He dimmed his vision.

The ghoul tried to set the bottle down, but fumbled and upset it. Amber brown liquid glugged out. He snatched up a pistol in its place. "You aren't supposed to be in here!" he said.

"But I am in here," said Sartak. "And we both know that if I decide to hurt you, the gun isn't likely to stop me."

"Oh, yeah?" said the ghoul, squinting.

He isn't sure what I am, thought Sartak, *even though he knew a minute ago. He's mad or drugged or something.* The Kindred lifted his upper lip and dropped his fangs. Then retracted them so he could speak. That was harder. They didn't want to slide back in their sockets. "Yes. See?"

The big man swallowed. "I see, but you don't scare me. I've got my own power."

Sartak said, "I'm here for information. No doubt you are strong, compared to kine. Perhaps you even know a trick or two. Still, deep down, you must realize you're no match for me. Does machismo or the strength of your Bond require that you defend your mistress's secrets anyway? If so, it's a pity. You will tell in the end, after a few minutes or hours of pain." He glided forward.

Expecting the ugly man to fire, he was poised to dodge. The ghoul startled him by whipping the tarp off the stack of cages instead.

The four ghastly creatures inside awoke at once. Perhaps the ghoul could goad them with his mind. Chittering, red eyes blazing, they threw themselves against the wire-mesh cage doors, which popped open instantly, then launched themselves at Sartak. In the gloom, it wasn't until the first one smashed into his chest and knocked him down that he made out what they were: malformed rats grown big as dogs. No doubt they fought in the special matches the old man had mentioned.

The instant Sartak hit the floor, the monsters were all over him, clinging, gouging with teeth like chisels, ripping with filthy claws. The ghoul circled the melee, shooting. The bullets cracked into the floor.

Sartak punched, kicked, guarded his eyes. He grabbed a handful of greasy, furless hide and threw a rat across the room. It banged against the wall, dropped to the floor, and scuttled back to the fight. He seized it again and tore it in half. Its viscera slid out of the pieces.

To dispose of that one, he'd neglected the other three. They'd gotten good holds and were *burrowing* into him, talons and muzzles sunk deep in his flesh. He pulled off another, hairless also, its hide a mass of bulging blue veins and oozing chancres, and snapped its body like a whip. Its spine shattered, and it convulsed.

With only two left, he managed to struggle to his knees. That should make it easier to do damage. He had more leverage.

Unfortunately, it also made it easier for the ghoul to shoot him. He didn't have to worry so much about hitting his hideous allies. A bullet stabbed into Sartak's side. He started to fall back onto the floor.

No! If he went down again, if he stopped fighting for an instant, the rats would shred him. Somehow he shook off the pain, wrenched off a third rat, this one a lopsided thing with both eyes on the left side of its skull, and twisted its head off. Outside the shack, people screamed.

The last rat had three tails, and a tiny second head sprouting from the base of its neck. He grabbed the creature, tore it off him, dug his fingers into its chest, and ripped it open from heart to crotch.

A bullet pierced the meaty part of his calf. Grateful it had missed the bone, his body ablaze with pain, he lurched to his feet. Blood streamed from his wounds and pattered on the floor. Wide-eyed, his mouth working soundlessly, the ghoul stumbled backward. Sartak grinned at his fear.

"How many shots do you have left?" the Kindred asked. "You'd better take them."

The ghoul fired. Sartak dodged. The big man tried again, but the pistol clicked.

Sartak sprang. The ghoul threw the gun at him, missing, then lunged to meet him.

They grappled. The ghoul tore at Sartak's wounds. Fresh pain slashed through them.

Sartak tried to hook the big man's leg with his own, dump him on the floor, but the other fighter evaded the maneuver. Somehow the ghoul tipped *him* off-balance and started slamming his head against the wall. Soot showered from the top piece of the broken stovepipe in time to the thuds. Black spots swam at the corner of Sartak's vision, and he realized he was on the verge of passing out.

He summoned the last of his inhuman strength. Lashed his arm in a circle, breaking the ghoul's hold, then struck him a backhand blow to the face. Bone cracked, and the big man reeled back. Sartak punched him in the forehead, caught him as he began to fall, and buried his fangs in his neck.

The Cainite thought, *I have to hold back. I want to question him. And he may be on drugs.* But he was in too much pain, too enraged, and too thirsty to restrain himself. The Beast and the Hunger were in control. He gulped the big man's vitæ till it stopped spurting.

And, despite a subtle nastiness, it was good. Better than last night's. But not, of course, good enough.

He dropped the corpse and collapsed on a moldy sofa. His body drew on the power he'd just imbibed. In a few seconds, his lightheadedness passed, and his wounds began to close. Sometime after that, he remembered the shrieking outside.

He listened. At this point, no one was screaming nearby, but a few cries still rang in the distance. He'd better find out what was going on. He staggered to the door and looked on carnage.

Meg screamed and thrashed. Zane lost a precious moment staring in horror, then started kicking Gyp. The pit bull kept right on biting her, until Zane had the nightmarish feeling that nothing he did could incapacitate or distract it.

Then, without warning, it let her go and lunged at him.

He scrambled aside, but stumbled on the uneven ground. He was still trying to regain his balance when the black-and-white terrier drove at him again. It clipped his leg, knocking him down, wheeled, and surged at his throat.

Reflexively Zane whipped his left arm across his body. The pit bull caught it in its foaming jaws. He jammed it in as far it would go, so the yellow fangs couldn't rip it so badly.

But it didn't help much. The back teeth still clamped down, tearing, crushing. Panic yammered through his mind.

But then something from boot camp came back to him. Sergeant Hillyard had been a martial arts nut. He hadn't been satisfied to teach the recruits their basic unarmed-combat maneuvers. He'd told them what to do in a bunch of special self-defense situations, including dog attack.

Zane reached around the crop-eared terrier and, pressing the bony edge of his forearm into the back of its neck, jerked its head backward and rolled. Gyp's spine snapped.

He yanked his arm out of the pit bull's mouth, losing more skin in the process, sprang to his feet, turned to run to Meg, and froze in dismay. The crowd from the bleachers was pouring out of the pavilion, blocking his path like a lurching, shoving, shrieking wall.

He tried to push through. A big man in a motorcycle jacket stiff-armed him and knocked him reeling back.

A short, fat guy fell. Feet trampled him. Zane grabbed the chubby man's flailing arm and dragged him out of the stampede. The action sent other people staggering, interrupting their rush forward and creating a gap.

Zane lunged into it. Bodies slammed into him. A leg shot into his path and tripped him. Somehow he stayed on his feet and blundered clear.

Meg was gone.

He pivoted, squinting against he darkness. "Meg!" he called.

No one answered. All around him, people screamed, and yelled each other's names. Two-legged shadows ran until four-legged ones shot out of the dark and pulled them down.

Zane yelled, "Sartak!" The vampire didn't answer, either.

Zane started for the cars. Surely Meg had fled in that direction, the same as everyone else. He had to keep making himself slow down. He desperately wanted to be out of the clearing himself. But a head-long dash seemed more likely to attract the pit bulls than a deliberate stride. And he needed to make sure that Meg wasn't one of the ravaged bodies strewn along the way. Some of these lay motionless, while others twitched and whimpered.

He tried his best to watch out for pit bulls. Nevertheless, in the dark, he almost walked right into one. During the first moments of the attack, the terriers must have taken down one human, then moved right on to another. Otherwise, there'd be fewer bodies. But now, with their masters routed, some had begun to feed. This one was worrying a squirming man with muddy boots and a ponytail.

Though Zane had already passed by a number of the wounded, he felt a compulsion to help this guy. He started forward, but, as he did, the dog's head jerked up from its prey's throat, tearing loose a strip of flesh. A geyser of blood shot into the air. The man bucked, then stopped moving. The stink of feces tinged the air.

Sickened, Zane swung around the dog, giving it a wide berth.

Behind him, something snarled.

His heart pounding, he looked around. Two pit bulls. Two *more*, stalking him *again*, when the people here must outnumber the dogs ten to one. For a moment, anger at the sheer unfairness of it almost blotted out his fear.

The trick he'd used to kill Gyp wouldn't save him from a pair of animals. He ran. Heard the terriers charge. Draw nearer. Evidently even a short-legged dog was faster than a man.

He wondered if he should turn and face them. Maybe he could at least hurt one before the other nailed him. Then he noticed the torches on poles, still burning at the edge of the clearing.

Sore, gasping, somehow he managed another iota of speed. Zigzagged, hoping that would keep the pit bulls from biting him. Unseen teeth snagged the leg of his jeans. For an instant he was sure the race was over, but then the denim tore. He pounded on.

Nearing a torch, he didn't slow down, just stuck out his hand. The pole whacked his palm, then snapped off close to the ground. He wheeled and swept the burning end around inches above the grass, slashing a blue-and-gold arc on the night.

Get back! he thought. *You bastards are supposed to be afraid of fire.*

And for a moment, the dogs shied. Then they began to circle, each trying to take him from behind.

Zane locked his eyes on one pit bull, a fight-ring vet with scarred haunches and a missing ear, and edged toward it, jabbing with the torch. When he sensed its companion darting in, he whirled and thrust.

He was lucky. The blazing torch plunged straight into the dog's jaws. He lunged, driving it down its gullet. When the terrier fell, his weight pinned it to the ground, fire crackled around its head.

Fangs like a bear trap snapped shut on Zane's ankle. The one-eared dog wrenched him off his feet, gnawed and shook his leg.

The pain was excruciating. It felt as if the dog was tearing off his foot. He kicked, but couldn't shake the animal loose. Tried to bring his weapon to bear, but the sudden deadweight of the other dog immobilized it.

Zane heaved with all his might. The shaft broke again, leaving him with a double-pointed stick. Frantically he stabbed at his remaining attacker.

His thrusts scored the pit bull's face. Popped an eye. It still wouldn't let go. Screaming, he shifted his aim to the juncture of its neck and shoulder.

The makeshift spear stabbed deep. Grunting, he rammed it deeper still. The one-eared dog fell, and its grip slackened. Blood gushed out of its mouth to mix with his.

For a while, Zane could only slump on the grass, gasp, and shudder. Then he remembered Rose—Meg. He couldn't pass out, couldn't just lie here, not when she was in danger. Gritting his teeth at his aches and pains, he sat up to inspect his ankle.

It wasn't as bad he'd feared. As far as he could tell, no bones were broken, nor was blood pumping from a cut artery. Perhaps his pant leg, sock, and shoe had protected him. He tore a strip of cloth from his shirt, knotted it awkwardly around the bite, and cautiously stood up.

The world revolved, then stabilized. He tried to walk. His ankle throbbed, but it supported him. Leaning on what remained of the pole, he looked around.

Things had quieted down in the immediate vicinity. Nothing scurried or slunk across the grass. Bone crunched as pit bulls ate, and one or two of the fallen still wailed for help. The air smelled of charred meat and hair.

Farther away, in the direction of the cars, engines roared to life, people still screamed, and occasionally a gun banged. Evidently some of the terriers had pursued their victims down the trail. Zane limped after them.

"Rose! Meg!" he shouted. No one answered.

A few yards farther on, he spotted a break in the wall of foliage on his right. A trampled space, where someone had shoved through. Drops of blood clung to the stiff, blade-shaped palmetto leaves.

Zane swallowed. He almost wished he hadn't noticed. In the open, where he could see another pit bull coming, he might stand a chance against it. Floundering through the brush, he probably wouldn't. Hell, why would Meg have run into the woods anyway? Why wouldn't she press on to the cars?

He had no idea. But like himself, she'd been hurt, yet managed to move on. He doubted that many others had. If they hadn't avoided attack altogether, they'd wound up maimed or killed. He took a deep breath and pushed past the bloodstained palmetto. The long leaves dragged across his arm.

At once the trees shut out the moonlight. Even if there was more sign, he wouldn't see it. All he could do was go where the brush looked thinnest, on the theory that whoever had come in here before him would have chosen the path of least resistance. Twigs scratched him and snagged his shirt. Dead leaves rustled under his shoes. An owl swooped over his head and made him jump. "Meg!" he shouted. "Rose!" The shouts echoed.

The noise from the parking area faded. Realizing he'd been subconsciously using it to keep himself oriented, he grimaced. His ankle throbbed.

He must have been crazy to think he could find anyone in here at night. Maybe Sartak could, with his sharper senses, but an ordinary person didn't have a prayer. He'd better retrace his steps before he got lost, maybe come back when it was light. But as he started to turn, he caught a whiff of blood.

He spun back around. Scrambled forward. Rounded a thick old oak draped in Spanish moss and found Meg lying under it.

When he crouched beside her, he winced. She was bitten from head to foot, and the moss and gnarled roots beneath her were soaked with blood. And she was so *still*. Trembling, he put his hand to her face to see if she was breathing.

Feebly she batted it away. "I'm alive," she moaned. "Barely." She smiled, her teeth white in the dark mask of her tattered face. "Not that you look so good yourself."

"Didn't you hear me calling?" he asked. He looked her up and down, trying to decide which of her wounds looked most desperately in need of attention. Even in the light, it would have been a tough call.

"Sure," said Meg. "But I couldn't answer for fear of leading him to me."

"'Him' who?" Zane realized he didn't know where to begin. He couldn't imagine anyone but a doctor or an EMT actually being able to help her. His hands opened and closed.

"The one that made the dogs run crazy, stupid." She sucked in a sudden breath. Her body arched. "Oh, God!" she breathed. "He's close, I feel him, but I'm too torn up to run any farther. God damn it anyway! Why couldn't Partridge have given me the car keys? I wouldn't have had to hide in here. I could have gotten away!"

Zane looked around. Didn't see anything but the shadowy forms of the trees. Maybe she was delirious. "Don't worry," he said. "Somebody must have run to a phone and called 911. There must be cops and ambulances on the way. With this ankle, I might not be able to carry you back to the path. Maybe I shouldn't move you anyway. But I can bring help here. If I yell again, answer." Using the broken pole for support, he started to get up.

Meg's hand clamped around his wrist, jabbing pain through Gyp's bite marks, then, just as quickly, let go again. "Yeah. Go. No reason for you to get caught in the shit storm."

"I'm coming back," he said. "I promise."

"I know. You're the type." Her body stiffened. "Oh, jeez," she said, her voice fainter. "But do you have a gun, a knife, any kind of weapon you can leave me? Just . . . you know, just in case."

Zane realized he did. The black-handled Swiss Army knife on his key ring. It was the smallest one they made, virtually useless for self-defense, but maybe it would comfort her to have it. He fumbled it out of his pocket. "I have this."

"Please," she said. He pressed it into her palm, gently squeezed her bleeding hand in both of his, clambered up, and scuttled back the way he'd come.

At first the woods seemed even darker than before. Invisible branches lashed his face, while bumps and dips did their best to pitch him off his feet. But then a shaft of moonlight swam out of the gloom. Maybe it marked the beginning of a stretch of clearer terrain, a faster route back to the path. His body clammy with sweat, he gimped toward it.

And then he froze. Because it *wasn't* a ray of moonlight. It didn't extend up into the sky. It was a *blob* of light, gliding along, moving roughly parallel to him but in the opposite direction.

Zane threw himself behind a pine. It didn't help. A chilling sense of malevolent scrutiny, the same thing he'd felt by the pier, rolled over him. The glowing thing seemed to stare through the tree trunk as if it had X-ray vision.

All right, thought Zane, *come on then!* He gripped his crutch like a spear, then felt the shining thing's attention slide away.

Because it wasn't interested in him. It wanted Meg.

Zane didn't doubt it could find her, even in the dark. And he wasn't quite terrified enough to let that happen. Drawing on his grief and hate, he screamed, "Hey! Wait, you bastard! Come back and fight!"

The thing just flowed on, deeper into the trees. Now he noticed a subtle rhythm to its progress, like the roll of an animal's gait. Glimpsed a hint of shifting limbs inside the veil of light.

Cursing, he chased it. But he could already see that, worn out and with a bad foot, he wouldn't catch it before it reached Meg's refuge.

A thunderous bellow split the air. Zane dropped his spear-crutch and fell to one knee. Even as he clutched his ears, he realized it wouldn't do a lot of good. The roar was only partly sound. Another aspect of it drilled directly into his *mind*.

The bellow died away. The bubble of light crumpled in on itself and winked into nothingness.

Zane stared, bewildered. Why would it give up the hunt? Why had it sounded so angry? One terrible answer popped into his head. Now oblivious to his pains and exhaustion, he ran.

Meg had managed to sit up with her back against the tree, the better, perhaps, to keep watch. One hand, with the discolored blade of the pocketknife sticking out of it, lay at her side. Evidently it had landed there when it fell away from her throat. A bib of fresh blood covered her breasts.

Zane told himself it wasn't Rose, just a look-alike.

But he couldn't help feeling that he'd lost her all over again. He sank down beside her and sobbed.

Something cool wafted against his face. When he opened his eyes, the air was full of steam.

Meg's body and blood were evaporating into pearly vapor, her features blurring like those of a weathered statue. Her clothing crumpled in on itself as the flesh inside boiled away. Soon all that remained was a softening, sagging skeleton in rags. Then even the bones disappeared.

A hand fell on Zane's shoulder. His heart jolting, he lurched around to see Sartak, his clothes shredded to bloody tatters but the wounds beneath already half-healed.

"Did you see?" asked Zane.

"The end of it," the vampire replied. He looked Zane over. "You won't die without immediate assistance. Get up. I think that with luck I can get you away before the authorities arrive. I'm sure you wouldn't find them any more congenial than before." He stooped and picked up the knife and keys. The clean metal gleamed.

10

Alexander Blake awoke trembling, sweaty, and sick to his stomach. Groaning, grateful that no one was here who could see him like this, he rose from the rumpled bed and shuffled across the room. The linoleum chilled his bare feet. He flipped the switch and the fluorescent lights pinged and flickered on. The harsh glow made him squint.

His gaze fell on a nightstand, and for a moment, he wanted to kick it over. How had the operation gone so wrong?

As soon as he'd arrived, he'd seen the strange Kindred. Sartak, if that was really his name. And it had rattled him enough to impair his control when he went to work on the pit bulls. None of the dogs was supposed to attack Meg. They were just supposed to generate enough chaos for him to pick her off without interference.

And afterward, stalking his quarry through the woods, he'd noticed the same rangy, brown-haired young man he'd seen at the pier. Perhaps Sartak had only come for the dogfights, just as he'd claimed, but the mortal's presence couldn't possibly be a coincidence. Who was he? What did he know? Surely not much. How could he? But what was he trying to do with whatever information he did possess?

It also galled Blake that Meg had killed herself before he could reach her. He'd never anticipated that. Perhaps he ought to count his blessings. At least she was dead. But he hated to see the power go to waste.

He looked at his motionless companion, secured with four-point restraints to the other bed. As was often the case, he was tempted to pick up a pillow and smother her. If it solved his problem, it might be worth sacrificing the fringe benefits just to put all the aggravation behind him.

But given the peculiar turn that things had taken, it could just as easily backfire. Bring on the crisis. In Blake's experience, that was the trouble with visions and premonitions. They never told you enough.

Well, if he was going to let the bitch live a while longer, he might as well get some use out of her. He walked over to her and pressed his hand against her head. Her auburn hair felt greasy beneath his fingers.

He wasn't really going inside her, not this time. He was examining a new and undigested facet of himself. Still, the physical contact made it easier. Without regaining consciousness, she squirmed.

First he saw a parade of sketches and cartoons. Rose Cooper's art. *No*, he thought. *I need real faces*. Identities. From the last two months.

For a moment, he felt a feeble, reflexive resistance—perhaps some sort of feedback from the woman on the bed had triggered it. He quashed it and began to sift.

Rose had never met Sartak. But the young man—Zane Tyler—had been her lover. Flashing through her memories, Blake kissed him, walked through a mall with him, dived with him through a rainbow of fish in clear Caribbean waters. But he/she never told him any secrets. In fact, until the end, Rose hadn't even *remembered* them. So how the hell had the boy traced Meg?

Blake would have to find out. If not with his psychic abilities, then by cruder methods. He lifted his hand.

Now goose bumps covered his naked body, partly because of the draft from the vent—the AC was too cold again—and partly because he'd burnt up so much energy. As he started for the closet to retrieve his clothes, the black phone on the wall rang.

He wanted to ignore it, but it could be important. Grimacing, he picked it up. "Blake here."

A husky female voice chortled. "Hey, you scrumptious love muffin. Why did the Polack lick go to the porno flick?"

Blake sighed. The fastest way to get her to come to the point was to play along. "I don't know, Ellen. Why?"

"To see the Toreador do a trick!" Ellen shrieked with laughter.

It would be pointless to try to work it out. Except for the fact that they rhymed, all her jokes were non sequiturs. "That's cute. Was there something else?"

"Uh-huh. Your midnight appointment's here. And your sweetie pie is on the line. I am *so* jealous. Would you give me a break, if I dragged my knuckles and barked like a dog?"

"Tell the Prince I'll be with him momentarily. And put Miss Carlyle on."

Ellen giggled. The phone clicked, and a different voice came on the line. "What happened to Henry?"

Blake had to admit, she did sound like a dog,

barking and snarling. During the first six months of their acquaintance, he'd had to skim the surface of her mind to understand her. "And a pleasant evening to you, Judith. What are you talking about?"

"He called to tell you he spotted one of your friends, isn't that right?"

"Yes. And I suggested he remove himself and your property from the line of fire, so to speak. I needed to create a diversion."

"Well, a minute later he phoned *me* to say that some strange Kindred—a Chinese or Japanese—had recognized him for a ghoul and accosted him. Now he doesn't answer. When I agreed to help you, you didn't tell me I'd be putting my people in danger."

Blake saw no point in explaining that, in his eagerness to kill Meg, he might have left Henry in an awkward position. "To the best of my knowledge, whatever happened between your man and this Chinese has nothing to do with my business." He hoped that was essentially true.

"Indeed. Well, I'd feel more confident about that if I knew what your business really is."

"I wonder. After all, you truly don't need to know. If I told you, wouldn't you worry about me being similarly indiscreet with our *mutual* secrets?"

Judith laughed. It had also taken Blake a long time to realize what the noise was. It sounded like the same huge hound, choking on a bone. "Very nice, my darling, glib as ever. Very well, we'll let it drop. Henry *was* just a servant, and it's not as if I have to worry about hostile Kindred turning up on *my* doorstep. But someone ought to alert His Nibs."

"As it happens, I'm going to see him in a few minutes. I'll take care of it." They said their good-byes and he rang off. Quickly wiping off the sweat with the damp washcloth he'd brought, he pulled on his clothes and grabbed the Mars bars he'd stashed in his jacket pocket.

Feeling much refreshed, he made it to his office at ten after twelve. Roderick Dean stood by one of the bookshelves. He seemed to be reading the leather-bound volumes' spines, though he hadn't bothered to turn on a lamp.

The Prince of Tampa Bay was a slim Kindred of medium height. His attire was subtly archaic, with a bow tie, vest, pocket handkerchief, cuffed slacks, and cuff links. His ivory-headed walking stick lay across the arms of a green leather chair. The clan Ventrue elder's features were intelligent but essentially nondescript. If he'd been a mortal, people might have said he looked like an accountant or librarian. But there was something commanding in his bearing, something instantly magnetic about his smile and gray-green eyes. Blake knew this was due to the vampire's charismatic powers. He could invoke a similar effect himself.

"I can't abide lateness even in my fellow Cainites," said Dean. "I wonder why I tolerate it from you."

"Because I'm a unique person and we have a special relationship," said Blake. "Are you angry that I'm late."

Dean smiled wryly. "No. What would be the point? You'd just explain it away as transference." He settled on the couch, while Blake took his customary chair.

"Before we begin," said Blake, "there's something you should know. Judith Carlyle"—Dean's mouth twisted at the name—"just called me. One of her ghouls ran into a strange Asian Kindred in the wilds of south Hillsborough County. She can't get the ghoul on the phone anymore, and she thinks the Asian probably killed him." He wouldn't mention any more about his own involvement in the matter unless it became necessary. He was no more inclined to confide in Roderick than he was in Judith. Except for a few neonates, all vampires were paranoid, and anyone who sought to walk among them was well advised to adopt the same stance.

Dean asked, "What was his name and clan?"

"I've told you everything I know," Blake lied.

"Maybe he was a Ravnos or Gangrel, just passing through."

"I wouldn't be surprised," said Blake.

"And perhaps Judith's ghoul provoked him. He might have been nearly as abrasive as the woman herself."

"Very possibly."

"On the other hand, the Chinaman could be an agent of the Sabbat, scouting us out. Or God knows what. In any case, I can't let Cainites wander around the fief without permission. I'd better tell everyone to keep an eye out."

Blake nodded. "Whatever you say."

Dean snorted. "In other words, you agree. You'd let me know subtly but unmistakably if you didn't."

Blake smiled. "Nonsense. This humble minister would never presume to second-guess you. Besides, you know my approach is purely nondirective. I'm going to have a kine taken up, too. A young man who seems to be sticking his nose in our business."

Dean shrugged. "Fine, if you think it's necessary. You know whom to use. Who's a ghoul and who isn't. Shall we start now?"

Blake suppressed a smirk at the plaintive note in his voice. "Certainly. What kind of week have you had?"

The Prince leaned back on the couch. "Good, until you dropped this mysterious Oriental on my plate. The Beast was quiet . . ."

11

Sartak wrapped tape around Zane's bitten forearm. "There," he said. "That should do it."

"Thanks," muttered Zane.

"Why so mournful?"

"Because people *died*. *She* died."

"Unfortunate, I suppose, but thousands of people die every day without upsetting you, as long as they're strangers. And these were. Even Meg, despite the resemblance." Sartak rose from the kitchen table and began to pace around. "I do regret losing the information she might have given us, but we're still leagues closer to the solution than we were before. At least we can now infer that Rose definitely *was* murdered, but the corpse melted into smoke."

Zane stared at Sartak. He'd bought the Kindred more than one outfit, but the little man hadn't bothered to change yet. The wounds inside his bloody rags had all but disappeared. Zane compared the rapid regeneration to his own bandages, bruises, and pains, the Mongol's cold-blooded cheer to his own grief, and a kind of rage surged through him. "God damn you," he said.

Sartak lifted an eyebrow. "Many people would say He has. But I don't see the relevance."

"I'm tired of you treating this like a game."

"But to me, it is," Sartak said reasonably. "I told you that from the start. And it isn't just that I never met Rose. I could never have doted on her the way you did, even if I'd known her while I was breathing.

"We Mongols were a hard people. We killed without pity, and we required our own folk to suffer and die as needed, without complaint. We even drank blood. I've often thought I was half-Kindred even before my sire Embraced me.

"And centuries of preying on you kine, of fending off witch-hunters, Lupines, and rivals among my own breed, made me even stonier than before. I simply can't feel the things you feel. Accept that, exploit me for your ends as I'm exploiting you for mine, and we'll get along."

Zane realized that his resentment, if not his sorrow, had faded. "Okay. Fair enough." He noticed he was thirsty. He guessed that blood loss and violent exertion would do that to you. He went to the refrigerator for a bottle of spring water. "What else do you figure we've learned?"

Sartak said, "At the risk of belaboring the obvious, that Rose's murder wasn't in any sense an ordinary crime. The whole affair involves what you'd call the supernatural."

Zane shook his head. "I know you must be right, but it's hard to get a handle on. I'm still having trouble believing in you."

Sartak smiled. "Did you think I was the only Cainite in the world? Or that all the rest live in Transylvania?"

"I hadn't thought about it. But if I had, I would've figured that vampires are so rare that it was pushing the odds to meet one in a lifetime, let alone two."

"We aren't numerous compared to kine," said Sartak, "partly for the same reason there are fewer lions than antelope. Neither are the other dark peoples, faeries, Lupines, and the like. But we aren't all that rare, either. You're like a man who's spent his whole life in a soundproof, windowless house in the middle of a rain forest. When at last he goes outside and glimpses a parrot, he's astonished, and a second one amazes him even more. But the birds have been there in quantity all the time."

Zane took a drink. The cold liquid felt good going down. "How can that be?"

"Because in large measure, we run things. At one time, when I was young, we ran them more or less openly. But then the kine rose against us. To survive, we had to go into hiding, convince you that you'd killed us all, or better still, that we'd never existed in the first place. But we still kept our hands on the reins. How else could we structure society in a manner that would support our Masquerade?"

Zane smiled skeptically. "You mean the president's a vampire?"

"Probably not," said Sartak. "But I wouldn't be surprised if he's a ghoul, or has a trusted Kindred advisor. Look, why do you suppose those policemen arrested us all the other night? Who do you think ordered those particular streets cleared at that particular time, and never mind how much manpower it diverted from other needs or whose rights were trampled in the process?"

Zane shrugged. "I don't know."

"Neither do I. But since it didn't seem to serve any

rational human purpose, perhaps it served the *in*human one of some being who can order the Tampa police around like a private army."

Zane said, "Trying to understand this is like trying to go crazy. I have to decide that almost nothing I believed is true. It's like switching over to thinking the world is flat. Or that matter isn't made of atoms."

"Science isn't true," Sartak said gravely. "If it was, your enemy and I couldn't wield the powers that we do." He smiled. "I'm joking. Of course it's true. But it's only one truth among many, and different creatures are bound by different verities. A mage I met in San Francisco in the 1860s explained that to me."

"Okay," said Zane. "I guess I do believe every crazy part of it. When it comes right down to it, what choice do I have? The world is *lousy* with you spooks, and one of you killed Rose. Where does that leave us?"

"In all likelihood, heading deeper into the hidden realm. I doubt we can unmask the killer without talking to the local Kindred, and perhaps certain other beings too. I warn you, it's going to be dangerous."

Zane chuckled. "You mean, as opposed to getting mauled by pit bulls?"

"Yes," said Sartak. He peeled off what remained of his jacket and dropped it in the wastebasket in the corner of the kitchen. "Since our existence is supposed to be a secret, few Cainites would want you to return to the other side of the curtain alive and unchanged. I'll do my best to protect you, but my own status is equivocal."

"Meaning what?"

"I'm an Autarkis, a sort of outlaw. I drop in and out of Cainite society as it suits me. I've been known to disobey the Six Traditions, the Kindred's most fundamental laws. I broke the First when I showed you what I am. I haven't lived this long to be bound by any code but my own."

"In other words, they're going to want to kill you as much as me."

"Actually, I hope not." He stripped off his bloody shirt. "It's not as if we have to advertise what a despicable felon I am. And if we claim you're my ghoul, no one should take exception to you, either. But if someone penetrates our own little Masquerade, things could get ugly very quickly." He looked at Zane expectantly.

"In other words, do I want to quit while there's still time? No." He shook his head. "It's funny, the things you learn about yourself. I never thought I was the kind of person who'd care much about revenge. But here I am, risking my life to get it."

"Perhaps your motives are a bit more altruistic than that," Sartak said. "Don't you want to protect the other—shall we call them the Sisters?"

Zane blinked. "What?"

"I'm sorry, I assumed you'd worked that part out. If Rose had one doppelgänger, perhaps there are more. If so, I imagine your glowing friend must want to kill them all."

12

Zane's head throbbed. He'd chalked it up to lack of sleep. He wondered how much longer he could go on like this, running around with Sartak all night, then doing legwork by day. Of course, getting beaten up and chewed on probably aggravated the problem.

The phone at the other end of the line buzzed a third time. *Come on*, he thought, *answer. Tell me what I want to know, so I can take a nap.*

Someone picked up the other phone. A woman's voice said, "Hello."

"Hello," said Zane. "May I speak to Mrs. Partridge, please?"

"My mother's resting. Her husband—my father—died last night." The woman sniffed.

Zane felt a pang of guilt for disturbing them. He did his best to quash it. "I know. And I'm sorry. But this is Sergeant Hillyard from the Sheriff's Department. I need to speak with her for just a moment, concerning the investigation."

"All right," Partridge's daughter said reluctantly. "But remember, you promised to keep it short." Her receiver clunked down on a hard surface.

It took Mrs. Partridge a while to reach the phone. Zane imagined a teary-eyed, feeble old woman creeping painfully along, perhaps with the aid of a walker, and felt like a jerk again. At last he heard her fumble up the receiver. A scratchy voice quavered, "Hello."

"Hello, Mrs. Partridge. I'm very sorry to bother you—"

The old woman snorted. "That's all right. What, did Lydia tell you I was too bad off to talk? That girl! I don't know if she honestly thinks I'm as fragile as china, or if fussing over me is what keeps *her* from falling apart. But listen. If you want to sue, like that fool that jumped me at the undertaker's, you need to have your lawyer call mine. And I warn you, mine knows how to make things go slow. I'll be in the ground before the case comes to trial."

"It's nothing like that, Mrs. Partridge. This is Sergeant Hillyard—"

"That's what Lydia said. But what happened to Deputy Miller, that talked to me before?"

"I work with him." The doorbell rang. Zane grimaced and decided to ignore it.

"Oh. Well, give me your number and extension at the station house and I'll call you right back."

Zane sighed. "All right, you caught me. My name is Zane Tyler, and I'm not a policeman. I just said that to get your daughter to put you on the line. I called because I need some information. It's not for a lawsuit, or anything like that."

"How'd you get my number?"

"The newspaper printed your husband's full name, and that he lived in Arcadia. That made it easy to find."

"Damn newspapers. Just a lot of gossip and trash. Mind you, the television is even worse. What is this about?"

"Mr. Partridge had an employee named Meg Irons."

"Yes, but she ain't here. The deputies didn't find her body, so I guess she run off. Probably figured she'd better, since by all accounts our Rebel killed John, and it was her job to control the dog. Not that I blame her, really. You breed and raise animals to fight, and sooner or later they're going to take it into their heads to fight you. I warned John of that, but he wouldn't listen, any more than he listened to anything else I said in forty-seven years of marriage. And I'll bet I don't sound much like a grief-stricken widow to you, do I?"

"I guess not really," Zane admitted. The doorbell chimed again. The person outside started knocking.

"Well, I'll tell you. When you first hook up with a man, you think he's God's gift. But after you've lived up close to him for a while, the new rubs off, and you see that he's pretty much like everybody else. I never thought that was much of a deal, but at last I see some good in it. What's your interest in Meg?"

Zane couldn't think of a good lie. "It would take forever to explain, and you wouldn't believe it anyway. But I promise, I'm not trying to hurt her." Not that anything could, not anymore. He blinked back a tear.

"All right," said Mrs. Partridge. "I'll trust you. No skin off my butt anyway, is it? What do you want to know?"

"When did she start working for you?"

"Six, seven weeks ago. Just showed up here at the farm one day. She'd seen an ad John tacked up at the feed store." The knocking pounded on. It was making Zane's headache worse.

"Where did she live before that?"

"I don't know. She was closemouthed, that first day and later. Ordinarily, we might not have hired somebody like that. But you could see she was good with animals. We felt sorry for her, trying to act so tough when anybody could tell she was homeless and starving. And I don't imagine it bothered John that she was pretty."

"Did she ever get mail or phone calls? Did she have any friends?"

"No."

"Did she show you any ID? Or fill out an employment application?"

"She didn't need to. We paid her off the books."

Zane tried to think of another question. He couldn't. At least he'd established that Meg, like Rose, had appeared out of nowhere about two months ago. That must be important, though God knew what it meant. "I guess that's it then. I'm sorry about your loss."

"Thank you. If you see Meg, tell her she can come back if she wants." Mrs. Partridge hung up.

The front door clicked and opened till it hit the end of the chain. Dazzling afternoon sunlight shone through the crack. Zane squinted. His brother Ben called, "Zane? Are you here? Are you asleep?"

Zane got up and headed for the living room. "I'm here. I was on the phone before. Why didn't you use your key in the first place, instead of trying to beat the door down?"

"Because I'm polite. And it wouldn't have gotten me in anyway, would it?" Zane opened the door. With his brown hair, brown eyes, and long legs, his big brother looked like an older, bespectacled, and slightly paunchy version of himself. Judging from his gray suit and maroon tie, he'd come from court or his office. His eyes widened, and his mouth fell open. "Jesus Christ!"

Zane was only wearing cutoff jeans. He realized his lack of clothes showed off his bandages and collection of black-and-yellow bruises to maximum effect. "It looks worse than it is," he said.

Ben came into the living room. "If it was as bad as it looks, you wouldn't be able to walk. What happened?"

Zane knew he couldn't tell Ben, either. Even his brother wouldn't believe him. The thought made him feel lonely. "I was walking and I got hit by a car. Fortunately, it wasn't moving very fast."

Ben eyed him suspiciously. "You had yourself checked by a doctor, didn't you?"

"Sure. Sit down, if you want." Ben took a chair, and Zane flopped down on the end of the couch. Rose's sketches were still strewn across the coffee table, with the spear resting on top of them.

Ben stared down at his folded hands for a moment, seemingly collecting his thoughts. When he looked up, he said, "I'm worried about you."

"I understand why," said Zane. "And I appreciate it. But I promise, I'm going to be okay."

"Your boss phoned me. He said he hasn't heard from you since Rose disappeared. You should have at least called in. I had to give him a real song and dance to convince him not to fire you."

"I appreciate that, too."

"Can you go back tomorrow?"

Zane sighed. "No. I've got other things to take care of first. If worst comes to worst, selling snorkels and jet skis isn't the only job in the world."

"What things do you have to do?"

"Just . . . stuff. What would *you* have to do if you lost Tracy?"

"I'd be devastated," said Ben. Ripples of reflection oozed across the lenses of his glasses. "But I wouldn't let what was left of my life fall apart." He hesitated. "Besides, it wouldn't exactly be the same thing. Tracy is my *wife*. I've known her since seventh grade."

Zane grimaced. "You mean, since I only knew Rose a couple months, and we were just living together, I didn't really love her."

"No. I know you did. And I understood why. She seemed like one of the nicest girls I ever met. But now that you know she lied about her past, now that she's vanished without a word—"

"She didn't run away. She *died*. I told you that, the morning after it happened."

"You also told me what you found, or didn't find, when you went back to the scene. And what the policeman said."

Zane grimaced. "Fair enough. If I was in your place, I guess I'd think I was crazy, too. But I'm not."

"That's *not* what I think," said Ben. "But when Mom died, it hit us both pretty hard. Then, a year later, you're in Somalia. Everywhere you look, people are starving. Bandits try to kill you. They do kill two of your friends—"

Zane surprised himself by laughing. His brother jumped. "Somalia wasn't that bad. I thought so at the time, but I know better now. At least"—he realized he was on the verge of blurting out too much—"skip it."

Ben shrugged. "Whatever. I don't want to argue. I came to invite you to stay with me for a while. It might help you feel better."

The hell of it was, it probably would. But Ben wouldn't tolerate his brother sneaking off every night, nor did Zane want to lead Sartak to his family. He trusted the Kindred within limits, but it would be stupid to tempt fate. "Thanks for the offer. But I need to be by myself right now."

Ben scowled. "Nobody who got a look at you would agree. I don't know—"

The doorbell rang. Grateful for the interruption, Zane jumped up to answer it.

Two Tampa police officers stood on the landing. One was a moonfaced white man whose belt looked as though it was buckled too tight. His belly bulged over it. The other was a willowy, light-skinned black woman. She said, "Good afternoon, sir. Are you Zane Tyler?"

"Yes," Zane said hesitantly. Had they identified him as one of the prisoners who'd broken out of jail? Was it even worse than that?

The woman said, "We have to ask you to come with us."

"Am I under arrest?"

"No, nothing like that," she said soothingly. She reached for his arm.

Zane's mouth was dry. He backpedaled and tried to close the door.

He wasn't quick enough. The cops pushed their way in after him, then faltered. Zane realized they'd seen Ben.

"This is Ben Tyler," Zane said. "My brother. My *attorney*." He turned his head. "They're trying to arrest me. Do something."

The male cop grimaced. "I thought you said he'd be alone," he muttered from the corner of his mouth.

"I said he *lived* alone," the black woman replied. "I'm not God, I can't predict everything. Shut up and let me handle it."

Ben stood up. "Like he said, I'm his lawyer. Would you please tell me who you are, and what this is all about?"

"I'm Officer Newman," said the black cop, "and this is Officer Patterson. We have a court order to transport your brother to a mental health facility for evaluation."

"Why?" asked Ben. "The family didn't petition for any such action."

"I don't know," said Newman. "We didn't have anything to do with taking out the order. We're just executing it. Maybe the neighbors had some kind of complaint."

"The hell they did," said Zane.

Ben turned to him. "Maybe you *should* go with them. I know how this works. If the psychiatrist thinks you're okay, he'll let you go."

"And if he doesn't, he'll lock me up?"

Ben sighed. "They'll hold you in the hospital pending a hearing. But that's the worst-case scenario."

Zane stared him in the eye. "Even if this is on the up-and-up, I can't afford the time. Not now. Look, I know you're worried about me. But please, unless you're absolutely, positively, one-hundred-percent sure that I've lost my mind, give me the benefit of the doubt and get me out of this. At least make sure they're doing it by the book!"

Ben bit his lip. He looked as if he wished he were somewhere, anywhere else. "Okay. You're right, I can at least do that." He held out his tanned, slightly pudgy hand. "May I see the order, please?"

Newman handed him a folded piece of paper.

Ben opened it and scanned it. "It looks like a standard order for involuntary—" He frowned. "There's no seal."

"I guess the clerk left it off," Newman said. "You know how it is. Sometimes somebody makes a mistake with the paperwork. We can go back and get the stamp if we have to, but I really hope you won't ask."

Ben squinted at the bottom of the order. "Whose signature is this supposed to be, Judge Threadgill's? If you don't mind, I'd like to call his office, just to make sure there hasn't been a misunderstanding." He turned and headed for the kitchen and the yellow wall phone.

"Great," said Patterson, sneering. "You really handled it."

"Like you could have done better," Newman replied. She reached for the strap that secured her revolver in its holster.

Zane yelled, "Watch out!" He lunged at her.

She sidestepped and gave him a push, maybe some kind of judo or aikido move, that threw him off-balance. Patterson grabbed him and threw him onto the floor. Despite the carpet, the impact jabbed pain through his cuts and bruises, and knocked the wind out of him. The beefy cop dropped on top of him, hurting him a second time, and snapped handcuffs on his wrists. The hard steel rings were painfully tight.

"Run!" Zane croaked, then realized Ben couldn't. The cops were between him and the only exits.

Glaring, fists clenched, Ben started back into the living room. Newman drew her gun. "I figured it would come to this," she said. "But you can't say I didn't try to give you a break. You'll have to come with us, too."

"Why?" Ben demanded. "What's the charge?"

Newman said, "Obstructing police officers in the performance of their duties."

"Will you cut the bullshit?" said Patterson. He was still on top of Zane, his knees digging into his back. "Just subdue him already, and let's get out of here."

"This is ridiculous," said Ben. A sheen of sweat

glistened on his forehead. *"You're* the ones breaking the law. You'd better put the gun away and let Zane go before *you* wind up in jail."

Newman glanced at Patterson. "I hate it when you're right," she said. She lowered the revolver to her side and eased forward. "Mr. Tyler, please bear with us. I know this seems a little out of line, but—" The blue-black gun flashed in an arc and smacked against Ben's face. His aviator glasses flew off.

Ben reeled back, jerking up his arms to protect his head. Newman went after him, swinging, cornering him against the back wall of the kitchen. The blows cracked. Zane thrashed, but couldn't buck Patterson off. He just gave himself rug burns.

When Newman stepped back, Ben's hands were covered with welts, and two of his fingers bent at peculiar angles. "I'm sorry I had to do that," she said, breathing heavily. "But you have to get it through your head. You're in a different place now, where there are different rules. Where nobody freed the slaves. If you don't want to get hit again, let me cuff you."

Trembling, Ben lowered his hands, revealing a pulped nose and a chin red with blood, and turned his back.

13

Last night Sartak had taken refuge in a vacant apartment near Zane's, so he reached his ally's home shortly after sunset. When no one answered the doorbell, he frowned.

Zane's Mustang was still parked in its usual space. Perhaps its owner had taken a walk. Or was fast asleep. But Sartak's instincts told him it wasn't so. He sharpened his senses, but didn't hear anything stirring inside the apartment. He wished fleetingly that he had a credit card, to pry open the spring lock on the door. Or that he was a shape-changer, so he could turn to mist and flow under it. Lacking such resources, he stepped back and kicked.

With a bang, the door flew open. He charged through at maximum speed. Just because he hadn't heard anything, that didn't mean nothing was lying in wait for him. Over the centuries, he'd met plenty of creatures at least as good at hiding as he was at ferreting them out.

But nothing leaped out at him. The boom echoed and died. When he was satisfied there was no immediate danger, he shut the door. Then, not bothering to turn on the lights, he began to prowl around.

Instantly he caught the scent of blood.

He followed the aroma into the kitchen. Drops of vitæ had spattered the linoleum, walls, and counter, as if someone had been beaten. He touched the stains and found that they were dry. He scraped one, then touched his finger to his tongue. Kine blood. Quite possibly Zane's, though he couldn't really tell. Even his senses had their limits.

In all probability, Rose's killer had come and taken Zane away. Sartak grimaced. Why hadn't he realized that the enemy might know who Zane was? That he might strike at him?

He could feel the Hunger burning and seething inside him again tonight. Maybe the blood thirst was impairing his judgment. Or perhaps, as he sometimes suspected, he didn't really seek out challenge to fend off boredom but to end it forever, by giving danger repeated opportunities to destroy him. That too could explain his recklessness and lack of calculation. But whatever he desired in the depths of his silent heart, it didn't give him the right to be careless with Zane's existence.

Sartak blinked. What was he feeling? Did he *like* Zane? Did he feel *guilty* that he hadn't protected him?

He examined the strange emotion. In a moment, it seemed absurd. Abstract. Artifical. He didn't truly feel anything, except perhaps annoyance at the enemy for outwitting him, and a renewed determination to bring him down. He was merely imagining the way he might have felt, long, long ago.

How could it be otherwise? He knew kine too well

to grow attached to them. Even relatively inoffensive specimens like Zane were *petty*, blindly preoccupied with cravings, vanities, and grievances of the most trivial kind. And even should one prove otherwise, what was the point of cherishing walking dust?

Still, assuming Zane was still alive, Sartak would do everything in his power to rescue him. His principles demanded it. And he'd learned it was important to uphold them, even if the feelings which had given rise to them were dead. It helped keep the Beast, the madness that festered in every Cainite, from annihilating the Man.

The wall phone rang, jarring him out of his reverie. To his heightened hearing, the shrill sound was painfully loud.

He wondered if he was under observation. Perhaps the enemy was calling to taunt him, or to threaten Zane's life. He picked up the receiver and said, "Hello."

For a moment, no one answered. Then a hesitant female voice said, "Who is this?"

"My name is Sartak," replied the Kindred. "But this is the Tyler residence. Zane is out at the moment."

"This is his sister-in-law," said the woman. "Do you know where he went? Is he with his brother?"

Sartak frowned. If Zane's brother had been here at the wrong time, perhaps the enemy had abducted both of them. "I'm sorry, I don't know. I just got here."

"Well, Ben was going to invite Zane to come stay with us. Till he feels better. But that was hours ago, and neither of them has shown up."

Sartak realized it was pointless to waste any more time on her. She couldn't tell him anything.

But he knew Zane cared about her. And something— *not* guilt, but perhaps its ghost—told him he had to

make at least a token effort to look after her. That to
do otherwise would be a breach of faith.

Another asinine conceit. He'd never promised to
protect the kine's relations. Still, he said, "Where are
you?"

"Twelve fifty-five Mainhardt Lane. It's in
Carrollwood."

"Stay there. I'm coming over. I have something to tell
you, but I think I should do it in person." He hung up.

Zane's keys lay beside his black leather wallet and
a glass jar of pennies, on his dresser. The Swiss Army
knife was missing from the ring. Maybe the kine
couldn't bear the sight of it anymore. Sartak shook
his head. *Don't be so modern*, he thought, *so soft.
Otherwise, you won't survive till I reach you.*

He took the keys and the wallet too. It might be
convenient to have some cash. He considered taking
a spear gun as well, but it seemed a puny, awkward
weapon, not worth the trouble. He'd arrange for better before the night was out.

The Mustang started at a touch. In the minute that
followed, he discovered he still felt at home behind
the wheel. In fact, after eight years as a hobo, driving
seemed a pleasant novelty again, though nowhere
near as much fun as riding a horse.

He stopped at a convenience store for directions,
then located Carrollwood easily enough. It turned out
be a housing development for parvenus. Or, as people called them in this place and time, yuppies.
Traffic choked Dale Mabry, the principal highway,
even though rush hour had ended long before.
Endless chains of strip malls and shopping plazas,
full of trendy, interchangeable shops and restaurants,
lined both sides of the road. The glare of neon signs
washed away the stars.

Sartak scowled. He hated places like this. It wasn't the lack of taste. He was no aesthete or Toreador. The Moulin Rouge, the Barbary Coast, Prohibition-era Chicago, and 1960s Bangkok had all been raw and gaudy, but they'd suited him well enough. It was the sterility. The lack of soul.

Or perhaps, he thought sardonically, the problem was that he was finally losing the ability to adapt. Perhaps in a few years or decades he'd resemble some mad old Ventrue, living by candlelight, prancing around in a periwig or a doublet.

Ben Tyler lived in a brick ranch house on a quiet side street. An oak tree and a glass ball on a pedestal stood in the front yard. Sartak drove on by, looking for police cars. He didn't see any, so he parked and loped to the front door.

Mrs. Tyler answered as soon as he rang the bell. She was a buxom, slightly chubby woman with startling aquamarine eyes. He decided she was probably wearing tinted contact lenses. "Are you Mr. Sartak?" she asked.

"Yes," he said. "May I come in?"

A little boy with straight brown hair like Zane's and chocolate ice-cream stains on his T-shirt appeared behind her. "Is it Dad?" he asked.

"Not yet," said Mrs. Tyler. She peered at Sartak's face, then said, "It's a friend of mine. Go watch TV in the Florida room."

The boy frowned. "Do I have to?"

"Yes." He grimaced and trudged away.

Mrs. Tyler ushered Sartak into a living room with an off-white carpet and a silver-gray sofa and chairs. Pewter collectibles from the Franklin Mint and an array of framed photos lined the shelves bracketing the fieldstone fireplace. Glancing at the pictures, the

Cainite recognized the same eye responsible for the ones in Zane's apartment. Evidently Ben, or the woman before him, was the family photographer. A white grand piano stood in the corner, and the air smelled of lemon Pledge.

"I sent Davy away because I was afraid of what he'd hear," said Mrs. Tyler, sitting down on the sofa. "I hope I was worried about nothing. But I don't think so. It's silly, Ben's only been gone a few hours, but I can *feel* something's wrong."

Sartak said, "I don't know for certain, but I believe it is." He took a chair. "I think Ben and Zane have been kidnapped. I found bloodstains in the apartment. And I have other reasons for thinking so, ones I'm not at liberty to divulge." He wanted to protect the woman, but not enough to breach the Masquerade. He'd defied the First Tradition on occasion, when the whim took him, but didn't feel moved to do so now.

She stared at him. "Why can't you tell? Who *are* you?"

"I'm sorry. I can't explain that, either."

Mrs. Tyler shook her head. "If this is a joke . . . but it's not, is it? Whatever happened, you were part of it, conscience made you come to me, but you're afraid to say any more. All right, then it's time to call the police." She started to stand up.

"No." He sprang out of his chair. Evidently startled, she flopped back onto the sofa cushions. "That would be unwise."

"Why?"

"In this situation, they can't help you. And if you pry into the disappearance, or urge others to do so, the kidnappers might decide to make you vanish as well, to make absolutely certain no one will interfere with them. I've seen it happen. If I were you, I'd take

Davy and go away for a while, just in case someone has already decided you represent a loose end."

"That's crazy. Kidnappers make ransom demands. They don't keep coming back and carting off family members until there's nobody left to pay them."

"If the motive is profit, that's true. But here, it isn't."

"Then what is it?"

Sartak sighed. "I can't tell you that, either."

"I can't believe this. If I weren't so scared, it would sound like a comedy routine. You can't possibly expect me to take you seriously when you won't say *anything*. I'm going to make my call." She stood up slowly, quivering almost imperceptibly. He wondered if she was afraid he'd restrain her by force. "If you don't want to talk to the police, you'd better leave."

"Stay where you are," said Sartak. He walked to the edge of the room, the thick carpet compressing beneath his feet. "Now clap your hands."

"Why? *Is* this a trick? Is everybody going to jump out and yell surprise?"

He shook his head. "I wish they were. Humor me, please."

Frowning, she tried to obey.

Sartak evoked his inhuman speed. Suddenly her hands were moving in slow motion. They made him think of insects trying to drag themselves out of gummy strands of spiderweb. He lunged forward and grabbed her wrists.

She gasped. "How did you do that?"

"The important thing is that I *can* do it." He moved to the piano and lifted it off the floor. "And this." A pang of Hunger burned him from mouth to belly. The use of his powers had sharpened his thirst. His head swimming, he set the musical instrument down.

Mrs. Tyler goggled. "No one could do that," she said. "You just took hold of the side. You just used your arms. You didn't have any *leverage*."

Sartak didn't recall sharpening his senses, but abruptly he could feel the heat of life radiating from her body. Smell the scent of her flesh. If he wanted to drink, all he had to do was reach out and take her.

But he'd come to warn her, not prey on her. He closed his eyes and took a deep breath. Though his undead body didn't need air, the gesture steadied him, just as it might have if he were still alive.

"You're right," he said. "No ordinary human being could do it. And this is no ordinary human affair. Now that you know that much, will you take my advice?"

"I don't know," she said. "Somebody still has to do something. Are *you* going to try to save Ben?"

"No," Sartak said. "I'm going to try to rescue Zane. If I stumble across your husband along the way, if it's convenient to free him as well, I will."

"*Convenient?*"

"I don't owe you or him anything, Mrs. Tyler." The Hunger squirmed in his stomach. "I'm leaving now." He turned and started for the door.

She scrambled after him. "No! Promise to help!" She grabbed his arm.

Even through the sleeve of his sports coat, the touch of her flesh enflamed him. His fangs dropped. He wrenched himself free, shoved her reeling across the room, and strode into the night.

14

The cell's padded walls muffled sound, but if Zane strained, he could still hear the occasional scream, or bray of laughter. When Newman and Patterson had brought him and Ben into the huge old building, only the click of their footsteps, echoing down the long, gloomy corridors, had broken the silence. Apparently the Tampa Bay Institute for Psychiatric Research and Intervention slept by day and lived by night.

The cops had forced Ben to remove most of his clothing. Now dressed only in his slacks and bloody shirt, he sat huddled in the corner, cradling his swollen hand in his lap. He kept blinking. Maybe it was because he didn't have his glasses, or maybe he was trying to hold back tears. "Why doesn't somebody come?" he asked.

"I think someone will, soon," Zane replied. "Now that it's dark."

"What's that got to do with anything? Oh. Right. They're vampires."

In the hours since their capture, Zane had told Ben his story. He'd figured he owed him that much.

"Maybe," said Zane. "Or maybe something else just as strange."

Ben shook his head. "I can't believe that you, of all people, fell for this. When I was interning with the State Attorney's Office, they prosecuted a Gypsy con man who could make anybody believe in curses, lucky numbers, and any other kind of mumbo jumbo. Your friend Sartak must be just as slick."

Zane sighed. "You're locked in a padded cell with broken fingers, and your nose mashed all over your face. Doesn't that show that something weird is happening?"

"It tells me that we've been the victims of police brutality and medical malpractice, not the bogeyman."

Zane decided to let it drop. Let Ben believe whatever he liked, whatever lie would dampen his fear, for as long as he could. Reality would shatter the illusion soon enough.

As if in response to the thought, voices murmured in the hall. Zane clambered to his feet. His pulse beat in his neck. Ben got up, too.

The door clicked open, and three people walked in. The two in the lead, a burly man with a black goatee and a petite blond woman, wore nurses' white. Both had a waxy pallor, and Zane wondered if they were vampires. The tall, thin man behind them had a fine-boned, aristocratic face with luminous copper-colored eyes. His hair was sculpted silver, almost the same shade as his expensive-looking double-breasted suit.

And he was probably the man who'd murdered Rose. Zane almost sprang at him, even though he realized the bastard wouldn't have come in if he hadn't been confident that he and his helpers could control the prisoners.

Ben squinted at the man in the suit. "I know you. I've seen you on TV, explaining why there can't be any such things as ghosts, or witchcraft."

The gray-haired man smiled. "Yes, that was me. My name is Alexander Blake."

The male nurse said, "My name is Alexander Blake."

The female nurse said, "My name is Alexander Blake."

"Only one of these people is the real Alexander Blake," the male nurse said. "The rest are impostors, and will attempt to fool this panel, on—"

Blake held up his hand. "Enough."

"Oh, all right," said the male nurse. "But it's not fair. You *always* get to be Alexander Blake."

Ben looked as if he was bewildered, but trying not to let it throw him. "Are you in charge here?" he asked.

"Yes," said Blake. The blonde mouthed the words *in his dreams* at Zane.

"Well, there's been a mistake," said Ben. "A whole series of mistakes, actually. My brother and I were brought here illegally, and savagely assaulted in the process. I don't hold you responsible for that. I'll take that side of it up with the Tampa police. But we've been waiting for *hours*, without seeing a single member of your staff, even though it's obvious I need medical attention. You should know that I'm an attorney. If you release us immediately, I'll *consider* letting the matter drop, even though your facility is guilty of gross negligence."

Blake said, "If you truly weren't a part of this situation, then I regret the bad luck that brought you here. Still, you are here, and I'm afraid I can't let you walk away with your free will intact, if, indeed, I let you go at all. Now please be quiet. I have a lot to do this evening."

"I will *not* be quiet!" Ben said furiously. "I demand—"

Blake glanced at the male nurse. The bearded man grabbed Ben, swung him around, glared into his face, and said, "Quiet!" Ben's words seem to catch in his throat. He made a choking sound. "Sit!" Ben's knees buckled, dumping him on the floor.

Instinctively, Zane lunged forward to help him. The blond nurse said, "Back!" Despite his intent, he floundered to a halt, then backpedaled till his shoulders pressed into the padded wall. "Stay!" He tried to throw himself at her, but his muscles wouldn't obey him.

Blake said, "Thank you."

The blonde smiled crookedly. Her cheeks dimpled. "You could handle these little situations yourself, if you weren't too high and mighty to do your own dirty work."

"I couldn't do it as efficiently," said Blake. "My talents work a bit differently." He looked at Zane. "So. Mr. Tyler. Why so quiet? Oh, I see. You were busy resisting the impulse to attack me. That was rather intelligent, though I can't honestly guarantee it will spare you any grief."

"Why?" asked Zane. "Why did you kill Rose? And Meg?"

"Would it make you any less angry if I claimed it was self-defense? That, in time, they might have posed a threat?"

Meanwhile, on the other side of the cell, the bearded nurse knelt beside Ben. "Hey," he said, "your nose and fingers do look pretty bad. I guess I'd better do something. After all, this *is* a hospital." He took hold of the injured man's wrist.

Zane sneered at Blake. "You're a liar. Rose wasn't doing anything but living her life. And she wouldn't have hurt a fly."

Blake nodded. "Isn't that the truth. And you chose her, out of all the women in the world. We could explore the reason why, and gain insights that would help you in future relationships. But I normally charge a hefty fee for that service, and who knows if you'll even *have* any more relationships. Now, it's time for me to ask the questions. What do you know about Rose's background?"

"Why should I tell you?" Zane replied.

The male nurse said, "Let's take a look at this." He lifted Ben's hand. Ben tried to pull away, but the nurse grabbed his other arm and threw himself on top of him.

Zane strained to hurl himself forward. "Stay, stay, stay," chanted the blonde.

The bearded man opened his mouth, exposing fangs like Sartak's, and sank them into Ben's hand. Ben screamed.

"There's one answer," said Blake, raising his voice. "We can torture your brother. Or you. But the truth is, we don't have to. When I ask a question, you can't help thinking of the answer, and that's all I need." He turned to the male nurse. "Please do that somewhere else. I can't hear myself think."

The male vampire lifted his head. "Roger dodger, Doc. I'll give ol' Ben some really *aggressive* treatment." He surged to his feet and hauled Ben out the door, leaving a pungent trail of blood behind. The shrieking faded as he manhandled his captive down the hall.

"God damn you," said Zane, shuddering with rage, horror, and exertion. "If anything happens to him—"

Blake smiled. "You'll kill me? Not much of a threat,

when I know you're hell-bent on avenging Rose in any case. Even more to the point, you're helpless to carry it out. Or are you expecting the Asian Kindred to appear and save the day?" Zane had hoped Blake didn't know about Sartak. He tried not to let his dismay show on his face. "Oh, I'm afraid I know almost everything, and your thoughts are steadily filling in the gaps. Since Rose didn't tell you what sort of creature she was, how did you find Meg? Ah, a clue in one of her drawings. Very clever. Have you involved anyone else in this affair? Only Ben. Good. That's everything, I think."

"How can you read my mind?" Zane asked. "Are you a vampire, too?"

"Not yet," said Blake. "Until I feel old age closing in on me, I'll be content to be their ally. An ally with certain godlike abilities of his own. I've been called a psychic and a mutant, and I suppose both terms are accurate. Good-bye. Perhaps we'll see each other again." He turned.

"Hey," said the blonde. "What are we supposed to do with them?"

"It turns out they're not important," said Blake, "so do the usual. Anything you like."

15

Sartak wanted to get out of Carrollwood. Find a darker, lonelier hunting ground. But the heavy traffic on Dale Mabry combined with his own impatience to make it impossible. Finally, with a curse, he pulled the Mustang off the road and into a shopping center.

He got out of the car and began to prowl the parking lot. The Florida daytime heat had finally begun to bleed out of the air. Pink lamps on tall poles cast an unfortunate amount of light. Soon he spotted a man, a woman, and two little girls climbing out of a station wagon. The girls giggled and chattered about an actor named Tom Hanks. It took an act of will to let the family pass, even though he generally preferred not to hurt children. He supposed it seemed too easy and thus vaguely dishonorable. An irrational notion, considering that no unarmed adult kine was a match for him either, but he appeared to be stuck with it.

Minutes crawled by. The Hunger writhed inside

him. He'd nearly decided to stalk someone on the sidewalk in front of the shops, or even inside a store, when two people rushed out of a Chinese restaurant.

The one in the lead was a dark-haired thirtyish woman in a green suede jacket. She was crying, and so smelled of mucus as well as the spicy beef and mixed-vegetable dish she'd been eating. A chunky man in a shiny turquoise silk shirt lumbered a pace behind her. "You're acting stupid," he said.

"Get away!" she said, pausing to yank at a ring. It wouldn't slip over her knuckle. "You said you don't want to be with me, so leave me alone!" She scurried on, off the curb and across the asphalt. Sartak trembled, forcing himself to stand still and let her move farther away from the brightest lights.

The man in the blue shirt kept pursuing her. "I *didn't* say that," he said. "I said I thought we ought to see other people, too. There's a difference."

"Not to me!" she said.

"Where do you think you're going?" he asked. "*I* drove. Why don't you come back inside—"

Sartak decided they'd come close enough, or perhaps he simply couldn't bear to wait a second longer. Fighting the impulse to run, he sauntered toward them. "Excuse me," he said.

The man scowled at him. "Can't you see we're in the middle of something?"

"I'm sorry," Sartak said. "But this is an emergency." Now the couple was only a few yards away. Despite his eagerness, he took a final look around. As far as he could tell, no one was watching, so, drawing on his inhuman speed, he charged.

The man slowly recoiled, his foot drifting over the blacktop with an almost stately grace. His chin began to droop, while his hands floated upward. To Sartak,

it seemed to take a long time for the woman to realize anything was wrong. Finally she began to turn.

But by that time the Cainite was on top of them.
He punched the man in the jaw. Felt the bone shatter. Grabbed the woman's neck as her companion
began to fall. Threw her on the ground between two
parked cars and squeezed her carotid arteries until
she passed out.

He dragged the unconscious man between the
cars, too. It was the last bit of caution he could
muster. At some point during the attack, his fangs
had dropped. He plunged them into the male kine's
throat and guzzled.

For a while, he knew nothing but the rich, alcohol-
laced taste of the vitæ, and the delicious tingle as it
suffused his body. But gradually, as the Hunger
began to relax its grip, he heard the kine's heart fal-
tering.

He didn't really care. But if he killed the man need-
lessly, with another helpless vessel lying conveniently
at hand, the Beast would score a victory over the
Man. He forced himself to stop drinking and lick the
kine's neck. The fang wounds closed and disappeared. When he'd cleaned off every trace of blood,
he turned his attention to the woman.

After several swallows of her vitæ, the Hunger vanished, or nearly so. A sort of vestigial ache remained
in his belly, and a slight rawness lingered in his
throat. He'd just have to put up with them until he
found the fare his system actually craved.

He retracted his fangs and wiped his mouth. As
usual, his hand came away bloodless. Even in frenzy,
he generally managed to feed without smearing vitæ
all over his face.

He stood up and looked around. No one seemed

to be paying any attention to him. He ambled back to Zane's car and drove away.

A block farther south, he spotted a Circle K convenience store with a pair of pay phones hanging on the brick facade. He parked in front of them, then got change from the clerk inside.

It had been eleven years, but the number came back to him instantly. He'd noticed that, with centuries of experience crammed into their heads, Cainite elders either became forgetful or developed razor-sharp memories. He'd done the latter.

The phone at the other end of the line rang twice. Then a woman said, "Hello." It was Julia's voice. She sounded older. The realization made him vaguely uncomfortable.

"Hello," he said.

She gasped. Evidently she recognized his voice, too. "My God," she said. "I'd given up hope. I was afraid you were dead. Why didn't you call before?"

"There was no reason to."

She sighed. "I thought that after all we went through together . . . well, I didn't really think it, but it was nice to imagine. Where are you? How are you?"

"I'm in Tampa. And I'm the same, I suppose. How are you?"

"I'm good. I own a computer store. Randy's fine, too." Randy was her son. On a whim, Sartak had helped the two of them escape from a murderous religious cult her husband had dragged them into. The fanatics had turned out to be vigilant and heavily armed, and despite his Cainite powers, they'd nearly killed him. "He's a junior now, and he wants to play baseball. Professionally. And he's good. People are already scouting him." Her voice grew softer. "He still remembers you, too."

Sartak grimaced. The exhilaration of feeding had ebbed away, leaving a kind of heaviness behind. "That's too bad. He'd be safer if he didn't. I need the things I left with you. Can you ship them to the post office at the Tampa airport?" It was the one branch open at night.

"I can bring them myself," Julia said. "If you're in trouble, if you need help—"

"It's Randy who needs you. Just send the parcels, and stay safe." He hung up.

As he climbed back into the Mustang, he felt ancient. Or perhaps it was the world that felt old, withered and used up, as if he'd sucked it dry.

He tried to shake off the mood. Surely there was no need to fall prey to melancholy tonight, not with an old, reliable remedy at hand. He pulled back onto the highway and sped south.

16

The cell door closed. The petite vampire smiled at Zane. "Well, well," she said. "Anything I want."

Zane's bladder throbbed, and for an instant he was afraid he was going to wet his pants. He clenched his fists, but he was sure the gesture was futile. How could he defend himself when he had to do whatever she commanded?

The nurse's fangs lengthened, indenting her lower lip. Then she cocked her head, as if listening to something Zane couldn't hear. Her teeth retracted, leaving two tiny holes in her layer of bright red lipstick. "I'm sorry," she said. "I've got to go, but I'll be back soon. Stay." She turned and left the room. The lock clicked.

Panting, Zane slumped down on the blood-spattered floor. Thank God she was gone.

But he soon discovered that being left alone was a kind of torment, too. The horrors and atrocities of the past few days replayed themselves in his mind. He saw Rose's mangled body, and Meg's. Nightsticks and pit bull teeth flashed at him. The bearded vampire sank his fangs into Ben's hand, again and again.

And unpleasant as the memories were, his dread of what was to come was even worse. He almost wished the blond vampire would come back and attack him, just to get it over with.

Then he scowled at himself. He was thinking like a coward. A loser. Maybe there *wasn't* anything he could do to help himself, but he shouldn't assume that. He owed it to Rose, Ben, and even Sartak to try to find a way out of this hellhole. He crossed the room to inspect the door.

He pushed it, then rammed his shoulder against it. It felt as solid as stone. An impulse prompted him to stoop and look at the keyhole, even though he didn't know how to pick locks, and didn't have a tool to pick this one with anyway. As he'd expected, he didn't notice anything helpful.

Well, if he couldn't break out, he'd use this time to sort out what he'd observed. His cuts itching and his bruises aching, the air cold on his bare chest and shoulders, he sat back down to think.

He couldn't make much out of anything Blake had said or done. But he found he could figure out the vampires' mind control, not the underlying principle, but the mechanics. To exert it, they'd stared their victims in the eyes. The effect had worn off quickly. And they'd needed to speak aloud to make their wishes known. Maybe, if he made the right moves at the right moment, he could keep them from using it against him.

Of course, they might have a thousand other tricks to fall back on, including overwhelming him by sheer weight of numbers. Still, the insight that their gifts had limitations made him feel a little better, at least until he heard footsteps ticking down the corridor.

His mouth went dry, and he wanted to cower against the back wall. Instead, he made himself stand in the center of the cell. Intuition told him it was a bad idea to show that he was afraid.

The lock clicked, and the door swung open. The blond vampire walked in with a covered tray in her hands. "Supper," she said.

It was so unexpected that it blunted his fear. "Are you calling me that, or did you bring me some?"

She laughed. "Good one." She stooped and set the tray on the floor. "I grabbed a bite somewhere else. And it occurred to me that you're probably hungry."

His stomach ached, and he realized he hadn't eaten since yesterday. But he was reluctant to accept a gift from the enemy. He eyed the tray uncertainly.

"If I were you, I'd eat it," she said. "Sometimes the cuisine around here is a little peculiar, but this is just regular food."

He sat down, and, half-expecting to find something disgusting, peeled back the cloth to reveal a burger and fries. The scent of grilled beef made his mouth water. He picked up the sandwich and took a cautious bite. It tasted fine.

"There," said the nurse, "isn't that better? My name is Marilyn. And I know you're Zane."

"I don't understand you," he said. "Why feed me? Why pretend to be nice all of a sudden?"

"Why, Zane," she said reproachfully, "I *am* nice. I'm your *nurse*, your angel of mercy." She giggled. "Actually, I have different moods, and my current one is friendly. Besides, you won't be very useful or much fun either if we don't keep up your strength."

Zane wondered how much information he could get out of her while she was feeling chatty. He wolfed down a french fry, then said, "Where's my brother?"

"I don't know," Marilyn said. "But I've decided that if you behave yourself, you can have the run of the place, except for what's on the other side of the locked doors, of course. Maybe you'll find him." She smirked. "Maybe you'll even enjoy it."

He shook his head. Every time he thought he had a handle on his situation, it got stranger. "I don't have to stay in the cell?"

"Of course not. We aren't inhumane, just pragmatic. Yet prone to zany antics."

He jumped up with the half-eaten burger in his hand. "Then I want out now." Before she changed her mind.

"All right." Despite her tight white skirt, she flowed to her feet with a feline grace. He'd seen Sartak move like that. "I'll show you around."

The corridor outside the cell looked even gloomier by night. The weak yellow glow of the ceiling fixtures left inky pockets of shadow. For a moment, pale, broken rainbows danced around the lights. Zane blinked them away.

The air was cold in the halls, too. It smelled musty. Occasionally, shrieks, groans, and sobs echoed out of the dark. Marilyn led him past one room after another, and around turn after turn. Either the place was laid out like a maze, or she was trying to make him feel lost. Maybe both.

Forms swam out of the dimness. An alabaster Cupid in an alcove. Towering, dingy portraits. An inert grandfather clock, its pendulum shrouded in spiderwebs. Intricately carved molding above an open door. And beyond the threshold, a music room, where a violin lay atop a piano.

The decor was amazingly ornate, in a somber, decaying, antique sort of way. Zane realized that the building must have been some rich person's mansion before it became whatever it was now. Probably it had been the inspiration for the haunted house architecture in Rose's sketches, also. It seemed unfair that he'd made the discovery too late to do him any good.

Something twanged. Startled, he pivoted to look through the music room door. Nobody was inside. The violin still lay where he'd seen it last.

Marilyn chortled. "Nervous?"

"Did you hear that?" he asked.

She spread her hands. "Now that the moment is gone, who can say? Come on, one of the big, open areas, where people tend to gather, is just ahead. Maybe you'll feel more comfortable in the crowd, though I wouldn't count on it."

"How can this place exist?" he asked. "I mean, I've heard of it. There have been stories about it in the newspaper. They said it was a normal, modern hospital."

"Part of it is," Marilyn said. "The part reporters and visitors see. The part where a patient goes if people know he's here and care what happens to him. And then there's this part. The *fun* part. The part kindly Dr. Blake set up to make us Malkavians feel at home." She waved her hand. "Check it out."

The corridor opened into a cavernous chamber that might once have been a ballroom or sumptuous parlor. A few scattered candelabra provided the only illumination. For some reason, the flames burned green. Some of the figures in the sickly light stood, sat, or lay motionless. Zane couldn't tell if they were catatonic, unconscious, or dead. Others were being restrained. A white-haired woman in a straitjacket hung by her feet from the swinging, tinkling chandelier. Two little boys were tied to chairs, and a black man in grubby rags had his hands nailed to a tabletop. The rest—vampires and ghouls, Zane supposed—were engaged in bizarre and often cruel activity. A pale, naked woman tickled the black man with a feather duster. Another, equally bare under a hospital gown that gapped in the back, kept screaming into an immobile man's ear. A guy in a baseball cap slid down the banister of the stately staircase on the far wall. Arms outstretched, a teenage boy with straw-colored braids spun around and around.

Zane felt as though he was looking into hell. But he still didn't want to show any fear. He clamped down on a shudder. "What's the point of this?" he asked.

"I told you. To us Malkavians, it's cheery. Homey. We're the *mad* clan of Kindred, don't you know. Except, now that we're the ones in charge of the asylum, the hypo's in the other butt cheek, isn't it? We're the sane ones, by definition." She winked.

The screaming from the big room jabbed into Zane's ears. He winced and retreated a pace down the hall. "Then this is some kind of revenge?"

"I'd rather call it inspired comedy. Can't you find any pleasure in the irony? No, I suppose you can't." She sighed. "Actually, there is more to it than entertainment. This is an all-you-can-drink blood bar. As long as we keep it stocked with nuts and the homeless, every lick in Prince Roddy's domain can gulp gore to his wormy little heart's content. It also makes it easy for us kooks to find people to Embrace. We prefer crazy recruits, and here we have a primo selection. And if we take a liking to an inmate who isn't loco, it's easy enough to *drive* him out of his mind."

Zane's vision blurred. He blinked the haze away. "Were you this cruel when you were human?"

She grinned. "I resemble that remark. Seriously,

you shouldn't judge me by kine standards. It doesn't bother you to eat a lower animal, does it? You sure sucked down that burger fast enough. Well, I'm higher up the food chain than you, so nyah. And as far as driving people crazy goes, we're doing them a favor. Insanity is the only wisdom. Reason is just blinders. A pack of lies."

For a moment, Zane had the queasy feeling that she might be right. Common sense had never warned him about killers cloaked in silver light, or vampires. He tried to push the thought away. "Maybe you are acting according to your nature," he said. "But Blake isn't Kindred, he's a man. An *evil* man. There's no excuse for what he's doing. If I promised to leave your clan alone, would you help me kill him?"

She crowed. The sound spiked pain through his skull. "Wouldn't that be a hoot! But he's too useful. My sire would have a cow."

"Then tell me how to get out of here. Give me a *hint*. Just because it's the crazy thing to do."

She shook her head. "Sorry. Just because I'm insane, that doesn't mean I'm stupid."

"All right." He slumped, trying to look dejected, then threw a punch at her head.

He expected her to block or duck, but she didn't. Maybe she wasn't fast like Sartak. The punch cracked against her nose. She stumbled back. Zane wheeled and ran back down the hall.

As big as the place was, if he could only get away from her, he ought to be able to find a hiding place. He'd hole up until sunrise, then look for a way out while the vampires slept.

Behind him, Marilyn yelled, "Stop!" Her voice was a nasal honk. The call didn't affect him. He grinned and ran on.

Then the floor bounced beneath him, like he was running on a mattress or a sheet of rubber. He fell to one knee. As he tried to jump back up, the corridor spun, and he lost his balance. He fumbled at the wall, trying to haul himself to his feet. The wainscot yielded under his fingers like wax.

Marilyn loomed above him. Her nose was mashed flat, like Ben's, and blood trickled out of her left nostril. "I like your nerve," she said, "but did you really think it could be that easy?" Each word came in a burst of fragrance. Perfume. Hot metal. Ammonia.

"You drugged my food," mumbled Zane.

"Maybe so, maybe no," said Marilyn. She squeezed her nose like clay, molding it back into shape. "The important thing is that you're starting to fit in. And that now you can give me a sweet, refreshing hit of madness."

As her canine teeth lengthened, her body both split and became transparent, until he was surrounded by a ring of Marilyns, their forms clear and iridescent as soap bubbles. They bent over him. He tried to throw another punch, but his coordination was gone. All he could do was flop, like a fish in the bottom of a boat.

17

Blake found Carmelita where his latest informant, another of Judith's ghouls, had said the fugitive would be, Dumpster diving behind a McDonald's on Fowler Avenue. She was scraping the residue of a milk shake out of a cup with her forefinger. Since her grease-stained coveralls were far too large for her, she'd rolled up the sleeves and legs. The soles of her bare feet were black with grime, and her auburn hair was matted. She looked as if she hadn't washed since she escaped.

He wasn't surprised to find her in such miserable straits. Psychologically speaking, she was one of the runts of the litter. She didn't have a trace of Meg's grit, or any of Rose's talent and charm. It was a wonder she'd survived at all.

He perched on the roof above her, then began to clothe himself in flesh. Years ago, when he was still learning about his talents, he'd set up a video camera to record what his body did while he was absent.

Thus, he knew that, back at the Institute, a mask of squirming, silver-gray ectoplasm had formed on his face. Now tendrils of it were streaming into the air and disappearing, somehow reaching him here without traversing the intervening space.

He swiftly wove the substance into bone, muscle, fang, and claw. As the body took shape, his hearing grew sharper. Now he could make out the hiss of cars passing on the highway, the squawk and crackle of the speaker in front of the drive-through window, and the rustling as Carmelita rooted through the trash. His senses of taste, smell, and touch, hitherto absent, came on-line. He caught the reek of the Dumpster, and felt the rough shingles beneath his feet.

He was a little worried that Carmelita would notice him materializing, but she didn't. Evidently she didn't have any of Meg and Rose's sensitivity, either.

When his form was complete, solidified, he stretched, reveling in his strength. Then he hissed, like the colossal cat he vaguely resembled. He wanted her to know that death had come. He wanted to see her expression.

She looked up. Her face turned white beneath its coat of dirt. Her eyes widened. He pounced on her.

His weight plunged her head and shoulders under the surface of the garbage. She kicked the side of the bin, and the metal bonged. He tore at her chest, scattering shards of rib, and ripped her heart to rags.

Eagerly he yanked her head back into view, cracked open the skull, and dug out the brain. As he gobbled it down, it occurred to him that the prospect of eating half-submerged in refuse would have nauseated Blake the human being. But Blake the gargoyle didn't mind a bit. Since the two were one and the same, it was an interesting paradox.

Her essence flowed through him, and he sifted it for power. As he'd expected, there was only a trickle, but he could use every bit he could scavenge. It had always been exhausting, managing his mundane affairs all day and dealing with the Kindred all night, and in recent weeks the demands on him had grown phenomenally.

He decided not to waste energy by remaining in this form any longer than necessary. He allowed it to dissolve, then, a creature of pure mind, soared into the sky. Below him, Carmelita's tattered remains began to steam.

In a few seconds, Blake was back in his body. Weariness washed over him. He could feel that if he only left his eyes shut for a few more seconds, he'd drift into a natural sleep.

Since there was no time for that, he pried them open. As always, he looked immediately, reflexively, at the woman on the other bed.

How he hated her. But he could feel that there were only one or two more to catch. It shouldn't be long until he could get rid of her.

His mouth twisted. No, it *shouldn't* be, but perhaps the last fugitives had remained at large this long because they were good at hiding. If so, it might take *months* to flush them out. That was why the interview with Zane Tyler had disappointed him so, though he'd done his best not to show it. He'd hoped that the meddling idiot knew where the others were.

He wondered again if he ought to enlist *all* the Kindred in the hunt. Before he did, before he even *hinted* at a vulnerability that someone could use against him, he'd better make absolutely certain that his relationship with Prince Roderick was on as firm a footing as ever. So, even though he cringed at the thought of using his psychic abilities any more tonight, he went to the nightstand and removed an inlaid snuffbox from the drawer. Then he dialed Judith's number.

As always, a ghoul answered. She considered it beneath her dignity to pick up a phone for herself. When the servant put her on the line, Blake said, "Hello, love. Do you have time for a lesson tonight?"

18

The *Tötentanz* throbbed through the hall. To Roderick Dean, the cry of the piano seemed to rise and fall on the dark chorus of the orchestra like a ship floating on the swell of the sea. He leaned back in his seat and closed his eyes.

It felt grand to get away. To lay down his scepter and all the aggravation that went with it. His Ventrue didn't give him any trouble. They'd better not—most of them were his Progeny! But the rest of his subjects, the deranged Malkavians and hideous, secretive Nosferatu, were a constant trial. How pleasant it would be to reign over, oh, say, a population of art- and music-worshiping Toreadors instead.

But as Alexander had pointed out on more than one occasion, the perversities of his subjects made his own achievements all the more impressive. And no matter what else went wrong, at least he could count on hearing Liszt performed on a monthly basis. When one supported an orchestra as generously as he did the Tampa Symphony, they tended to play one's favorite composers.

The music stopped abruptly.

Dean's eyes flew open. He was *standing*, on one of the concrete walks *outside* the Performing Arts Center. Horned gargoyles leered down at him from the roofline. Ahead and to his right, the illuminated jets at the top of the elaborate fountain splashed and gurgled, while beyond them, the water cascaded down a series of marble steps. Below those lay the black expanse of the Hillsborough River. Two will-o'-the-wisps floated down the middle, the running lights of a small boat otherwise invisible in the dark.

Dean still had his cane. He glanced around. Naturally enough, now that the concert was well under way, no one was nearby, not even the valets who parked the cars. He twisted the ivory handle, carved in the shape of a stylized eagle, and pulled the slim sword out of its scabbard. Even in the darkness, the oiled blade gleamed. It was clean.

He sheathed it, then inspected his hands. They were clean as well. Last of all, hesitantly, he checked his mouth. It didn't *taste* like blood, he could feel that his fangs were in their sockets, and when he touched his lips, his fingers came away dry.

He felt a combination of dread and relief. It was always jarring to discover he'd had an episode. But at least this time, he'd come out of it without doing any harm. Obviously, the psychotherapy was doing him some good, senseless and humiliating as the process often seemed.

But how he wished he didn't need it! His predicament was utterly unfair. Other Kindred could resist the pull of madness by force of will. Summon forth the Man to fight the Beast. But not him. When insanity beckoned, he slipped into what Alexander called a fugue, a dreamlike state in which he didn't know what he was doing. His greatest fear was that someday a blackout would blur into wassail, the final frenzied descent into savagery, and he'd lose all Humanitas forever.

He grimaced at the turn his thoughts were taking. No, blast it, he would *not* go mad. He was growing stronger, not weaker. One day, with Alexander's help, he'd achieve Golconda, the ability to balance Hunger and reason effortlessly, which many Cainites sought, but which no one he knew had ever attained. Who would have thought one could solve the Riddle through psychiatry?

Dean realized that he felt composed enough to go back inside. No doubt, by now, he'd missed the end of the Liszt, but there was still the Mendelssohn. He straightened his tuxedo jacket, shot his cuffs—

And found himself crouching behind an evergreen on the other side of the building. Apparently it was now intermission. People milled around the terrace and the grass, calling out as they spotted friends, critiquing the performance, admiring the landscaping, smoking, and sipping wine and cocktails from plastic cups. Dean stared at two young women. One was short, with long brown hair worn loose, round glasses, jeans, and a fringed buckskin jacket with beadwork trim. Her companion was medium height, blond, and wore an off-the-shoulder midnight blue velvet gown. A string of sapphires glittered around her neck.

Dean was appalled to feel himself drawing on his charismatic powers. He'd fed earlier tonight, on one of Alexander's lunatics. He was free of the Hunger. It was utterly reckless to take prey on the edge of such a crowd. And he wouldn't have wanted to hunt in the vicinity of the symphony in any case. It was gauche, and a disservice to those he'd taken on as clients.

He tried to remain aware, in control, but his conscious mind plunged into oblivion again. The next thing he knew, the two women were pressing themselves against him. Fondling him. His hands unlocked the sword cane. Apparently the Beast wouldn't be content merely to drink. It wanted to kill or mutilate, just for the vicious joy of it.

Dean sensed that this moment was his last chance to reestablish control. Employing the technique that Alexander had taught him, he imagined his dark self, a shadow with blazing eyes, gleaming fangs, and hands gloved in blood, and silently chanted, *No, no, no, no, no!* With each negation, a door slammed or a porticullis dropped in front of the creature, sealing it away in the depths of his mind.

A numbness tingled out of his flesh. He felt centered in his own body again. He relocked the cane.

Murmuring endearments, the two kine continued to paw him. Though he knew it wasn't their fault, their attentions sickened him. He felt an urge to use his charisma to strike terror into their hearts.

But that sort of cruelty would itself partake of the Beast. And it wasn't likely to help him slip away without causing a commotion. He called on his hypnotic ability instead.

The women blinked, then jerked back from him. They'd forgotten ever seeing him prior to that instant. He gave them a nod, then walked away.

He realized that he didn't care about the concert anymore. He wanted to be alone. He walked down the riverbank until he reached the base of the Cass Street Bridge. Graffiti—boasts, jokes, and salutations left by fraternities and sculling teams from the University of Tampa—covered the grimy brick pylons. He sat on the grass and listened to the whisper of the current. After a while, he removed his favorite of all his many snuffboxes, the engraved silver one his wife had given him on their first anniversary, from his pocket, and put a pinch of the contents between his cheek and gum. The familiar gesture soothed him.

19

Sartak parked the Mustang about a block from the doorway where he'd attacked the two men. The neighborhood looked as run-down and uninviting as before. Beer cans and candy wrappers littered the sidewalks. Strips of yellow police tape sealed the entrance to a carryout, and a roach crawled over a chicken hanging by its feet in a butcher's window. Somewhere, mariachi music played, but something was wrong with the stereo. The tempo dragged till the bright tune sounded as mournful as a dirge.

The Cainite considered the scene. Dismal, but not dismal enough. He suspected that he was only on the fringe of his quarry's territory. The interior would be even more desolate and deserted. He sharpened his senses. Suddenly colors glowed in the darkness, and the stinks of urine and garbage stung his nose. Underlying those scents was a hint of seawater and ozone. Out in the Gulf of Mexico, a storm was driving toward land. He headed down the sidewalk, then turned onto a narrower street with even fewer lights.

As he'd hoped, it led him into a part of town where nearly every building looked vacant and ruinous. Gas stations with no pumps in front of them. A grocery with a shattered wall, as if someone had begun demolishing it with a wrecking ball, then given up. A used-car lot, where all the vehicles had flat tires, and none had been manufactured within the last twenty years. Houses with flaking paint and boarded windows. Faded, tattered EVICTION, FOR RENT, and CONDEMNED notices stirred in the fitful breeze.

Behind Sartak, claws scraped on pavement. He turned. A large, shaggy mongrel was watching him from the shadow of an overturned school bus.

Fortunately, Sartak was downwind. Inhaling deeply, he caught the pungent scent of unwashed dog.

Though the animal was no more than it appeared to be, it might still have something to do with the business at hand. The people he was looking for had a special affinity with beasts.

The dog wheeled and ran away, as if it meant to warn someone of his presence. Hoping that it did, he slowed his pace and continued down the same street.

For another couple of minutes, nothing else happened. Perhaps he'd simply frightened the dog, or it had remembered some urgent but mundane bit of canine business. Then he spotted gleaming eyes, peering from behind an overturned trash can thirty feet ahead.

Sartak was upwind this time. He'd have to get close to determine what he was looking at. He strolled on. Soon he saw that the creature was another canine, gaunt as a greyhound, with upright triangular ears and mangy brown fur.

But that didn't help him. He ambled closer still. The animal eyed him intently, not moving a muscle.

When it was six feet away, he finally caught a whiff

of it. He smiled. It might look like a dog, but it smelled like a wolf.

As he walked past it, he imagined it swelling into a man-beast that walked on two legs but had fur, claws, and a muzzle full of fangs. He'd fought such creatures many times in his long existence, generally when he was on the road. Most werewolf tribes hated cities as much as most Kindred clans disliked open country.

Straining his ears, he heard the Lupine rise and skulk after him, still moving on four feet. Perhaps it was merely stalking him, but he suspected that it was cutting his line of retreat. That its pack mates were massing ahead.

Soon more eyes shone from the shadows on either side. Hearts thumped and breath rasped. Sometimes Sartak smelled a scent that was human, or nearly so, and sometimes the musky odor of wolf. The street bent, then ended in a cul-de-sac ringed by collapsing houses. Vague figures lurked between them.

"Hello, Bone Gnawers," said Sartak. "Why are you hiding? Are you afraid of me? I'm alone."

"Buck was right!" a high voice cried. Turning, Sartak saw a thin, bald woman with crooked shoulders leaning out a second-story window. "He *does* have Wyrm taint on him!"

Sartak didn't know much about Lupine mythology. But over the course of many encounters, he had gleaned that the Wyrm was their version of Satan, and that they believed that Cainites were its minions. It was one reason among many that they hated his people so. "Yes. I'm a vampire," he said.

"What do you want here?" the hairless woman asked.

"To play tag," Sartak said. "You flea-ridden, garbage-eating curs are it." He stooped, snatched a red-and-white Coca-Cola can off the ground, and threw it. It hit the woman on the forehead.

A collective snarl knifed through the air. Those
Lupines already in man-beast form charged. The others moved into the light more slowly, changing as
they advanced. Limbs and torsos lengthened. Worn,
filthy garments tore as the frames inside them
swelled. Fur erupted from grimy skin. Nails turned to
heavy claws.

Sartak turned, memorizing the appearances of particular individuals. Then, when the first werewolf was
mere inches out of striking range, he drew on his
inhuman strength and leaped.

In man-beast form, the average Lupine was half
again as tall as a human being. Though Bone Gnawers,
the despised scavengers at the bottom of the werewolf
social order, were usually smaller than average, many
of the monsters facing him were seven to eight feet
tall. They could easily have batted him out of the air.
But his maneuver caught them by surprise. He soared
over the heads of the nearest attackers and hit the
ground running.

Claws flashed at his head. He ducked, and the
blow only ruffled his hair. He dived between the legs
of a Lupine with a scarred chest, scrambled up, and
dashed on into the gap between two houses.

Most of the enemy had surged forward, but there
was still one man-beast blocking the way. Sartak
lunged, avoided the Lupine's strike, and kicked it in
the knee. Bone cracked. When the werewolf staggered, he grabbed its wrist and whirled it into the
path of the beasts charging up behind him.

He sprinted on. His superhuman speed was taxing
to use for more than a few seconds at a time. He
could virtually feel it burning up the stolen vitæ in his
system. But he didn't dare slow down.

He vaulted a rickety picket fence, nearly falling

when the rotten wood crumbled under his hand. He dashed down a street, then up an alley, fearful every instant that he'd run into another dead end.

But he didn't. And gradually, one hard-earned stride at a time, the Lupines fell farther and farther behind him. At last he turned down another street and realized that, for the next few seconds, the pursuers wouldn't be able to see him anymore.

Choosing the side of the street that was downwind of the pavement, he ran into an overgrown yard. The long grass swished against his calves. When he reached the vacant house at the back of the lot, he sprang onto the roof overhanging the porch, then jumped to a second-story dormer. Three bullet holes pocked the dirty windowpane. He flattened himself against the darker side of the structure, the one that was out of the moonlight.

An instant later, the Lupines pounded around the turn. They ran a few yards past his hiding place, then faltered. Spreading out, they began to look around. Some sniffed noisily, but it looked as if they'd lost the scent. A naked, hairless female with uneven shoulders pressed her clawed fingertips to her temples.

Sartak surmised that she was scanning for him psychically. He could only hope the attempt would fail. Perhaps he'd have a chance if she neglected to direct her attention upward. Remaining absolutely still, he closed his eyes and made his mind a blank.

After what seemed a long time, a rough voice said, "Now what?"

Sartak cracked his eyes open. The furless Lupine and a male who stank of cheap muscatel had shifted partway back to human form. Perhaps they'd needed to do so to talk. Now they looked like anthropoid, beetle-browed ancestors of modern man.

"We can't give up yet," growled the hairless Lupine. "He's still near. I can feel him. I just can't zero in. Let's split up and search."

"Sounds good to me," said the man. "We don't get many chances for payback." Some of the other Lupines snarled, evidently in agreement.

The company divided and stalked away. Sartak stayed where he was. Occasionally, a howl rang through the night.

Finally, when he was reasonably certain that all the hunters were truly gone, he jumped back to the ground. Senses straining, keenly aware that some of the enemy were at least as stealthy and perceptive as he was, he began to prowl from one shadow or piece of cover to the next.

The breeze whispered, and brought him the scent of wolf. He ducked behind a telephone pole. A moment later, a pair of Lupines loped out of the dark. Neither was one of the ones he wanted. He let them pass, then slunk on.

In another minute, he came to a chainlink fence. The boarded-up concrete block building on the other side had been a tire store. In fact, a stack of tires still sat on the tarmac.

On impulse, he decided to cut across the lot. He scrambled over the fence, effortlessly avoiding the strands of barbwire running along the top, then crept across the blacktop, staying in the shadow of the building.

As he drew even with one of the sealed windows, he heard a faint movement on the other side. He began to step away.

The window exploded in a hail of glass and splinters. A huge gray hand shot out at him. He wrenched himself aside, enough to keep from being grabbed, but the hand still clipped him and knocked him staggering. As he struggled to regain his balance, his attacker swarmed out at him.

It almost didn't fit through the window frame. Perhaps the typical Bone Gnawer was scrawny, but this one was an exception. It looked like it ought to belong to one of the berserker tribes, the Red Talons or the Get of Fenris. Sartak knew that he *was* a small man, particularly in this era, when the kine had shot up like weeds, but it rarely bothered him. A raging werewolf champion like this one, towering over him with eyes blazing and foam flying from its jaws, was one of the few things that could make him *feel* small.

But as he got his feet back under him, he realized that he was going to have to fight it anyway. It was too close, too long-legged, and too manifestly quick. If he turned tail, it was likely to strike him down from behind, his supernatural speed notwithstanding. And just to make matters even more interesting, he needed to defeat it without killing it. He'd wanted to provoke the Lupines, but they mustn't be *too* angry in the end.

The Lupine stooped and grabbed a scrap of wood, intended, no doubt, to stake him through the heart. It began to circle. Glass crunched under its feet.

Sartak extruded his fangs. He had no intention of biting the Lupine, but he wanted the creature to worry about the possibility.

The man-beast lunged. Its empty hand streaked at Sartak's face. He could tell that, in a sense, the strike was a feint, intended to set him up for the thrust of the stake, but it still would have torn out his eyes if he hadn't blocked it. He sidestepped, avoiding the second attack, then slammed his elbow into the Lupine's kidney as it blundered by. The creature grunted.

Sartak darted after it, staying so close that it would

have trouble seeing him, let alone attacking, using its own superior height and reach against it. He kicked at its knees and ankles. Snapped punches into its belly and spine. He could tell that he was hurting it, but try as he might, he couldn't knock it down.

Suddenly, the stake drove down like a dagger. He saw it coming an instant too late to twist aside. It plunged through his shoulder, shattering bone, and stabbed into his chest cavity.

Pain ripped through him. He crumpled. But before he could fall, the Lupine stepped away to strike him a backhand blow. Sartak's cheekbone shattered. He flew through the air and slammed down beside the building.

The werewolf raised its claws. Its legs flexed to spring. For a moment, Sartak watched it indifferently.

Then a flash of fear cut through his daze. The beast was about to kill him! He had to act!

He tried to shift his hand. It moved. Whatever damage the stake had done, it hadn't pierced his heart. The Lupine dived at him.

Sartak lurched up and threw himself forward, slamming his unbroken shoulder into the werewolf's shins. The impact brought another burst of agony. But the Bone Gnawer pitched over him. Its neck smashed down on the blades of wood and broken glass still clinging to the bottom of the window frame.

Sartak scrambled up, clung to the fur on the man-beast's back, and hammered on its shoulders, pounding the sharp debris deeper into its flesh. It thrashed, and blood sprayed.

After a few seconds, when the pain of violent exertion grew intolerable, he stepped back. He knew that he hadn't killed the Lupine. But it couldn't free and heal itself in time to detain him any longer.

Gritting his teeth, he pulled the bloody stake out of his body, then listened. The night was absolutely silent. He couldn't even hear the Lupine's feet drumming spastically on the pavement. He realized that he couldn't smell anything, either.

He struggled to heal his concussion. Honed his senses once more. The pungent tang of vitæ suffused the air. Howling rent the night in all directions.

The rest of the pack must have heard the fight, and now they were closing in. He didn't dare let them surround him a second time, especially now that he was wounded. He hurdled the fence and ran. Every stride brought a fresh jolt of pain.

A Lupine with mottled gray-and-black fur glided out of the shadows ahead. It was wearing a striped, coarse wool poncho, the kind tourists buy in Central America, and it had a pistol in its hand. The size of its fingers made the weapon look like a toy.

Sartak was still a little addled. He almost pivoted to run in another direction before he remembered that this was one of the Lupines he'd singled out before. Hulking and bestial as it looked now, in human form it was a skinny waif of a girl, fourteen or fifteen at the oldest. She'd probably Changed for the first time no more than a year ago.

He charged her, zigzagging in what he hoped was an unpredictable manner. She fired, but mercifully, none of the shots came anywhere near him.

The pistol stopped barking. She pulled the trigger three more times, then lifted the gun like a club.

Sartak sprang into the air and drove the edge of his foot into her face. She reeled and fell. He stamped on her head, and felt bone break. She sprawled motionless.

He grabbed her under the arms and dragged her

across the ground. His shoulder throbbed. But he wanted his back against a wall, so no one could sneak up behind him. And by the time more Lupines appeared, he was sitting on the stoop of the black, burnt-out shell of a post office, more or less holding his captive in his lap. It was bliss to be off his feet. He wondered wryly if he could muster the wherewithal to jump back up even if his gambit didn't work.

Excluding the girl, the nearest Bone Gnawers were about forty feet away. Sartak started to call to them, then realized his fangs were still sticking out. With a grimace, he retracted them. "Don't come any closer! You can't reach me fast enough to keep me from biting out her throat." And she wouldn't recover from that, any more than he could shrug off damage from a Lupine's teeth and claws.

Lost in frenzy, three man-beasts roared and ran forward anyway. But some of their pack mates grabbed them and hauled them back. Two of the enraged Lupines thrashed, but essentially suffered themselves to be restrained. The other sank his fangs into a captor's ear. A melee erupted. Five seconds later, the mad wolf lay stunned and bloody on the ground.

Sartak smiled. In his experience, Lupines were hard on their offspring. Evidently they thought they had to be, to prepare them to survive in a violent and unforgiving world. But they prized them, too, particularly now that, by all accounts, their race was dying out. Thus he'd gambled that if he could take a cub hostage, without causing unpardonable harm in the process, the Bone Gnawers would negotiate to get the youngster back. Supposedly, they were more reasonable and less bloodthirsty than other tribes. More concerned about getting by and less obsessed with lost causes and ancient hatreds.

The hairless Lupine stepped out of the crowd. She'd returned to human form. She was still nude, but seemingly no more concerned about it than she'd been as a beast. "You've had your game," she said. "Now let Lollipop go. We'll give you twenty minutes to get off our turf." Other Lupines snarled, apparently at the prospect of his imminent escape.

"Actually, I wanted more than a game," Sartak said. "I want information. If you'll give it to me, you can have her back." The hostage twitched. He surreptitiously ran his fingers over her skull to determine how quickly she was healing. It could be awkward if she came to prematurely.

"Information about what?" the hairless woman asked.

"The lay of the land," Sartak said. "Who's who among the dark peoples of Tampa. That kind of thing. I'm a stranger here, you see."

The Lupine who smelled of muscatel stepped forward and turned into a stooped, middle-aged man with an unkempt salt-and-pepper beard. "Don't make a deal with corruption!" he cried. "Kill his ass!" A number of the other Lupines bayed and growled.

"I wish we could," said the bald woman. "But the Wyrm will still be here tomorrow, whether we off this one cadaver or not. Lollipop won't be, if we throw her away." She looked back at Sartak. "We won't tell you anything that would endanger any of our people."

"I understand," said Sartak. "Is it a bargain?"

"Yes."

"Then take her." He rose, still cradling Lollipop in his arms, and moved forward. The giant Lupine he'd fought by the tire store, the fur on his chest soaked with blood and the cuts in his neck half healed, loomed out of the shadows. Sartak laid the captive in its enormous hands.

"I've got to admit, you've got balls," the bald woman said. "I expected you to hold on to her until this was over."

Forgetting his shoulder, Sartak shrugged, and regretted it. "I've generally found that Lupines keep their word." He took out Zane's wallet and removed the cash. Fortunately, the kine had been carrying quite a bit. "Shall we make this a dinner meeting?"

20

The Bone Gnawers had made a camp of sorts in a weedy vacant lot. Wavering yellow firelight illuminated pinched, grimy human and near-human faces, few of them older than middle-aged. A number of children and wolf cubs, about half of each deformed in some way, ran around or wrestled. The smells of wood, tobacco, and marijuana smoke, cheap wine and beer, roasting hot dogs, musky wolf, and sweaty kine suffused the air.

Spider, the hairless woman, Sartak, and Peewee, the giant Lupine, now in kine form also, hunkered down beside a heap of wastepaper and scrap wood. Spider stared at it, and it burst into crackling flame.

"I'm glad you didn't try that on me," Sartak said.

Spider smiled. "I almost did. But I couldn't have burnt you to ashes in a split second. You might still've killed Lollipop. Or, I could've accidentally torched her, too. My aim's a little shaky." She shook her head. "I can't believe you put us all through this,

just to find out a little basic info about our fair city."
She waved a callused, black-nailed hand in a gesture
that encompassed the blight on every side.

"If I'd simply asked politely, with no leverage,
would you have helped me?"

Spider snorted. "A slimy leech? Hell, no. We would
have ripped you apart. But if you'd just poked around
town, you would've eventually run into some of your
own kind."

"That 'eventually' is the problem," Sartak said. His
shoulder twinged, but not badly. It had nearly finished repairing itself. The trade-off was that the
Hunger was cramping his belly again. "A . . . comrade
of mine has been taken prisoner. Someone with
arcane talents is responsible, but I don't know who.
Since I'd like to rescue my ally quickly, I risked calling
on the only people I knew of who might be able to
furnish useful information."

Peewee impaled a wiener on a green stick, then
held it over the fire. "How did you know we were
here?" he asked.

"I saw your tribal insignia painted on a wall,"
Sartak said. "You shouldn't mark your territory if you
want to keep a low profile. Other Lupines aren't the
only ones who recognize your marks. Tell me, do
either of you know of a person or creature that shines
and can vanish in an instant? That's the entity I'm
hunting."

Spider smiled crookedly. Sartak noticed that one
of her incisors was chipped. "Did it ever occur to you
that maybe that's one of us? Maybe you just let us
know that we really do need to get rid of you."

Sartak grinned back. "That would make life interesting, wouldn't it, considering that we have a truce.
I wonder if we'd all continue to honor it. But my

instincts tell me that none of your earthy tribe is involved in anything this odd. You see, my enemy is hunting and killing a group of redheaded women who look almost exactly alike. When one of them dies, her body dissolves into vapor."

Peewee and Spider stared at him. "That *is* weird," said the hairless woman at last. "What's it all about?"

Sartak said, "I wish I knew. The ladies in question keep succumbing to the foe's attentions before anyone can get a straight answer out of them."

"Hm." She frowned thoughtfully, and her forehead creased. On a face without eyebrows, the expression looked peculiar. "No, I don't know of anybody who glows *and* turns invisible or whatever. Of course, different people know different tricks, and sometimes they keep them a secret. To have an ace in the hole if things get rough."

"Ah, well," said Sartak. "I didn't think you could hand me all the answers on a platter, but it was worth asking. What's the most powerful group in the city?"

Peewee scowled. "You damn leeches," he said.

"Specifically, the ones led by someone called Prince Roderick," Spider said. "I don't know his last name."

"And I don't suppose you know where he lives, either," Sartak said. "I assume that if he calls himself a Prince, he and his subjects belong to the Camarilla."

"I don't know what that means," Spider said.

"It's a Cainite Sect," Sartak said. "A philosophy or political faction, depending on how you look at it. The Camarilla seeks to preserve the Masquerade— keep our existence a secret from mortals—by cleaving to the ancient Traditions at any cost. As opposed to the Sabbat, which wants to rule the world as openly and brutally as Hitler did, or at least that's how it appears to me."

Peewee took his sizzling hot dog out of the fire and gobbled it off the stick. Reminded of how it had felt to burn his mouth on hot food, Sartak winced, but the big man didn't seem to mind the heat. "Which are you?" he asked through a mouthful of sausage.

"Neither," said Sartak. "I go my own way. I assume that Prince Roderick has influence with the government, and the police."

Spider shrugged. "How the hell would we know? But yeah, it looks that way from down here."

Four campfires away, a drunken woman got on her hands and knees, turned into a creature resembling a huge jackal, and began to howl.

"The police seem to be sweeping the homeless off the streets," Sartak said. "Do you know what they ultimately do with them? They can't warehouse them in the jail indefinitely."

"No," Spider said. "All we know is that if a bum gets rousted, he doesn't come back."

Sartak cocked his head. "I've been living the life of a hobo myself for quite a while. One or two of the bums I met had heard rumors about the Bone Gnawers. They said that you sometimes look after humans who are down-and-out. Have you tried to find out what's going on?"

Peewee glared. The hairs on his arms began to thicken and multiply. "What are you saying?" he asked.

"Nothing," Sartak said. "I'm asking."

"Do you think that we were too scared to do anything?" the Lupine asked. His nails lengthened. "Maybe *you* should take a shot, if you think that you can do better."

"Unfortunately, I doubt that I could," Sartak said. "I could get myself arrested to investigate. But if nothing interesting happened before morning, my little problem with daylight would rear its ugly head."

Spider laid her hand on Peewee's arm. "It's all right," she said. "He wasn't accusing us." He nodded jerkily, and the tension went out of his body. She looked back at Sartak. "We'd *like* to help. But these days, we need to keep a low profile. Put our own safety ahead of the homids'."

Sartak said, "I understand."

"No, you don't," she replied sharply. "Not if you think Bone Gnawers are gutless or weak. That's always been a damn lie!"

"I never thought that," Sartak said.

"Good," said Spider, "Look, two years ago, Tampa Bay was different. There was a what-do-you-call-it, a balance of power, between you leeches and us Garou. You were strong in town, but there was a pack of Silver Fangs just as strong outside the city limits. And we Bone Gnawers were pretty tough ourselves. We went where we wanted and we did what we pleased." Her mouth quirked. "Well, more or less. Anyway, it all started to fall apart when Trevor Stuart came to see us.

"You can bet that had never happened before. Maybe you know, the Silver Fangs are the Garou answer to the Rockefellers and the Kennedys. They don't ordinarily hang out with the likes of us. And Trevor was their best Theurge—their seer, someone who walks with the spirits.

"He told us that an Incarna, a messenger sent by the Falcon, the Fangs' Totem, had come to him and told him to start a holy war. Basically, all of us local wolves were supposed to kill all the cadavers. It would be a big victory over the Wyrm.

"Well, at first some of us Gnawers were skeptical. We were getting along okay, so why stick our necks out? But on the other hand, we do hate you guys, and we do honor the spirits. What's more, we knew that Stuart was the real deal, a Theurge with powers that none of our guys could match. And he was one hell of a persuasive speechmaker—the bastard may have used a gift on us. Toward the end of the confab, the Incarna itself appeared for a second. It was a huge bird made of light, the most beautiful thing I've ever seen.

"Anyway, bottom line, we all went off to fight. Supposedly, Stuart was using a plan the Incarna gave him. The leeches were having a meeting or a party in a ritzy beachfront hotel outside St. Pete. We were going to hit them by surprise.

"But when we got there, Prince Roderick, his people, and their flunkies were waiting for us. With grenades. Mines. Machine guns spraying silver bullets. We were the ones who got massacred.

"The Silver Fangs stood and fought till the last one dropped. Some of us Gnawers ran and got away."

Spider's mouth twisted. "And now we hide here, in the one part of town where we feel halfway safe, and wonder what went wrong. Did the Incarna mean for us to get ambushed? Was it some kind of punishment, or test? Did we fail Gaia by running away? If everybody had stuck it out to the bitter end, would we have won somehow despite the odds? Even our own special spirits can't tell us, maybe because all our best Theurges died in the battle."

Sartak felt a flicker of emotion, but it died before he could even identify it, let alone express it. "My condolences," he said with hollow courtesy. "You mentioned that there are other vampires. Ones that don't pay fealty to Roderick."

"Yeah," said Peewee heavily. He guzzled beer.

Foam ran down his square, stubbled jaw, and he belched a malodorous belch. "Near as we can make out. We don't have 'em over for tea. But supposedly there are some young bloodsuckers who won't take orders from the old ones."

Sartak nodded. "We Kindred call them anarchs."

"They'd better watch their step," Spider said. "If Roderick broke the Garou, he can certainly wipe them out if they get on his nerves. Not that I give a rat's ass. Anyway, I can tell you where to find *them*. They hang around in Ybor City. Figures, doesn't it, since it's the death-metal capital of the world."

Sartak raised an eyebrow. "Death metal?" He imagined a modern Krupp plant with molten steel glowing, machines roaring, and smokestacks fuming, cranking out cannons and shells.

"Rock music about death, doom, and the devil," Spider explained. "About critters like you and us."

Sartak smiled. "That does make sense. Do you have mages and faeries around here?"

"I've never run into them," said Spider, "so there can't be many."

"And are the true dead reasonably quiet?"

"As far as I know."

Sartak closed his eyes for a moment, thinking, then said, "I don't know what else to ask you. Thank you for your help and your hospitality." He rose.

Spider and Peewee stood up, also. "*Did* we help you?" the hairless woman asked.

"At the very least, you've reinforced my conviction that I need to talk to my fellow Cainites. And you've told me where to find some of them. Good-night."

"Don't come back," Peewee said. "The cease-fire ends as soon as you leave the neighborhood."

Sartak smiled. "I didn't think you'd decided to

adopt me into the pack." He turned and sauntered away.

Concerned that some of the Bone Gnawers might not be able to bear the thought of his safe departure, he sharpened his senses. He didn't smell or hear anything padding after him. After a block, he began to relax.

He wished he could press on with the search tonight. But it was already late. He needed to feed, steal money and fresh clothing, and find a new refuge before sunrise. Whatever Zane was enduring, he'd just have to hold out for at least another day.

As Sartak reached the Mustang, lightning flared in the west. A drop of rain plopped on his hand.

21

Two shadows dragged Rose down a dark corridor. As her heels bumped over the floor, pieces fell off her naked body. A toe. An ear. A nipple. Her left forearm, and her right foot. She screamed for help.

Zane chased after her, but sets of fangs, some ivory and some clear as glass, kept shooting out of the walls and nipping at him. And he had to gather up the fallen fragments, so he could reattach them. It all served to slow him down.

Sartak appeared behind him and gave him a shove. Zane staggered into a pair of the disembodied jaws, which ripped a chunk of flesh out of his thigh. He dropped the body parts. As he knelt to pick them up again, they began to steam and melt—to shoot out of his hands like wet soap.

Sartak kicked him. "Get up, soldier!" he said. Zane realized that, somehow, the vampire was also his drill instructor from basic training. "Move it! They're getting away!"

"Stop it!" Zane said. "This isn't helping!"

Sartak grinned. "It isn't supposed to. Did you really think I was on your side? I'm one of them." He bared his own fangs and grabbed Zane by the shoulders.

Zane thrashed, trying to break free. Then his eyes popped open. He was lying on the floor of a hallway not much different from the one in the dream, and a small, pretty blonde in a nurse's dress was shaking him. "Rise and shine," she said.

The terror of the nightmare faded, leaving a sort of indifferent confusion in its place. He blinked. "Where am I?" he asked.

"Still at the Institute," said the blonde. "I'm Marilyn. Remember me?"

In a way, he did, but the details wouldn't come clear. Another female voice said, "Why did the Brujah elder drink the British welder?" Zane turned his head. The voice belonged to a tall, dark woman with a heart-shaped face. She wore a conservative gray suit, like a lawyer or banker, but a jeweled ring hung in her left nostril.

Marilyn sighed. "I don't know, Ellen, why?"

"Because he smelled her!" Ellen paused, as if waiting for them to laugh. "Because he *smelled* her. Don't you get it?"

"Sure," Marilyn said. "That's a real knee slapper." She winked at Zane. "Can you get up?"

He took stock of himself. Now that she mentioned it, he felt weak, sore, thirsty, and sick to his stomach, though the discomforts were somehow dull and far away. It was like he'd been anesthetized. "I think so." He started to stand, and she took his hand to help him.

He felt as if he were floating upward like a balloon. As he rose, memories tumbled through his head.

Suddenly he remembered what kind of place this was. What kind of creature Marilyn was. And she'd bitten him!

A part of him was terrified, but another part didn't care about any of it. As he wrenched himself away from her, he almost felt like an actor playing a role.

"Hey, hey," Marilyn said. "Be nice. You might as well. What's done is done."

"What do you mean?" he asked. He touched his neck. The fang holes were gone. He guessed that she'd licked them closed, the same way Sartak could.

"She means she turned you," said Ellen, smiling. "You're one of us now. Welcome to the Family."

"I don't believe you," he said. A faint, protracted moan echoed down the hall.

"But that's how it works," Marilyn said reasonably. "We bite you and you join the club. Didn't you ever see *Dracula*? Heck, don't you *feel* different?"

He did. Numb and detached. Dead inside. Wasn't this what Sartak had described? For a moment, horror stabbed through his daze. He shuddered.

"Now, don't get upset," Marilyn said. "It was for your own good. Now you get to be young forever. And we'll teach you everything you need to know, you cute little childe, you. Think of me as your mom and Ellen as your aunt."

"Your sweet, *beloved* aunt," Ellen said. She reached out, apparently to stroke his cheek.

Zane jerked away from her. "This can't be. I need to help Rose! I need to find Ben!" But as he spoke, the deadness trickled back, and he wondered if he meant what he was saying.

"I don't know who Rose was," Marilyn said, "but I heard you and Dr. Blake talk about her in the past tense. Maybe Ben's dead, too. I know you boys only got here last night, but sometimes people just don't last. Even if he isn't, it's time to put down all that mortal baggage. The sooner you dump it, the happier you'll be. Let's worry about Zane. You feel parched and ill, don't you?"

He nodded.

"Well, it's only going to get worse till you take the cure," Ellen said, reaching for him again. "Come with us. Mommy and Auntie know best."

This time, he let her take his arm. It didn't seem like he had a choice. Her touch was pleasantly cool. Marilyn took his other arm, and they guided him down the hall.

"Where are we going?" he asked.

"Supper," Ellen replied.

The hallway bent unpredictably as it led past one doorway after another. Dust floated in the dull amber glow of the widely spaced fixtures in the ceiling. It tickled Zane's nose. Once he sneezed, and the two vampires laughed. For some reason, the sound reminded him of breaking glass.

And that brought a pang of anxiety. He almost tried to push it away, but some instinct, some desperate voice yammering deep in his mind, made him try to analyze it instead.

He and his companions strolled by a guy in platform heels and a lime green leisure suit. Judging by his milky complexion, he was probably a vampire, too, although everyone must turn pale in here, forever sequestered from the sun. Pointing his finger, he counted the faded roses on the mold-spotted wallpaper. "Three hundred forty-one, three hundred forty-two . . ."

"Twelve, thirteen, fourteen, fifteen!" Ellen said loudly.

The male vampire glared at her. "You are a horrible, horrible woman!" He grinned, grabbed her, gave her a long kiss, and then turned back to the wall. "One, two . . ."

Zane and his escorts walked on. The blonde and the dark-haired woman chattered, but he found that he couldn't listen and concentrate, too. Even when he ignored them, his thoughts tried to squirt away like the body parts in the nightmare. Fortunately, the vampires didn't seem to mind his lack of attention.

Why did the idea of glass disturb him so? Why had there been glass fangs in the dream? Suddenly an image of Marilyn dividing and turning transparent popped into his mind. And immediately after that, a vision of a hamburger on a tray.

She'd drugged him. He'd been sure of it. For another moment, his sluggish brain couldn't work out why that should matter now. Then it dawned on him that the way he felt, the haziness, the sickness, and all the rest of it, could be the aftereffect of what she'd given him.

If so, then maybe he was still a living human being. Maybe Marilyn and Ellen were playing a joke on him. They wanted to trick him into doing something horrible.

He wondered how he could find out for sure. He mulled it over until another wave of vagueness oozed over him. His thoughts broke up like a weak radio signal.

When he came back to his senses, the vampires were leading him through a musty-smelling library. Ranks of leather-bound books climbed up the walls. A ladder stood in the corner to provide access to the high shelves, and a dingy painting of Greek gods, obscenely defaced with slashes of Day-Glo yellow and pink, spanned the lofty ceiling.

"We're almost there," Marilyn said encouragingly.

Almost where? Zane wondered. Oh, that's right, he was a vampire headed for his first drink of blood . . . or maybe he *wasn't* undead. He supposed that he needed to decide quickly.

Finally it occurred to him that he could feel his heart beating. Pounding hard, as if his body was scared even though his head was having trouble feeling anything. And he was breathing. He *guessed* that meant he was still alive. He wished that he'd asked Sartak more about the mysteries of vampirism when he'd had the chance.

Ellen opened a door to reveal a small room. The candle on the mantelpiece burned blue. In the middle of the floor stood a bed, with a fat, middle-aged woman chained to the frame. When she saw them, she started to shudder.

Marilyn handed Zane a small bone-handled knife. "You'll need to use a blade until your fangs grow," she said.

A surge of revulsion swept away the haze. He *must* be human. Otherwise the prospect of drinking blood wouldn't sicken him this way.

But now that he was sure of that, he realized that he didn't know what to do about it. Attack Marilyn and Ellen? He still felt too dazed, too tenuously connected to his body. Even with surprise on his side, he could never overcome two vampires.

He could simply refuse to do what they wanted. But if he spoiled the game, they might get mad and hurt him. Or try to make him entertain them in some other way. At best, it would show them that he wasn't as confused and suggestible as they'd hoped. Then they might give him another dose of the drug, or lock him back in a cell.

On the other hand, if he let them degrade him, maybe they'd leave him alone afterward. To start searching for Ben, and a way out.

Trying to look bewildered, blank, he shuffled into the room. It was an effort just to put one foot in front of the other. The fat woman shook harder. Her shackles rattled. "Please," she whimpered. "You don't have to do this. I know about the sex rays, but I won't tell. Explain that to the CIA! I won't *tell*!"

Zane knelt beside the bed. Up close, the woman smelled of rot. Maybe she had bedsores. *I'm sorry*, he thought. *But maybe if I do this now, I can help us all later.* Hesitantly, his own hands trembling, he set the point of the knife against her meaty forearm.

She wet herself. Screamed and thrashed. He had to grip her arm with all his strength to immobilize it for the cut.

His first attempt was too gentle. It didn't break the skin. Gritting his teeth, he tried again, and the knife popped through. He wanted to make a tiny slit, but she bucked, and the blade jerked three inches down her arm. Blood welled out of the gash.

Zane pressed his mouth to the wound. The blood tasted warm and salty. He nearly choked. The woman's lurching arm battered his face. From the corner of his eye, he could see Marilyn and Ellen hugging each other, clasping each other's mouths to smother laughter. Except for Blake, he'd never hated anyone so much.

He drank for as long as he could stand it, then stood up and stumbled away. Without meaning to, he dropped the bloody knife.

Marilyn stooped and picked it up. "How did you like it?" she purred.

Remember you're dazed, Zane told himself. You

don't understand what's happening. "I don't know," he mumbled. "Did I do okay?" Behind him, the fat woman's shrieks turned into sobs.

Marilyn licked the knife. "You did good," she said. "*If* you really are Kindred. Of course, if you're not, you're one sick puppy. Serial killer material. It's a good thing they locked you up."

Zane stared at her. "What do you mean?"

"Think about it," Ellen said. "Maybe it will come to you. Meanwhile, have a wonderful time settling in."

"Don't leave me," he said. "I don't know what to do."

"Now, don't act like a *spoiled* baby," Ellen said. "Mommy and Auntie can't spend *all* their time with you. We have responsibilities. But I promise, you'll see us again real soon." Giggling, she and Marilyn flitted out the door.

Zane waited until the sound died, then warily peeked into the hall. It looked as if the vampires really had gone.

But he couldn't start exploring without trying to help the woman on the bed. Maybe he could make a bandage. He turned back to her. "It's all right now," he said. "I won't hurt you anymore. I—"

She started thrashing and shrieking again, over and over and over. The noise hammered into his head. At last, feeling helpless and guilty, he left her. Her screams followed him down the hall.

22

By the time Sartak picked up his parcels at the airport post office, he could feel that one of his problems had become acute. He'd fed immediately upon arising, but already his belly ached again.

He needed to take care of the situation tonight. Before his thoughts became cloudy, and his powers unreliable. He put his gear in the trunk of the Mustang, then headed east. A departing plane howled over his head. Beside the road, palm fronds lashed in the wind, and sheets of lightning flared across the sky. Evidently it would rain again tonight.

He got on the interstate. The Bone Gnawers' wasteland rolled past on his left, and the skyscrapers of downtown rose to his right. A few were gracefully shaped and fancifully lighted, but most were dark, smog-stained slabs. They looked like a tyrant's fortresses, or the tombstones of wicked men.

In contrast, Ybor City turned out to be an old and rather picturesque section of town, full of Spanish and Italian names, glazed tile facades, enormous murals, and bronze historical markers. Hooked black lampposts lined Seventh Avenue, the main thoroughfare, illuminating the entrances of bars, restaurants, art galleries, and boutiques. The amount of pedestrian traffic made it look as if the area was struggling toward renewed prosperity. But most of the narrow brick side streets were dark and empty, with vacant, vandalized storefronts, and heaps of trash bags clogging the sidewalks. Apparently no one had collected the garbage in weeks.

As Sartak parked beside a broken, plundered meter, it occurred to him that with its wrought-iron balconies and colonnaded walks, Ybor City looked something like the French Quarter in New Orleans. And, more to the point, it resembled the architecture in some of Rose's sketches. Perhaps the trail he was following was warmer than he'd thought.

But he wouldn't be able to get excited about it until he'd satisfied his craving. Until his head stopped throbbing and he'd loosened the knots in his guts. As he climbed out of the car, he sharpened his senses. The neon signs blazed, dazzling him. It was another symptom of his malnutrition. Wincing, he dulled his vision and set off down the sidewalk.

The wind was cool and moist with the promise of the storm. Trash skittered along the gutters. An alto sax moaned from the depths of a blues club, and he wished that he could stop and listen. Instead, he pressed on toward the music screeching and pounding a block ahead.

The racket came from a bar squeezed between a pawnshop and a tattoo parlor. A horned black skull with red LED eyes grinned from the center of the door. When Sartak opened it, the music blasted out four times louder than before. The lead singer ranted about killing his mother and hacking open her womb. The Cainite wondered if the lyricist was actually familiar with the life of Nero, or if it was simply a case of like minds thinking alike.

A thick haze of cigarette smoke shrouded the bar's interior. Thrashing forms jammed it from wall to wall. On the stage at the back of the room, people dived into the crowd, and the band hurled globs of something viscous.

Sartak doubted that he could pick a fellow Kindred out of such a mob, or that he could do anything about it if he did. He closed the door, leaned against the rough brick wall, and watched the black-clad patrons come and go. Most had satanic paraphernalia of one sort or another. A silver pentagram pendant. A 666 tattoo. A stencil of a batwinged succubus on an artfully tattered T-shirt.

Every age produced a few fools titillated by the trappings of devil worship. Dashwood and his Hellfire Club, for instance. But it seemed to Sartak that in this era, the affectation was becoming commonplace. Once, in a somber mood, he'd wondered if it was an omen that the darkness in which he'd dwelled for so long was about to swallow everything. If at last the kine, tormented and exploited since Caine murdered Abel, were becoming as heartless as their oppressors.

The matricidal song staggered to a halt. Sartak's ears rang, even though he'd listened to most of it through the wall. But he still heard a wail from overhead. From one of the windows above him, or the roof.

Knowing he wouldn't see anything looking straight up, he dashed into traffic and on across the street. A horn blared, brakes screeched, and someone yelled, "Watch it, slope!"

Sartak wheeled and raised his eyes. Shutters covered all the windows. But five stories up, on the flat roof, pale, thin columns of phosphorescence shone. Two silhouettes darted and circled in the glow.

The Mongol couldn't tell what was making the light. Perhaps it had something to do with the enemy. Or maybe the figures atop what was allegedly an anarch haunt were Kindred themselves. There was one way to find out.

Rather than try to locate a stairway in the crowded bar, Sartak ran back across Seventh Avenue, around the block, and down a rat-infested alley. Beady eyes glittered from the shadows. The sweetish stink of spoiled fruit tinged the air.

A rusty fire escape snaked down the back of the death-metal club, ending about eight feet above the ground. Sartak leaped, caught the guardrail, swarmed over it, and skulked up the steps.

Stopping just short of the top, he stuck his head up to look around. A swarthy youth in a black leather jacket stood in the center of the roof. A gold ring shone in his ear. A slim, white-skinned woman lay several feet beyond him, shuddering. Her long black hair and her hands masked her face. Blood oozed between her fingers. Crosses made of silvery light hung in the air around her.

"Okay," said the young man, "I guess that's enough. Come on out." Two crosses blinked out of existence, clearing a path. The girl scrambled forward. A new cross flared directly in front of her. She screamed and fell back. The man laughed. "Whoops! You got to be quick."

Sartak risked honing his senses. This time, it worked properly. Listening, he discovered that neither the youth nor the woman had a heartbeat.

He grimaced. He'd actually hoped to find one Cainite and one kine. He knew he ought to pause to ponder his options, but the Hunger wouldn't let him. He climbed the remaining steps. He tried to move silently, but perhaps his eagerness made him clumsy. One of the metal risers clinked.

All the crosses disappeared. The boy spun around. He had an impish face with black, lustrous eyes. Gypsy eyes. "Well, well," he said. "Did you come up here to rescue the damsel in distress? I think you're a little old for her."

Sartak surmised that the boy thought he was a kine. "You have no idea," he said, stepping onto the roof. "I take it that you're a Ravnos."

"Yeah," the young man said, suddenly wary. "My name is Milosh. Who are you?"

"Sartak." He moved forward.

Milosh fell back a pace. "Well, look, Sartak, I was just having a little fun with her. Trying to help her, really. She's got a phobia of crosses, did you ever hear anything so stupid? I thought I could cure it."

"I don't care about her," Sartak said. "Torture her to your heart's content." He kept advancing.

He was trying to look calm, but evidently the Hunger showed in his face. The Ravnos snarled, baring his fangs, and reached inside his jacket.

Invoking his inhuman speed, Sartak charged. A flash of light exploded in his eyes. He knew that it was only an illusion, a product of the Ravnos's powers, but that didn't make it any less dazzling. He tried to move even faster, compensating for his sudden blindness with speed. His outstretched hand brushed leather, but he missed his grab. His opponent had leaped aside. As the Mongol blundered past, something cracked into his left elbow. His forearm went numb.

Sartak whirled, blinking, shaking his arm back to life. Through floating spots of afterimage, he saw Milosh poised in a martial arts stance, spinning a set of nunchakus.

The Mongol lunged. Into another flash. He jumped and kicked, without connecting. The nunchakus whizzed past his left ear.

Now the night was completely black. He groped with his remaining senses. He felt the raging music of the band below, shaking the building. Heard the female Cainite panting, just as if she needed air. And then, at the last possible moment, smelled leather.

He sprang, then pivoted to the left. He grabbed, and his hands closed on Milosh's arms. His vision began to return, enough to provide a blurry glimpse of the Ravnos's astonished expression. "I'm sorry," Sartak said, "but blinding me isn't good enough. Not if you're always going to dodge in the same direction."

Milosh struggled futilely to break his grip, then snapped at his neck. Sartak jerked his head aside, avoiding the bite by a hair. He kicked Milosh's legs out from under him and slammed him down. The Ravnos's head cracked against the rooftop, and he stopped moving.

Sartak dived on top of him and plunged his fangs into his throat. A vitæ sweeter and richer than that of any kine welled out. The first taste enflamed him, and he drank frantically. Ecstasy burned along his nerves.

From the corner of his eye, he glimpsed the woman creeping toward a door that no doubt opened on a staircase. For a moment, drowning in pleasure, he couldn't even think about the implications. But gradually, hazily, he remembered that he'd wanted to question an anarch. Besides which, she might be going for reinforcements.

The hell with it. He could find and interrogate some other Cainite later. And why should he care if she fetched her friends? With his strength replenished, he could kill them all. He gulped another mouthful.

Then she brushed the raven hair out of her eyes. Just as he'd expected, she had fangs. Her face wasn't cut, she'd been weeping tears of blood, and red trails streaked her alabaster cheeks. But except for her teeth and her coloring, she was Rose Cooper's twin.

23

Thunder boomed, and the old mansion shook. Somewhere, someone screamed. The noise startled Zane, too, but he also found it comforting. It proved that the real world was still outside the walls.

He'd been sneaking through the prison for what felt like hours. Sometimes his mind drifted, and he had to fight to bring his thoughts back into focus. At other moments, he thought he saw faces smirking from the shadows, but when he turned, they disappeared. He kept telling himself that it was just the drug, and that the effects would wear off in time.

He couldn't find the door that the cops had brought him and Ben through. No doubt it was one of the locked ones, but he had no way of telling which. He couldn't locate any exit, or even a window. If he hadn't known better, he might have assumed that the whole place was buried like a pharaoh's tomb.

Rounding a corner, he saw the open door to a billiard room. Two trays of sandwiches sat on the table. The Tiffany lamp above it made the felt glow green. In another setting, the light might not have seemed so bright, but in this gloom, it dazzled.

Zane hurried inside. Shortly after he'd begun to explore, he'd discovered a bathroom, and drunk from the faucet. But he hadn't had anything to eat since the hamburger last night. He grabbed a turkey and Swiss cheese sandwich, lifted it to his mouth, then froze.

What if this food was drugged, too? Maybe that was one way that the Malkavians kept the inmates confused and incapable of resistance.

He smelled the aroma of the bread. His mouth watered. Hell, he didn't *know* the food was bad. Maybe if he ate, he wouldn't feel so queasy. So weak. So cold.

On the other hand, maybe he'd be throwing away his only chance at escape.

Grimacing, he started to put the sandwich back. Then a floorboard creaked, and a foul smell filled the air.

He jerked around, dropping the food in the process. The sandwich flew apart, scattering slices of bread, cheese, and turkey across the rail and felt.

Before him stood a wrinkled, gray-bearded little man in slippers and bloodstained pajamas. He'd tucked the baggy shirt into the pants. He snatched a ham on rye, managed to cram most of it in his mouth, and chewed noisily.

Despite the new, nauseating stench, it made Zane's stomach ache to watch him. "Are you sure this stuff is all right?" he asked.

The little man looked at him blankly, gulped the rest of the first sandwich, and grabbed another.

Zane said, "I'm new here. How about you?"

The little man gobbled the second sandwich. He started dropping others down the V-necked collar of his shirt.

"Please, talk to me," said Zane. "People must notice things. Where new prisoners are brought in, and how the vampires go in and out. If we all put our heads together, maybe we could figure out how to get away."

The little man gaped at him, exposing gapped teeth and bloody gums, then backed away. "Spy," he said.

"No," said Zane, following him. "I promise I'm not."

"You're talking *bad*." The little man kept retreating. "The ghost people will punish us."

"Not if we plan it right," Zane said. "If just one of us got out, he could bring back help." He caught hold of the little man's arm.

"No!" the hoarder screamed. He thrashed, trying to tear himself free, and his shirt pulled out of his waistband. Sandwiches tumbled to the floor. So did a human foot, severed three inches above the ankle, with some of the flesh gnawed away.

Shocked, Zane let the little man go. Still yammering "No," he knelt to gather up his stash. A thin, white-faced man stepped into the room. Pince-nez glasses perched on his long blade of a nose, and bushy side-whiskers framed his lantern jaw. With his wing collar, cravat, and claw-hammer coat, he looked like he'd stepped out of the nineteenth century.

Zane grabbed one of the fallen sandwiches and scrambled into the far corner of the room, trying to look nuts and thus unworthy of notice. The cannibal squealed and cowered against the wall.

To Zane's surprise, the vampire crouched and gently put his hands on the little man's shoulders. "Look at me," he said. Slowly, trembling, the human turned his head. "There's no need for all this screaming. No one is going to hurt you. You can take your food and go." He picked up the foot. "Except for this. It would make you sick." He threw it behind the table.

The little man grabbed two sandwiches and bolted out the door. The vampire straightened up, wiped his hand with a handkerchief, then tossed the cloth away. "There's no reason for all this chaos," he said. Zane got the feeling that he didn't expect a reply, or even understanding. He was talking to him for the same reason that a human might speak to a dog. "It's unpleasant, unsafe, and inhumane. If Roderick would listen to reason, we could sedate you kine into a permanent slumber." He peeled off his coat and laid it on the table. "Take this. You're all gooseflesh." He turned and ambled away.

Zane realized that he was holding his breath. Letting it out, he stood up, pulled on the coat, and went through the pockets. They were empty. He crept out the door and prowled on, wryly grateful that, for the moment at least, the sight of the amputated foot had killed his appetite.

Cries and moans echoed down the corridors. A woman fled at his approach. Behind the half-drawn curtains of a canopy bed, a hunchbacked shadow slurped at the throat of a motionless body. And in one of the larger rooms, an exercise class did jumping jacks by purple candlelight, ignoring the one man who lay wheezing on the floor.

The thunder cracked again, even louder than before. The lights went out, plunging the hallway into darkness. Zane bit back a cry.

In a moment, to his relief, the round yellow ceiling fixtures flickered on again. Ahead, down a branching passage, a deep voice said, "God damn it."

"It's okay," said a second voice, also male, but a reedy tenor. "Power's back. Hit it again."

Curious, Zane tiptoed forward, and found himself in one of the sections of the house that actually resembled a hospital. The first room he came to was another padded cell. The second was an examination room, with an anatomical diagram and an eye chart hanging on the back wall. The voices emanated from the third.

The bass said, "Nothing. You know, Doc Blake actually uses this thing. If it's broken, he's going to be pissed."

"So what?" said the tenor. "He's just a kine, isn't he? He can kiss my lily-white Malkavian ass."

"They say he has powers of his own, like a mage. And even if he doesn't, he's the Prince's *pet* kine."

"Those Ventrue faggots can kiss my ass, too."

The other man sighed. "I forgot, you're the baddest of the bad. But it would still be nice if we could fix this. Maybe we need to throw a breaker, or change a fuse."

"Where? I don't see anything like that."

"I don't know. Let's find Marilyn. She'll know." Floorboards creaked.

Zane lunged into the examination room and hid behind the door. He heard the two men walk by.

He waited until the click of their footsteps died away. It seemed to take a long time. Finally he skulked on to the next room.

Inside it, Ben lay strapped to a gurney. His injured hand had swollen to twice its normal size, and his face was a mass of purple bruises. His captors had jammed a wad of grubby foam rubber into his mouth, and stuck two prongs to his temples. Wires connected them to a squat gray console with switches, knobs, and a voltmeter. If Zane was right, it was a shock therapy machine.

His hands trembling, he pulled the padding out of Ben's mouth. "Thank God I found you," he said. "Are you okay?"

Ben blinked. "Zane?" he croaked.

"Yes." He pulled off the prongs.

"Honest?"

"Yes." Suddenly his mouth was dry. He swallowed. "Can't you see me? Did they do something to your eyes?"

"I see all kinds of things. I see the colors." Tears rolled down Ben's battered cheeks. "I don't think I'm real anymore."

Zane was so relieved that he had to stifle a laugh. "You're real. It's just that they drugged you. Your first high, Straight Arrow." He unbuckled one of the ankle restraints. There was a deep ligature mark underneath. Ben's foot must be completely numb.

"She's here," said Ben. "I should have believed you."

Zane freed his other leg. "Who's here?" he asked.

"Rose," said Ben. "The mad doctor was wheeling her out of here when the vampires were bringing me in."

Zane's heart leaped up. Grimly, he reminded himself that Rose was dead. But if Sartak's theory was right, Ben could have seen one of the "Sisters." On the other hand, he could have been hallucinating.

Thunder crashed. Ben flinched and gasped, and the power wavered. And something clicked in Zane's head.

Rose's sketches were full of storms and lightning. And Sartak thought the images were symbolic. Maybe they represented shock treatment. If so, then Ben probably *had* seen someone real.

Wondering what to do about it, Zane opened the leather strap around his brother's left wrist. It was even tighter than the ankle bands. Beyond the doorway, voices murmured.

Ben shuddered. Zane said, "Shit!" He frantically yanked on the remaining strap, the one immobilizing the hand with the broken fingers. Thanks to the swelling, it was the tightest of all, so tight that the buckle wouldn't give. The voices got louder. Now he could make out a woman's laugh, a sound like bits of crystal chiming together.

Ben closed his eyes. "Go," he said. "Save yourself."

No! Zane thought. *You wouldn't even be here if it weren't for me.* He ripped at the restraint. Ben hissed in pain. Finally the tongue of the buckle popped out of the hole.

Ben sat up clumsily. Zane shoved him down again.

"We've got to run!" said Ben.

"Pretend you're still strapped down!" Zane said. "Trust me!" He was sure that his brother couldn't run fast enough to get away, not with numb feet and the drug still screwing up his balance.

To his relief, Ben positioned his hands and feet where they'd been before. Zane grabbed the head of the gurney and shoved it into the corridor. Marilyn and the two male vampires were several yards away. He wrenched the bed around and dashed in the opposite direction.

The wheels clattered, noisy as he'd hoped they'd be. Behind him, footsteps pounded. Laughing, Marilyn said, "You are a bad, *bad* baby."

Zane wondered if *he* was fast enough to pull this off. Maybe. After all, he'd stayed ahead of Marilyn before, until the drug tripped him up. With luck, other Malkavians weren't inhumanly quick, either.

Paintings and doors flashed by. He veered around a fallen suit of conquistador armor. The gurney sideswiped the wall, tearing the paper, and Ben nearly tumbled off. A man wearing knee breeches and a powdered wig lounged on a staircase. Zane was afraid that he'd try to stop them, but he simply watched them pass.

Zane's heart pounded. He gasped for breath. He desperately wanted to know how much of a lead he had, but he didn't dare look back to find out.

He did know that he couldn't keep sprinting for much longer. His lungs burned, and his bandaged ankle throbbed. Finally, trusting to luck, he whirled the gurney around another turn and said, "Roll off!"

Ben dumped himself on the floor. Zane dashed a few more paces, then gave the bed a final shove. He blundered around, yanked his brother to his feet, and hauled him through a doorway.

He meant to hide behind something, but he didn't get the chance. A split second later, the hunters appeared.

He tensed, but they raced on by, pursuing the rattle of wheels into the darkness. He and Ben waited a few moments, then scurried out of the room and ducked around the corner.

24

With immense effort, Sartak lifted his mouth away from Milosh's throat. "Wait!" he said.

The Rose Cainite scrambled through the door. Calling on his speed, he leaped up and chased her.

The stairwell stank of beer and urine. The glare of a bare bulb illuminated the black-and-red graffiti, pentagrams, and HAIL SATANS on the walls. Sartak caught the Sister three steps down. He grabbed her by the arm.

She snarled and tried to shove him away. Her strength surprised him, but it was no match for his. Trying not to be too rough, he pinned her shoulders against the wall. "I don't want to hurt you," he said.

She thrashed. Though he'd satisfied the Hunger, the feral exhilaration of the act had awakened the Beast, and her struggles aroused it further. He felt a sudden desire to lick the bloody tear tracks off her face, simply for the fun of terrifying her further, and then tear open her neck. He strangled the impulse.

"I rescued you," he said. "Are you afraid of me because I stole Milosh's vitæ?" The practice of feeding on one's fellow undead was called diablerie, or, by elders, the Amaranth. Traditional Cainites, like those comprising the Camarilla, professed to consider it a heinous crime. He sneered at her. "I thought Ybor City was for outlaws. But I see that you're just a timid childe."

She made a visible effort to pull herself together. To answer his sneer with one of his own. "Fuck you. I'm not scared of anything. I've hunted Kindred myself, lots of times." He doubted that she'd ever even seen it done. "I just didn't want you coming after me." She grimaced. "Not while I was still weak."

"Even if I were still thirsty, I wouldn't attack you," Sartak said. "I've been looking for you, so I can help you."

She eyed him sullenly. "Just let me go. That's all the help I need now."

He released her. "That isn't true. Your enemy is hunting down your twins. He—or should I say she, or it?—has already murdered Rose, Meg, and possibly others. I wouldn't count on even your Kindred powers protecting you."

She shook her head. "Are you a Malkavian? You're making zero sense. Look, thanks for taking out Milosh, but now piss off, okay?" She started edging down the steps.

Sartak wondered if she was lying out of misplaced caution, or if she truly didn't understand. He said, "You joined the anarchs within the last two months, didn't you?"

Her dark eyes narrowed. "How did you know that?"

"I didn't. But I was able to guess, based on what I do know. Information that you need to know, too, if you don't already."

She hesitated. Hard as she was trying to look tough, he could tell that she was still afraid of him. But now

she was also fearful that she'd come to grief if she
didn't hear him out. "If you've got something to say, I
want my friends to hear it, too." So they could help her
if he decided to attack her after all, he assumed.

"That's fine. I'm Sartak. What's your name."

"Ligeia Dupres. Come on." She led him down the
top flight of stairs and into a candlelit apartment.

Inside, the air was hot and stale. Thick drapes covered the windows. Someone had painted the walls,
floor, and low ceiling black. The wan firelight illuminated posters, full of grotesque and satanic imagery,
for bands with names like Deicide, Cannibal Corpse,
and Obituary. Books by Goethe, Nietzsche, and LaVey
lay strewn about, along with underground and super-
hero comics. The music from the bar wailed through
the ventilation, while on the TV screen, a man in a
black hood hacked a bound, naked woman with an ax.
She shrieked, but silently. The sound was turned off.

Three Cainites, two male and one female, lounged
on rumpled pallets, laughing and jeering at the show.
As the door swung open, their heads snapped around.

"It's okay," said Ligeia. "This is Sartak. He's
Kindred." She looked at the Mongol. "These guys are
Roberta, Santa, and Reg."

"Where's Milosh?" asked Roberta. Like Ligeia and
the other anarchs, she looked young. She'd probably
still been in her teens when her sire Embraced her.
Her ears were pointed, and her bushy eyebrows met
above an aquiline nose. Sartak surmised that she was
a Gangrel, and, like many of the shape-shifter clan,
developing bestial stigmata.

"He hurt me," Ligeia said. "Sartak . . . made him
stop. I don't know if he'll be back."

"Let's hope not," said Santa. He was a rarity, a
chubby Cainite. He wore a spiked collar and had a

flaming swastika tattooed on the back of his left hand. A hand-rolled cigarette smoldered in his mouth. "I hate that Gypsy prick. I still say he stole my medallion. And as far as I'm concerned, he isn't really an anarch." He gave Sartak a challenging stare. "Are you?"

Sartak smiled. "I'm not much for meetings or organization, particularly organized disorganization. But I helped your founder a time or two, when he was getting started." Until he'd decided that the anarch movement was doomed to become as repressive as the regime it opposed. It was, after all, a *Kindred* insurrection.

"Right," said Santa skeptically. "You fought with Salvador. I'm sure."

Sartak shrugged. "Believe it or not. It doesn't matter. It's done. What's important now is that Ligeia is in danger."

"What do you mean?" asked Reg. He was a wiry, ash-blond youth with upraised scars on the inside of his left wrist. A chain linked the ring in his nose to the stud in his earlobe. He sat on a red beanbag chair, cleaning a .44 Desert Eagle.

Outside, thunder roared. Raindrops pinged on the metal shutter on the other side of the drapes.

Ligeia said, "He says that somebody wants to kill me."

"Somebody from her past?" asked Roberta. "You *know* about her past?"

"Not exactly," said Sartak. "Obviously, neither do you." He looked at Ligeia. "Why don't you tell us about it. I *have* to know, so I can help you."

Ligeia tensed. She shook her head. "Oh, no. You first. I still don't know how you found me, or why you even care about me. How can I trust you until I do?"

"All right," said Sartak. He sat down and told an edited version of the story. Everything he said was true, but he didn't mention breaking the First Tradition, or stealing Milosh's vitæ. Since Ligeia hadn't seen fit to mention his diablerie, he'd be equally discreet.

"And there you have it," he concluded. He smiled at Ligeia. "Your turn."

Rose's double quivered. She looked as if she wanted to jump up and flee the room. "You got involved in this for *fun*? To solve a puzzle? How can you expect me to believe that?"

"I believe it," said Roberta. "I've known other Kindred who went looking for trouble, just to give themselves a rush. I think that you believe it, too. You just want an excuse to keep your mouth shut. Look, Santa, Reg, and I are your family now. Whatever happened in the past, it won't make us stop caring about you. Hell, Reg told you about his dad molesting him."

Ligeia's body slumped. "Okay," she said. "It's stupid, I don't even know why I don't want to tell. Except that I have holes in my memory, and that scares me. I don't like to think about it.

"I grew up in Savannah, in a neighborhood of beautiful old houses by the sea. Last year, on my eighteenth birthday, a man named Sergei Romanov moved into the home across the street. He was handsome and charming, and he fascinated me. When he started visiting me in my room at night, I couldn't resist him. I don't think I could have done it even if I'd understood that he was drinking my blood.

"My parents could see that I was getting weak. They called the doctor, but he couldn't figure out what was wrong, or tell how serious it was. After a week, I died in my sleep, and Sergei stole my body out of the funeral parlor. The night after that, I rose as his bride.

"My new existence was wonderful. I knew that my soul was damned, but I didn't care. I didn't need God or Heaven, as long as Sergei and I could be together. But then, suddenly, we weren't."

Fresh red tears seeped from her eyes. "One night, I didn't wake up in my coffin. Instead, I was standing naked in an alley. I found out later that I was in Tampa. I attacked a girl, drank her blood, and stole her clothes. After that, I just wandered around and survived the best I could, until I ran into Reg."

"Now that you've told the story out loud," Sartak said, "do you see how absurd it is?"

She scowled. "What do you mean?"

"Your sire couldn't make you a Cainite simply by draining your blood. You would have had to drink his. Sergei could have loved you, but not as a 'bride.' Kindred lose the erotic impulse when they acquire the Hunger."

Ligeia glared at him. "Are you calling me a liar?"

"No," Sartak replied. "I think that you're telling the truth to the best of your ability. But that doesn't change the fact that what you've given us is a hackneyed piece of vampire *fiction*. Even the names smack of melodrama. Ligeia. Romanov. Dupres. You didn't want to share the tale because subconsciously you knew that any knowledgeable listener would pick it apart."

"I'm not crazy!" Ligeia said.

"No, you're not," Roberta said. She tried to put her arms around Ligeia, but the black-haired woman jerked away. The Gangrel looked at Sartak. "There's more to this than a screwed-up memory. She *operates* like a storybook vampire, too. She runs from crosses and garlic, and she can't go into somebody's home unless she's invited. I know, that could just be because of what's in her mind. But how much do you know about shapechanging?"

"I can't do it," Sartak said. "But in the abstract, I know quite a bit."

"Well, she can't use the lesser powers. Can't grow claws, see in the dark, or earth meld. But she *can* turn into a bat, just like a Gangrel elder. I watched her do it three weeks ago, and I've been trying to figure it out ever since."

Santa frowned. "Why didn't you tell me about it?"

Roberta shrugged.

"Could there be a *second* race of vampires?" asked Reg. "Licks like the ones in the movies?"

"The world holds plenty of secrets," Sartak said. "But if such beings existed, I imagine I would have run into them before now. No, I think the answer lies elsewhere."

"God damn all of you!" said Ligeia. She jumped up and threw open the door.

Sartak surged to his feet, grabbed her, and spun her around. She bared her fangs and he yanked her off-balance, so she couldn't bite him. He sensed the other anarchs leaping up behind him, then hovering uncertainly.

Ignoring them, he shook Ligeia until she stopped fighting. "Why are you running?" he asked. "Have we made the fragile little childe feel deranged? Like a freak? Well, welcome to the club. We feel exactly the same way. *All* Cainites are mad, unnatural creatures. Those strong enough to face the truths of their condition endure, while the weak ones perish. Which kind are you?"

Ligeia said, "I'm as strong as anybody! But how am I supposed to face *my* facts when I don't know them?"

"By discovering them," Sartak said. "I think I know how to do it, assuming you've got the nerve." He looked over his shoulder. "Can any of you control someone else's mind? Well enough to hypnotize her, if she doesn't resist?"

"I can," said Reg.

25

At first, Milosh felt too weak and dazed to lift a finger. But, gradually, his belly started to cramp. His skin itched, and his flesh burned as if he had a fever. The Hunger had arrived, and it soon became so excruciating that he *had* to move.

Sluggishly, he touched his neck. The fang wounds were still bleeding. The Asian bastard had jumped up in too much of a hurry to lick them closed. Or maybe he just hadn't given a damn. Hell, maybe he would have drained Milosh to death if Ligeia hadn't distracted him.

The Ravnos tried to close the bloody holes. They shrank, but he couldn't seal them. Vitæ kept seeping out. This fresh evidence of his debilitation intensified his fury and his shame.

Clutching his neck, he lurched to his feet. The stars spun around him, and he was afraid that he was going to fall down again. But after a moment, the dizziness passed. Trembling, he staggered toward the stairs. Perhaps the idiot anarchs would help him.

But when he warily pressed his ear against their

door, he heard Sartak's voice on the other side. No doubt Ligeia was in the apartment, too, and had already convinced her friends that Milosh was a scumbag. He was on his own. Resisting the urge to cry, he slunk away.

Clinging to the banister, he descended the remaining stairs, then shuffled out into the alley. A broken plastic crack pipe lay on the stoop. Rats scurried through the shadows. The air smelled of car exhaust and rotten produce.

Like most of his clan, Milosh took pride in feeding through trickery and charm. But now, he realized, he wouldn't have time. He'd have to stoop to the crudity of violence, one more offense to charge against Sartak's account.

He wanted to stop and lie in wait where he was. But for all he knew, it might be a long time before a kine came by. What if he passed out before one did? What if he was still sprawled here unconscious when the sun rose? He stumbled on toward the street. The fever gave way to chills. He tried to close his jacket, but his fingers were too numb to work the zipper.

Abruptly he realized that he'd left his nunchakus on the roof. He could never climb back up five flights of stairs. They might as well be on the moon. But a chunk of broken brick caught his eye. He stooped, picked it up, and blundered on. A sheet of lightning lit the sky.

Finally, after what seemed like an hour, he reached the street. At the moment, there were no pedestrians, but there were parked cars. Surely someone would come along soon. Someone had better, because he couldn't walk any farther.

He slipped into a shadowy doorway and slumped against the wall. Thirst seared his throat. His fangs chafed his dry lower lip, but he found that he couldn't retract them. One block away, on Seventh Avenue, kine chattered as they walked up and down. The sound was so tantalizing that it made him whimper.

Then two voices grew louder and more distinct. Two sets of footsteps scuffed nearer. Milosh held himself motionless until the prey came into view.

They were a middle-aged couple, pink-cheeked and overweight, walking hand in hand. The man was tall, wore chinos and a Who reunion tour T-shirt, and had a blond goatee. The woman was a bespectacled brunette, with sandals and a loose floral print dress. Since she was closer, Milosh sprang at her.

She jerked around. Her mouth fell open. She tried to raise her hands, but she was too slow. He slammed the brick against her forehead. Bone cracked, and her knees buckled. He tried to catch her, but her weight bore him to the sidewalk. He wound up pinned beneath her.

The male kine tried to pull her away. Milosh clung to her frantically. The man started kicking him. Ignoring the jolts of pain, the Ravnos bit blindly at the mass on top of him, ripping long gashes to make sure he opened a major artery or vein. Blood gushed into his mouth.

For a while, he forgot everything but the ecstasy. The relief. But eventually, when he'd guzzled his sickness and exhaustion away, he realized that his vessel's companion was still kicking him. The impacts now seemed insignificant, like gnat bites, but irritating nonetheless.

Grinning up at the bearded man, he created an illusion. The woman's body shriveled and blackened. Maggots writhed from its eyes and mouth. The stench of corruption filled the air.

Milosh rose with the corpse in his arms, then offered it to the man. He screamed, whirled, and ran back toward Seventh Avenue.

Laughing, the Ravnos allowed the illusion to dissolve. Then he carried the woman into the alley, leaving a trail of spattered blood. He crouched behind a Dumpster and returned to his meal.

When he was completely sated, he noticed with mild surprise that the kine was still breathing. He dropped her into the garbage bin, then, on a whim, squealed like a rat, beckoning the alley vermin to finish his leftovers.

And now it was time to plot revenge.

Milosh had practiced diablerie himself, many times. It was a fundamental part of the Path of Paradox, the Ravnos way, though the clan took pains to conceal that fact from outsiders. Thus, he supposed that, from a certain perspective, his outrage at finding himself on the receiving end was laughable. But perceiving the irony in no way blunted his desire to get even.

He'd never seen any Kindred move as fast as Sartak. The son of a bitch was obviously an elder. No doubt Milosh was ten times smarter, but he still couldn't defeat him without assistance.

He could gather other Ravnoses. They'd be happy to help him kill an elder of another bloodline. But they were also scattered across the country. In the time it would take to assemble them, Sartak could easily disappear.

Fortunately, there was another way to bring the Asian down. Humming a Gypsy song, Milosh sauntered down the alley. Behind him, the Dumpster clicked and rattled as rats scrambled into it.

26

". . . eight, nine, ten," Reg droned. "Are you asleep, Ligeia?"

"Yes," Ligeia said. She lay on the stained, dilapidated couch. Her face was slack and her eyelids closed. Outside, rain rattled the shutters.

Reg turned to Sartak. "Thank God," he murmured. "I *thought* I was pretty good at this, but that took forever."

"Because a part of her still wants to bury the truth," Sartak said. "I doubt that any kine mesmerist could have put her under at all."

Slumped in the beanbag, Roberta scowled. The expression made her face look even more brutish. "This isn't going to hurt her, is it?"

Reg shrugged. "It shouldn't. It wouldn't ordinarily."

"It can't harm her as much as having the brain dug out of her skull," Sartak said. "We *have* to go after the facts. I don't know how else to protect her."

"We anarchs protect each other just fine," said Santa. "Nobody messes with us twice."

Roberta rolled her eyes. "All right, get on with it," she said to Reg.

The blond Cainite nodded. "Ligeia, Sartak is going to ask you some questions. You answer him just like you would me, okay?"

"All right," Ligeia said.

Sartak shifted his rickety chair even closer to the sofa. "We're going to relive some moments in your past," he said softly. "Here's how it will work. No matter what time we visit, you'll see everything clearly, just as it happened. But you won't *feel* anything. It'll be like looking at a stranger's life. Like watching a show on television. Do you understand?"

Ligeia slowly nodded. "Like TV."

"Exactly," Sartak said. "First, we're going back two months, to your first night in Tampa. Are you there?"

"Yes," Ligeia said. "I'm outdoors *naked*. I don't recognize this place. Where's the house? Where's Sergei?" A red tear oozed from the corner of her eye.

"Don't be afraid," Sartak said. "It's over. It's not happening to you anymore. It's happening to another Ligeia."

"All right," she said, relaxing.

"Skip back another week," Sartak said. "What's going on now?"

Ligeia smiled. "I wake up in my coffin. So many candles, burning all around, filling the air with the scent of jasmine. I stand up, and see that Sergei woke up before me. We're going to the theater, and he's already dressed, in his gray silk suit. He"—she hesitated shyly—"he's so handsome, and he smiles at me with so much love, that I decide he'll have to undress again. I want to make love right now."

"Stop," Sartak said.

"Why?" said Santa, smirking. "It was just getting good."

"Shut up," Roberta told him.

Sartak said, "You did well, remembering that. But now I want you to find a different set of memories. The memories from your *other* life."

Ligeia trembled. "I don't know what you mean." Her voice quavered like that of a frightened child.

"Yes, you do," Sartak said gently. "Rose Cooper, Meg Irons, and a glowing killer are parts of that life. So are storms, and terrible jaws, or something very like them."

Ligeia said, "I can't see anything like that! Only Sergei!"

Sartak took her hand. She squeezed his fingers tightly. "Still, something else *is* there, and we have to look at it. Please, do your best to open the way."

The black-haired woman swallowed. "I'll try."

"Good girl," Sartak said. "I want you to imagine that Sergei and the room with the candles are a painting on a curtain. I'm going to count to three, and on three, the curtain will rise. Your other memories, the hidden ones, are waiting behind it. Do you understand?"

"Yes," Ligeia said.

"Good. One . . . two . . . three. The curtain is going up. What do you see?" The other anarchs leaned forward.

"The dark," Ligeia said. Four floors below, their shriek faint and tinny with distance, the bar band chanted, "Devil, devil, eyes so red—"

"Is everything dark?" Sartak asked.

"No," said Ligeia. "The flashes of electricity light things up. The monster shines. But the flashes burn us, and blast the house apart. And the monster is eating us."

" 'Us,' who?" Sartak asked. "Who are the others?"

"I don't know," Ligeia said.

"Are Rose and Meg there?"

"I don't know," she repeated. "I never hear their names. I just watch them run into the shadows, until it's my time to run, too."

"And you run to the alley, don't you?"

Ligeia's sighed. "Yes."

"Where is the house?"

"Not too far away. Other than that, I don't know."

"What is the monster? Who is it, or who controls it?"

She shuddered. "I don't know!"

"That's all right, you're doing fine. I want you to go back to a time before you came to the dark house."

Ligeia shook her head. "I can't."

"Please," said Sartak, "try."

"Really, I can't. There isn't any 'before.' I was born in the house. Or the house built me. It made me Kindred because it hoped that the monster wouldn't think to look for a Kindred. But it didn't know that much about licks, so it put me together wrong." Another drop of blood slid out of her eye.

"Why did it give you false memories?" Sartak asked.

"I don't know," Ligeia said. "Maybe that was supposed to throw the monster off, too. Or maybe I made them up for myself. I couldn't be a person without a past. With nothing inside."

Sartak tried to think of another question. He couldn't. Santa snorted. "This is total bullshit," he said. "She's just throwing out whatever garbage she thinks he wants to hear."

"I don't buy that," said Roberta. "Weird as it sounds, it means *something*."

"I agree," Sartak said wryly. "My intuition tells me that she just handed me every missing piece of the puzzle. It's a pity that I have no idea of how to put them together." He removed his hand from Ligeia's. Witnessing her distress, he'd felt a faint compassion. Or perhaps he'd merely feigned it, to encourage her. He wasn't sure anymore. Either way, the moment had passed, and now the gesture of sympathy felt awkward and hypocritical. "You might as well wake her up."

"Should I let her remember?" Reg asked.

"Why not?" Sartak replied. "She has a right to know what we know, such as it is."

"Listen to me, Ligeia," said Reg. "I'm going to count backward from five. When I reach one, you'll be awake, calm, and alert, and you'll remember everything that happened while you were asleep. Five, four, three, two, one!"

Ligeia's eyes fluttered open. For a moment, she looked about blankly. Then her face crumpled. "Oh, God," she whispered. "Oh, God."

Roberta rose from her chair, knelt beside the couch, and squeezed Ligeia's shoulder. Sartak noticed that the back of her hand was hairy from the nails on down. "It's okay," she said.

Ligeia shook her head. "No, it isn't. I'm not a real person." She laughed brokenly. "I'm two months old!"

"But you are real," Sartak said. "However you got here, you have a life and a mind, just like the rest of us. Look at your friends. Do they look as if they've decided that you're a mirage?"

Ligeia hesitantly peered around. "I guess not."

"Then stop whining!" Sartak snapped. Roberta shot him a glare. "We have work to do."

Ligeia's mouth twisted. Her fists clenched. "All right."

"Now that you're awake," Sartak said, "can you shed any light on what you told us?"

"No," Ligeia said. "Just that I know that it sounds completely crazy, but somehow, it was real."

"Right," said Santa. "Just like good old Sergei was real."

"Ignore him," said Roberta. "We believe you."

"We do indeed," said Sartak. He rose and began to pace, picking his way among the scattered books and comics. "And despite the fact that our glowing friend doesn't sound like any Cainite I ever heard of, I'm certain that one or more of our kind are involved in this. Otherwise, that ghoul talking on the phone just before the dogfight incident is far too much of a coincidence. I'd like for you all to tell me everything you know about—"

Someone pounded on the apartment door. "Open up in the name of Prince Roderick!" a male voice cried.

Sartak raised an eyebrow. "Never mind. Here they are, to tell me themselves."

27

Shivering, Zane tugged the musty-smelling blanket tighter around his shoulders. The coat the vampire had given him was better than nothing, but it didn't actually keep him warm.

He and Ben had hunkered down behind the sagging bed, so no searcher would see them even if he opened the door. All but invisible in the darkness, Ben murmured, "Maybe they were trying to do me a favor."

"Who?" Zane asked.

"The vamps with the shock machine," Ben said. "Maybe a fried brain, a brain that doesn't know what's happening, is the best that we can hope for."

Zane gripped his brother's shoulder. "You can't give up," he said. "Tracy and Davy need you."

Ben sighed. "Yeah. I know. I'm sorry. It's just that I'm scared, and my hand and my face hurt really bad. I feel like I'm stuck in a nightmare. Or in hell."

"Me, too," said Zane. "But it isn't hell, because there's a way out." Of course, if they didn't find it soon, before hunger forced them to eat more of the drugged food, chances were they never would.

"Do you think that Marilyn and her friends are still looking for us?"

"I don't know," said Zane. "But I'm sure that *they* don't believe that we can escape. So maybe they did quit hunting, if they got bored. I don't think Marilyn has a very long attention span."

Ben clambered to his feet. The floor creaked. "Then let's get moving. I can't stand just sitting here. Maybe the LSD is still in my system, because my imagination's killing me. For the last fifteen minutes, it's been trying to convince me that somebody's standing in that corner."

Zane stood up, squinting against the gloom. "I don't see him. Of course, when you're dealing with vampires, that might not prove anything."

Ben snorted. "Hey, thanks, bro. Comments like that are great for morale."

"Sorry. Look, I know we need to find the way out. I know I don't have any right to ask you to concentrate on anything else. But—"

"You want to look for the girl I saw," Ben said.

"Yeah," said Zane. He felt guilty enough to squirm.

"I guess if Tracy had gotten killed, I'd feel the same way. All right, what the hell. No reason we can't look for her and an exit at the same time. But if we find a way out first, we'll use it, agreed?"

"Sure," said Zane. "And thanks. You're a great brother."

"Remember that on Christmas and my birthday. Remember the name Rolex. Do you have any bright ideas about where to look?"

"As a matter of fact," said Zane, "I do. Let's assume that Blake is giving the Sister a *series* of shock treatments.

He wouldn't want to wheel her a long distance every time. I'm betting that he's got her in that same hall."

"Makes sense," said Ben. "Let's go see if you're right."

Zane pressed his ear to the door. He heard the usual echoing screams and moans, but nothing that sounded close at hand. He peeked out. The corridor was empty. After the near-total darkness of the bedroom, the widely spaced amber lamps seemed almost adequate. Maybe, after months or years of captivity, their dim glow would look as bright as sunlight. The thought made his skin crawl.

Still wrapped in his blanket, he skulked down the passage. Ben followed.

Their bedroom hiding place was on the third floor. As they crept back down the staircase they'd ascended, they met a man and a woman coming up. Both were gaunt, pale, and dressed in institutional pajamas. The man had strands of fake pearls braided in his bushy, graying beard. The woman wore a black velvet blindfold, but carried a candle with a bloodred flame. Strings of melted wax encrusted her hand.

Zane and Ben cringed, trying to look demented, frightened, and harmless. The strangers inclined their heads to them, then walked on with regal dignity.

"Do you think they were vampires?" Ben whispered. "Or ghouls?"

"God knows," Zane said. "The important thing is that they didn't mess with us. Come on."

As they neared the hall with the shock machine, Ben grabbed Zane's arm, startling him badly. "Do you hear that?" he said.

Zane listened. Somewhere, someone was whistling "Amazing Grace." "You mean the hymn?"

"No," said Ben. "Another sound, underneath it. A

hum. I think they fixed the machine. I think some-body's in there using it now."

Zane strained his ears. "I still don't hear it. I'll sneak up and see. Wait here."

Ben's grip tightened. "Don't leave me!"

"One can sneak quieter than two. I promise, I'll be right back." Ben nodded stiffly and released him.

Zane tiptoed forward. Even when he was right out-side the shock therapy room, he couldn't hear the hum. He peeked around the doorjamb. As he'd expected, the room was vacant.

He hurried back to Ben. "Nobody's home," he said. "Do you still hear it?"

"No," Ben said. "It died away. I'm sorry. Things are bad enough without me freaking out."

"You're doing fine," Zane said. "You should've seen how flaky the drug made me. Come on, let's find the Sister."

They slunk down the hall. Zane checked the doors on the left and Ben the ones on the right. None of the rooms was locked, and none was occupied. When the passage turned, the medical rooms—a radiology lab and a surgical theater among them—gave way to shadowy parlors and pantries furnished with molder-ing antiques.

"It was a good guess," said Ben, "but it looks like you were wrong. Should we just keep looking for her?"

"No," sighed Zane. "If she's not here, she could be anywhere. It could take us days to find her. We'll just have to get ourselves out, and pray that she'll still be alive when I come back. Wait, maybe not!"

"Do you have an idea?"

"The Sisters are important to Blake," said Zane, "or why is he bothering to hunt them down? So this pris-oner is important. If you were him, would you leave her in plain sight, where any crazy Malkavian or human psycho could mess with her? Or would you stash her in a *hidden* room?"

Ben shrugged. "If there was ever a place that looked like it ought to have dungeons and secret passages, this is it. But even if the room is here, how do we find it?"

"Let's look at the size of the hospital rooms," said Zane. "Maybe we can spot a gap between the walls."

They started retracing their steps. When they were halfway back to the shock room, a long-legged man in a fedora and trench coat strode down the hall. His wide hat brim, upturned collar, and round dark glasses masked his face so thoroughly that he reminded Zane of the Invisible Man. As he approached, a stench like that of the severed foot filled the air.

His stomach churning, Zane tried to look dazed and lost. Ben fumbled at the rosebuds on the wallpaper as if he thought he could pluck them free. The man in the hat marched by without giving them a second glance. Just as he turned the corner, Zane glimpsed movement under the back of the coat. Could the guy really have a *tail*, switching restlessly under the fabric? Maybe it was only a trick of the shadows.

Ben left out a shaky breath. "How many times can we be lucky?" he said. "How long before we run into somebody—or something—that wants to hurt us?"

"I don't know," said Zane.

Peering into doorways, they pressed on. "Hey," said Ben, half a minute later, "I don't think this office is flush with the little library next door." He scuttled back down the corridor, then rapped on the wall. The knock sounded hollow.

Zane looked at the lay of the two rooms. "You're right." He raised his voice. "Is there anyone in there? We're friends! Humans! We want to get you out!"

No one replied.

"What do you think?" asked Ben.

"If she's gagged, or drugged, maybe she can't answer. Look for a latch."

They pressed and pried at the wallpaper and the wainscot, without success. "Okay," said Zane. "I'll go down the office wall, and you do the library."

Ben hesitated, then said, "All right."

"I don't want to split up, either," Zane said. "But if we don't, this will take us twice as long. And if something happens to one of us, the other will only be a few steps away."

Ben smiled wanly. "I know. I'm okay." He turned and disappeared through the library doorway.

Zane felt an impulse to scramble after him, just in case something *was* lying in wait inside, even though he'd just seen for himself that the room was vacant. Grimacing, he went into the office and started probing his way along the wall. Occasionally he heard a faint thump, reassuring evidence that Ben was still at work on the other side.

Zane examined a cracked mirror and an oil painting of a schooner battling a stormy sea, without finding anything unusual. But then a piece of the scotia molding at the top of the wainscot gave under the pressure of his fingers. A section of the wall clicked and swung inward.

He dashed out the door and around the corner. Ben was on his knees, pulling fat volumes out of a towering bookshelf. "I found a door!" Zane said.

Ben jumped up. "Is she in there?"

"Come on, and we'll find out."

The space beyond the hidden entry was utterly dark. Zane groped, and found a light switch. Fluorescent tubes pinged and flickered on. They were the brightest lights he'd seen since Marilyn had taken him out of the padded cell. He flinched from the glare.

When his vision cleared, he saw a space that looked like a patient's room in a general hospital. A black phone hung on the wall, and two wheeled, steel-framed hospital beds gleamed in the center of the linoleum floor. One was empty, but a woman lay strapped to the other, just as Ben had been fastened to the gurney. Zane couldn't see her face. It was turned in the wrong direction. But a spray of auburn hair burned across her pillow.

As he ran to the bed, he caught the stink of urine, and when he got there, he found fat brown roaches crawling on the wet, stained sheet. With a cry of disgust, he tore it off and threw it aside. The woman under it was naked.

He crouched. Peered. Caressed the blank, emaciated face on the pillow with a trembling hand. "Rose," he whispered.

"No," said Ben. "The resemblance is incredible, and I'm sorry, but it still isn't her. Rose is dead. This is just one of the doubles. Stay in reality."

"Yeah," said Zane heavily, "I know. For a second, I forgot, like when I saw Meg, but I'm okay now."

He wondered if he was telling the truth. He really did understand that Rose was gone. Yet he couldn't quite dismiss the idea that, if vampires could return from death, perhaps she, who'd apparently been a magical creature in her own right, could do the same. In fact, a part of him didn't want to wake the woman before him. As long as she was asleep, she wouldn't do anything to prove that she was a stranger.

Pushing aside his reluctance, he gripped her shoulder and shook her, gently at first, and when that didn't work, more vigorously. Finally she opened bloodshot green eyes. She looked up at him dully, and then her eyelids drooped again.

"No," he said. "Stay awake. We're here to help you."

The Sister shook her head. "Nobody helps Robot," she said.

"Robot?" said Ben. "Is that a nickname?"

"No. It's who I am. Who I was. Dead Robot." Her voice was absolutely flat.

Ben shot Zane a puzzled glance. Zane shrugged. "We really do want to help you," he said to Robot. "For Rose's sake."

"You loved her," said Robot.

"Yes," said Zane, "very much."

"That was her job," Robot said, her eyelids drooping again. "To get love, and have fun. So she turned out sweet and charming, with no meanness or anger inside her. Meg's job was to be tough, so she was mad all the time. It helped her fight. The others—Ruby, High Q, Carmelita, the Cook, Ligeia, and the rest—did other things. My job was to take the pain, so they left me here when they ran away."

"We don't understand," said Ben.

"It doesn't matter," said Robot. "They couldn't hide well enough. Dr. Blake found them and ate them, one by one. Now only Ligeia's left, and when she's gone, he'll kill me, too. Dead, dead Robot."

"Not if we get you out of here," Zane said. He unbuckled the strap securing her right arm.

"Don't do that," said Robot. "I have to get hurt and stay tied up. It's what I'm for. Robot the victim. Robot the punching bag."

"I can't believe that you want to die," said Zane.

"I do now," she droned. "He burned too much. He gobbled too many parts. Ligeia is holding me together somehow, but after she's gone, I'll fade away, even if he doesn't finish me. Bye-bye, Robot." Her eyes closed.

"Stay with us!" said Zane. He shook her again, hard, but she didn't stir. He felt a sudden, shameful urge to slap her.

"Poor kid," Ben murmured. "Did you understand any of that?"

Zane shook his head.

"Then it's unanimous. But I do have an idea about how to get out of here. Let's see if we can do it the easy way." He picked up the phone. Stooping, peering myopically at the buttons, he dialed one number, then another, then a third. A moment later, he hung up. "No good. I can't get an outside line. Come on, we need to start looking for an exit again." He hesitated. "You know that we can't take her with us, don't you?"

"Now that we've found her, we can't just leave her!"

"We have to," said Ben. "Even if you could get her walking and motivated, she looks as weak as a starving kitten. She'd slow us down too much."

Something twisted in Zane's chest. "Then we don't want it to look like anybody was in here." He buckled the leather cuff back on Robot's wrist, though he couldn't bring himself to cinch it quite as tight as it had been before. "I promise, we'll come back for you," he told her.

She didn't respond. When he turned off the lights and shut the door, he felt as if he was abandoning Rose herself. As if he was burying her alive.

For the next few hours, he and Ben checked one door after another, hiding from voices and the clack of footsteps, or acting timid and bewildered when a passerby surprised them.

Zane's stomach growled. He shook with cold and fatigue, and his cuts and bruises ached. He was sure that Ben, with his broken bones, must feel even worse.

Finally he said, "This is getting us nowhere. The exits are either locked, well hidden, or both, and that's all there is to it."

Ben frowned. "You said it yourself. We can't give up."

"No, but a few minutes ago, I thought of another approach. The catch is that if it doesn't work, it could kill us and all the other prisoners, too."

"We'd all be better off dead than trapped in here," Ben said. "Whatever it is, let's do it."

28

Reg rammed the clip into the Desert Eagle and jacked a round into the chamber. Santa looked frantically about, as if he expected a costumed champion to rise from one of the comic books to defend him. Ligeia scrambled into the kitchen and returned with a snub-nosed revolver. Sartak wished that he had his own weapons. It was unfortunate that they were too large to carry concealed.

"Chill!" snapped Roberta. "If they wanted to fight, they wouldn't knock. They'd just bust in. Everybody stay calm." She opened the door.

In the hall stood Milosh and three other men. Rain had plastered their hair down, and dripped from the hems of their coats.

The thin man in front had the snowy pallor of a Cainite. His side-whiskers framed a bony, long-nosed face. With mild amusement, Sartak noticed that his pince-nez glasses had no lenses. Evidently the Kindred had grown so accustomed to them in life that even today he'd feel uncomfortable without them.

Seemingly unfazed by the guns pointed in his direction, the thin man said, "Good evening. I'm Malachi Jones, one of Prince Roderick's advisors. The two gentlemen in the black raincoats are my retainers. Milosh, I believe you know."

Reg glared at the Ravnos. "You bastard. You led them to our *haven*. You were supposed to be on our side."

Milosh smiled. "I guess I did give you that impression, but really, people like me don't take sides. We try to make friends with everybody. That's how you hear things. Like who's hunting for who."

"Perhaps you shouldn't be too hard on him," said Jones. "He didn't give away so very much. Your elders have known where you sleep for a long time. May we come in?"

"I guess," said Roberta reluctantly. She stepped away from the door.

As the intruders filed in, Sartak sharpened his senses. He heard two heartbeats thumping. Evidently the burly "retainers" were ghouls.

Then he noticed that the taller of the pair, a shaven-headed black man with scar tissue on his knuckles and a cauliflower ear, was staring at Ligeia. The hairs on the back of Sartak's neck stood on end.

"Are you Sartak?"

Startled, the Mongol pivoted. Jones was looking at him. "Yes."

"Then Milosh is right," said Jones. "We have been searching for you. The Prince commands your presence, to answer certain charges."

"We don't take orders from him," said Roberta. Her nails lengthened.

Milosh said, "Don't stick your neck out for this bastard. He's a diabolist. He drank *my* blood! Ask Ligeia, she saw it."

Santa glared at the black-haired woman. "Why didn't you tell us?"

"He had it coming!" she said. "And we had other stuff to think about."

"Whatever Sartak is," said Roberta, "Roderick's goons can't just drag somebody out of *our* place."

Jones extended his hand, and his tan raincoat fell open. Beneath it, he wore antique clothes, a weskit and cravat, but, to Sartak's surprise, no suit coat. "Let's talk frankly," the Prince's deputy said. "You may not recognize Roderick's authority, but he reigns here nonetheless, and you profit from his management of the city. He tolerates your disrespect where many other rulers wouldn't, because he hopes that you'll outgrow your impudence in time. But you mustn't defy his orders, or mine, when I speak for him. You mustn't try to thwart his justice. Otherwise, he'll destroy you."

"Maybe," said Reg, "but I bet we can destroy you guys first." He aimed his pistol.

Milosh and the shorter of the ghouls, a squat, narrow-eyed man going prematurely bald, tensed, but Jones merely sighed. "Possibly so, but afterward you wouldn't fare as well against the reinforcements waiting outside."

He shifted his gaze to Sartak. "Why don't you come with us voluntarily, and spare these childer the consequences of their folly?"

Sartak said, "I think not."

"Roderick is a decent man. He'll give you a fair trial."

The Mongol grinned. "That's the most discouraging

thing you've said so far. The last thing any elder can afford is justice."

Jones ruefully smiled back. "Isn't that the truth." He looked at the anarchs. "Here's how it will be. You have fifteen minutes to decide whether to stand with this rogue, or step aside. Then I'm coming back for him. Please, make the sensible choice. Whatever our differences, we're all Kindred. I'd hate to have to kill you." He turned toward the door.

Milosh scrambled after him. Evidently he was afraid of being the last one out. As opposed to the black ghoul, who seemed to have difficulty tearing himself away. Still staring at Ligeia, he backed into the hall and closed the door.

Santa scrambled across the room and engaged the locks and chain. "What are we going to do?" he wailed.

Sartak chuckled. "Strike a blow for the revolution, I assume."

"Do you think that he really has an army out there?" Roberta asked.

"Believe it," Reg said. "I knew Malachi before I came over to the anarchs. He doesn't bluff."

Santa said, "Then the Chink has got to go. Jesus, he's just a stranger, and a headhunter, too! It's no skin off our ass!"

"You're wrong," Sartak said. "Did you notice how the black ghoul studied Ligeia?"

"So what?" said Santa. "She's pretty, and he's still breathing."

"I doubt that he was thinking about romance in such a tense situation. He's connected with the shining hunter."

Ligeia trembled. Outside, wind howled, and rain drummed against the wall.

"You don't know that," said Santa. "You'd say anything to get us to help you."

Roberta dragged her claws through her coarse, tangled hair. "I hate this," she growled. "Maybe if the rest of our people were here . . . but they're not. We're in this by ourselves. Let's vote. How many want to fight?"

Hesitantly, Ligeia raised her hand. No one else did, though Reg hung his head and looked ashamed. Santa said, "No way in hell! Even if we could shoot our way out, or hold them off, old Roderick would call a Blood Hunt against us."

Sartak looked at Ligeia. "You aren't bound by their decision. You can try your luck with me."

She shook her head. "I'm sorry. These are the people that I know. If Sergei and my mom and dad weren't real, then they're the only people I've *ever* known."

"You're on your own," said Santa with a sneer.

"So it seems," said Sartak. "I should have remembered that rebellion has its charlatans and dilettantes, the same as any other art." He sighed. "I apologize. That was unfair. We're Kindred. Predators and survivors, not heroes and martyrs. No one knows that better than I."

Looking Ligeia in the eye, he said, "Stay on your guard, and flee this place as soon as the coast is clear. Now, assuming that you have extra guns, could one of you spare one? I won't tell the Prince where I got it."

Reg gave him the .44, and Ligeia handed him the revolver. "Good luck," she said. He stuck the smaller gun in his jacket pocket, then pulled apart the drapes, raised the window, and cracked open the black steel shutters.

Cold rain stung his face. Lightning flared. Employing his inhumanly keen senses, he scrutinized the street. By now, most businesses had closed, and the storm had driven any innocent pedestrians indoors. Only the enemy remained, half a dozen figures lurking in doorways, and several more, sharpshooters, evidently, in upper-story windows. If, as he assumed, others waited on the stairs, in the alley, and inside the death-metal club, then the odds against him were long indeed.

He rather enjoyed wild weather. As he recalled, he'd liked it even when he was breathing, and thus was susceptible to chills. He savored it for a few more seconds, until another thunderbolt split the sky, then hurled himself into the night.

Twisting in midair, he fired at a silhouette in a window. It pitched backward. As the sidewalk rushed up at him, other guns boomed and chattered. Thunder roared, adding to the din.

He landed hard, but rolled, absorbing the shock. As he scrambled to his feet, red dots of light danced around him. Some of the enemy had laser sights. Chips flew from the brick wall behind him, and the pavement. Someone equipped with a bullhorn yelled, "Stop! Stop! Stop!" Obviously it was a Kindred, trying to dominate him, but he wasn't afraid of that. Over the centuries, he'd developed a resistance to mind control that was virtually a power in itself.

Drawing on his speed, keeping low, Sartak ran in the direction of the Mustang, snapping off a shot whenever he glimpsed a target. He killed a rifleman crouched behind a van, then fired a round into a woman's chest. She fell, but jumped right up again, blasting away with her Uzi. Evidently she was a Cainite, too.

Sartak shot her in the head. That wouldn't kill her, either, but it ought to do a better job of slowing her down.

She dropped in a puddle and flailed, splashing up sheets of oily water. He pivoted just in time to see another rifleman, armed with an AK-47, lean around a telephone pole. He tried to shoot him, but the Desert Eagle only clicked.

A bullet burned through his forearm. Blocking out the pain, he dodged to the side and threw his pistol. It didn't hit the rifleman, but it cracked against the telephone pole and the enemy flinched backward. The barrel of the AK-47 jerked to the side.

Before he could redirect it, Sartak charged. He grabbed the assault rifle, tore it out of the man's hands, and drove the stock into his face. Bone crunched. The enemy reeled and fell on his back.

Sartak sprinted on. Bullets whined around him, almost as plentiful as the pounding raindrops. The hole in his arm closed.

He grinned. Obviously, though some of the hostile Cainites seemed to be quicker than kine, none could match his speed. In the dark and the rain, even those with automatic weapons were having trouble hitting him. Unlikely as it seemed, perhaps he was actually going to get away.

He was nearing a window. One of the few at street level unprotected by burglar bars. He decided to dive through it and duck out the back of the building. Maybe that would shake the hunters off his trail.

He veered, and an explosion of light seared his eyes. Dazzled, he staggered. His foot landed in a hole in the sidewalk. His ankle twisted and he fell, banging his elbow. Pain jabbed up his arm. His finger twitched on the trigger of the AK-47, and the gun blazed.

Enemy fire hammered the pavement. A bullet stabbed into his thigh. He leaped up and whirled, shooting blindly, then launched himself at the window.

He slammed into brick, not glass. Even as he floundered backward, he understood what had happened. Milosh had cast an illusion to make it look as if the window was in the wrong part of the wall.

Pain ripped through Sartak's head and torso. As he collapsed, he heard the clatter of the guns, but he blacked out before he hit the sidewalk.

When he came to his senses, he was lying on his side, watching the rain wash his blood over the curb and down the gutter. The pain of his injuries was as excruciating as any he could remember. His wounds clenched in a kind of peristalsis, trying to eject the slugs.

"Was *that* good enough?" Milosh asked.

Sartak strained to turn his head. Milosh stood about eight feet away, grinning down at him, an Uzi cradled in his hands.

"Good enough if you have a few dozen genuine warriors backing you up," Sartak said. When he'd fallen, the AK-47 had tumbled out of reach, but he still had Ligeia's revolver in his pocket. He tried to reach for it surreptitiously, but his arm lurched spastically. Before he could even touch the gun, Milosh fired.

The first shot slammed into Sartak's forehead. He lost consciousness again. When he woke up, he was wearing leg irons, and a steel harness that hoisted his arms behind his back. Even if he were unhurt, and drew on every bit of his inhuman strength, he'd probably be unable to break free. As Mrs. Tyler might have remarked, the apparatus was well designed to deny him any leverage.

Malachi Jones looked down at him. "You shouldn't have run," he said.

"Considering the result, I'm inclined to agree. But you never know until you try. Now that you have me, satisfy my curiosity. Tell me about the glowing hunter. The thing stalking the young women who resemble one another."

"I don't know what you're talking about," Jones said. "Perhaps you're delirious. You were shot in the head at least three times." He nodded to the ghouls who'd accompanied him to the anarchs' haven. They grabbed Sartak under the arms, lifted him, and hauled him toward an olive-colored van waiting in the middle of the street. The idling engine rumbled. Down the block, other members of the Prince's force climbed into other vehicles.

"I'll admit that my head still hurts like the devil," Sartak said, "but I think my brain has already healed. Perhaps you don't know about the hunter, but this man does." He nodded at the black ghoul. "He couldn't take his eyes off Ligeia—the dark-haired girl—and she's one of the women I'm talking about."

"That's ridiculous," said Jones. "Phillip is Blood Bound to me. He can't possibly have divided loyalties, or any sort of hidden agenda. Do you, my friend?"

"Hell, no," said the ghoul. He and his partner started to manhandle Sartak into the van.

Sartak looked into Phillip's maroon eyes and decided that he was telling the truth. "Do you *remember* seeing the anarchs?" he asked.

"Sure," said Phillip. "I guess."

Jones frowned. "What do you mean, you guess?"

Phillip shrugged. "I know that we went there. It's just kind of . . . fuzzy."

Jones looked at Sartak. "Can you account for that?"

"Frankly, no. But ride with me to wherever we're going, and I'll tell you what I do know."

29

Bodiless, Blake floated over the black, hook-shaped lampposts of Seventh Avenue, watching the pursuit. He felt a glow of satisfaction when Sartak went down. He didn't think that the Asian Kindred had ever posed a true threat, but it was still a relief to know that the meddler wouldn't be poking his nose into matters that were none of his business anymore.

Of course, the real triumph of the evening was finding one of the missing alters. According to Milosh, her name was Ligeia. Blake had to admit, it had been clever of her to take on Kindred form. No wonder none of his Nosferatu agents had spotted her. They'd all been looking for fugitive mortals.

But her slyness wouldn't protect her now. He flashed back up the wet, gleaming street, through sheets of pounding rain he couldn't feel, and flitted through the grimy brick wall of the building in which she'd taken refuge. Settling in the hall outside the anarchs' apartment, he began to weave himself a body.

In seconds, it was complete. Grinning, he bashed the door, and it flew off its hinges.

He leaped into the room, jaws and talons at the ready, not at all daunted at the prospect of facing four Kindred at once. They were only childer. Jones, priggish fool though he was, had been right about that much.

But the messy, candlelit living room was vacant. Dropping to all fours, Blake bounded through the rest of the apartment. It was unoccupied as well.

He snarled in fury. He'd assumed that the anarchs, having abandoned Sartak to his fate, would cower here until they were certain that the Prince's soldiers had departed. Instead, they'd apparently decamped as soon as the chase moved down the street. He could only assume that the Asian had sensed him looking out of Phillip's eyes, and warned them. Perhaps he should have watched the parley as a disembodied phantom, but he'd wanted to make certain that he could hear the conversation clearly.

Be that as it may, what mattered now was that Sartak might somehow know more than he'd supposed. Perhaps even enough to make his appearance before Roderick awkward. Fortunately, Blake knew how to defuse the problem, but he meant to eliminate Ligeia first. Now that he'd found her, he was damned if he'd let her get away.

Sniffing, he caught the scent of the four anarchs. The smell of Roberta, the Gangrel girl, was particularly distinctive, musky and subtly inhuman. Through a mesh of other odors—blood, cheap white wine, marijuana smoke—he followed it down the stairs. The silvery sheen of his flesh cast smears of glow on the graffiti-covered walls.

When he slunk onto the stoop, rain hammered his

head and spine. Lightning blazed, illuminating the alley. Fifty feet away stood a mangy, emaciated collie, tearing into a mound of trash bags. It turned its head to look at him, then dashed off.

Blake laughed silently, wishing that he had time to run the mutt down and kill it. But his amusement turned to disgust when he inhaled. The rain had washed away the scent trail.

He scanned for Ligeia psychically. He should be able to find her, now that he'd gotten this close. He knew the shape and texture of her mind, or at least of fifteen minds just like it.

But even so, he couldn't sense it. With a pang of regret for the energy he'd wasted creating it, he let his gargoyle form dissolve. His scanning talent worked better when he was out of body. His senses of taste, smell, and touch seemed to dampen it somehow.

Drifting up toward the storm clouds, he groped for Ligeia again. For another few frustrating moments, he still couldn't lock onto her. But then he felt her, a distinctive tang, a resonance, to the southeast.

He flew to her. Circled her like an imperceptible gnat. She and her fellow anarchs were walking down a narrow residential street. Like most of the houses in Ybor City, the crumbling shacks and duplexes had no front yards. Their front doors, or, in some cases, sagging porches, abutted the sidewalks. Televisions glowed behind a few of the curtained windows. The muted bray of laugh tracks mingled with the hiss of the rain.

Hardier than humans, Kindred were often indifferent to bad weather. But with his shoulders hunched, and water streaming over his head, the plump vampire called Santa looked miserable anyway. "This is stupid," he said sullenly.

"Just shut up," said Roberta. "We'll be at Jack's place in a minute."

"I still say, we're running from nothing," Santa replied. "The Jap was crazy."

"No," said Ligeia, glancing over her shoulder. Blake hovered inches in front of her eyes. *You still can't see me, can you?* he thought mockingly. "I really do remember."

"Sure you do," said Santa. "You're crazy, too, babe."

Reg sneered. "At least she isn't gutless."

"Fuck you," said Santa. "You didn't fight it out with the Prince's gang, either."

Blake decided that he'd seen enough. He shot halfway down the block, landed behind a dilapidated house, and reassembled the gargoyle.

Crouching, he waited under the eaves. A miniature waterfall gurgled from the clogged rain gutter. His luminescence made it sparkle.

The anarchs shuffled past his hiding place. He charged, fast as the cheetah he vaguely resembled, hoping to strike them down before they even sensed his presence.

But Ligeia turned and screamed. Perhaps the gargoyle hadn't moved quite as silently as usual. Or maybe she'd sensed him psychically. Either way, it didn't matter. Nothing could save her now.

Reg jumped in his way, pointed a pistol, and yelled, "Drop!" Perhaps he felt compelled to make up for the cowardice—which had actually been sound judgment, in Blake's opinion—that he'd displayed earlier.

If so, he was about to pay a heavy price for his atonement. No Kindred could hypnotize Blake. Through his schemes and talents, he controlled them, not the other way around. Unhindered, he ran on.

Reg's eyes widened. He fired. One shot stung

Blake's shoulder. A pinprick, nothing more. He sprang, knocked the Kindred down, and raked him with his talons.

Reg thrashed, but couldn't get out from under Blake. He caught the boy's neck in his jaws, bit down hard, and wrenched his head away from his shoulders. Blood gushed, not the rhythmic spurt of a mortal's severed arteries, but a steady flow.

Pain burned down Blake's flank. Spitting out Reg's skull, he whirled to see Roberta. Her eyes glowing red and her fangs bared, she slashed at him with pointed claws.

Since her nails were the product of her Kindred nature, the gashes hurt worse than the bullet wound. But not badly enough to slow him down. He reared and punched at her head. Bone cracked. She reeled, and he pounced on her, hurling her backward. They landed on the narrow strip of weeds and sparse grass between two shacks.

He ripped at her face, popping her eyes and flensing the flesh from her skull. He spread his jaws to decapitate her, too.

Then she lurched beneath him, throwing him off-balance. In an instant, she sank into the soft, rain-soaked ground. Her red, fanged skull grin seemed to widen as she disappeared.

She'd escaped him by merging with the earth, another application of her shape-shifting power. But that was all right. She wasn't the one he wanted, anyway. She was merely an obstacle, and now she'd removed herself from his path.

Something jabbed his hindquarters. He spun around. Her feet planted wide and a pistol gripped in both hands, Ligeia stood plinking away at him. Santa was nowhere in sight. Evidently he'd run away.

Blake roared and charged. And Ligeia's body flowed into the form of a huge black bat. Leathery wings beating, she spiraled into the sky.

Blake gaped up at her, dumbfounded. He'd never dreamed that she had enough power to counterfeit such an extraordinary feat, particularly since none of the few Nosferatu, Malkavians, and Ventrue she'd encountered prior to her escape from the Institute could do it. If, as he'd assumed, she'd modeled herself on them, she shouldn't possess the shape-changing power at all.

Perhaps he'd understand it when he'd absorbed her. In any case, he didn't have time to wonder about it now. He had to catch her, and that meant that he had to sprout wings of his own.

Reshaping his ectoplasmic body took almost as much effort as abandoning it and creating yet another. He grunted and shuddered with the strain. But gradually, his pelt turned to feathers, and his muzzle to a hooked beak, until he became a gigantic, radiant owl.

Wings pounding, he rose into the air and streaked after her. Jagged blades of lightning stabbed the earth, and thunder shook the sky, as if some god of the hunt were cheering him on.

He could tell when Ligeia realized that he was on her trail. She swooped low, skimming over deserted, rain-swept alleys, wheeling around one turn after another. Trying to lose him. Apparently she didn't realize that, now that he'd zeroed in on her, he could track her with his mind.

For a time, enjoying the chase, he simply tried to overmatch her endurance and speed. But eventually his wings began to ache, and he found himself struggling to stay aloft against the pressure of the rain.

The game was too strenuous. Too time-consuming, when, as usual, other matters demanded his attention. It was time to cheat.

He'd already tethered himself to her mind. Now he whispered across the link: "You're getting tired. Terribly tired. Exhausted. You have to slow down. Your wings are cramping . . ."

Except for those occasions when he actually took up residence in a victim's head, his powers of influence worked more slowly and insidiously than a Kindred's ability to control minds. Unlike many of his Ventrue and Malkavian associates, he couldn't enforce obedience with a single word. Yet given a little time, his own talent could be equally effective. And after a few minutes, the steady pulse of Ligeia's wings began to falter. Soon, she virtually stumbled through the air.

Now, ignoring his own fatigue, he beat his way higher. When he'd climbed two hundred feet above her, he furled his wings, extended his talons, and dropped.

Perhaps Ligeia didn't sense him plummeting at her, or perhaps she was too spent even to try to dodge. In any event, his claws plunged squarely into her torso, and they hurtled down at a rooftop locked together.

He spread his wings a little. They still landed hard—shingles crunched beneath her—but not hard enough to stun him. Clenching his talons in her flesh, trying to immobilize her, he ripped at her with his beak.

Ligeia thrashed, fighting to break free. Her body rippled, warping back into human form. He pecked at her head, and punched through bone. Her struggles, and the transformation, ceased abruptly.

Blake knew that if her metabolism was as robust as that of a genuine Kindred, she might only remain immobile for a second. He grabbed the edge of the wound, then wrenched his head back. A piece of her skull snapped free, exposing a section of crimson brain. He thrust his beak into the hole and began to feast.

Power coursed through him, replacing the soreness and fatigue with exhilaration. Reading their minds, he'd discovered that it felt very much like this when the Kindred fed.

Just as he'd expected, given her shape-shifting, Ligeia had possessed far more psychic strength than Carmelita. A great deal more personality, as well. It was a bit unfair, really. Carmelita had existed for at least twelve years, whereas the bogus vampire was a last, desperate improvisation. A final message in a final bottle, hastily committed to the sea.

Picking through her essence, he discovered how it was that she'd been able to change form. In her ignorance, she'd based herself on *fictional* undead, not actual Kindred. Inwardly, he smiled, pleased with himself for solving the petty mystery. He snapped down the final scrap of brain.

Illumination, vivid as the lightning flashing overhead, flamed through his mind. Abruptly he *knew* that she'd been the last. There were no more fugitives running free, only the woman imprisoned at the Institute. Only passive, pathetic Robot, whom he could finish devouring at his leisure.

The danger was over. When he returned to his flesh-and-blood body, he found that it was grinning.

30

Sartak had all but healed his many wounds, but he'd burnt up most of the vitæ in his system doing so. Now the Hunger gripped him. His gut cramped, and his mouth was dry and raw. Jones's ghouls had laid him on what appeared to be a comfortable bed. Yet the silk sheets chafed like sandpaper, while his steel bonds cut into him like swords. His arms ached as if they were pulling out of their sockets.

The bedroom door opened, and Jones walked in. He'd put on a frock coat. Four grubby, malodorous tramps, looking thoroughly out of place in such plush surroundings, shuffled in after him. From their vacant expressions, Sartak assumed that they'd been mesmerized. Phillip and his comrade brought up the rear, each carrying an Ingram M10 submachine gun.

Jones peered at Sartak through his pince-nez frames. "You look as if you're recovering nicely. Good." He took a key out of his weskit pocket. "I'm going to remove the shackles for a little while. Don't try anything foolish. Even if you somehow got past the three of us—and I'm more formidable than the people you overcame on Seventh Avenue—you're in the heart of the Prince's stronghold. You'd never make it to the street."

"Don't worry," said Sartak. "I feel a little weak for strenuous activity."

"We're going to remedy that." Jones stooped and unlocked the leg irons, then the harness. "The kine are for you."

Sartak squirmed out of the chains. The links clanked, and fresh pain jabbed through his shoulders and elbows. "Really? I'm surprised by such hospitality."

"It's standard procedure. I told you that Roderick was a fair man. He wouldn't require you to defend yourself with your mind clouded by the Hunger."

"But why supply so many?"

"You'll drink a lot," Jones said. "I don't believe in killing unnecessarily."

He beckoned. One of the kine, a tremulous old man wearing a battered panama, and a pea coat several sizes to large for his shrunken frame, knelt stiffly beside the bed. Sartak gripped his bony shoulders and sank his teeth into his neck.

By the time he finished with the third vessel, the pain had gone, and he felt reasonably fit. He wondered if he *should* try to fight his way out, but prudence dissuaded him. Besides, if he spoke with the Prince, he might learn Zane's whereabouts, or the identity of the glowing hunter. He licked the wounds he'd inflicted, closing them. "Have you thought any more about what I told you?" He'd given Jones a partial account of his recent activities, omitting any mention of breaching the Masquerade, or consorting with Lupines.

"Yes," said Jones. "Your tale is troubling, but also utterly vague. Still, if I were you, I'd tell it to Roderick. If you can convince him that you've discovered a potential threat to the domain, or even pique his curiosity, he might be lenient with you."

Sartak grinned. "Remember, I'm innocent until proven guilty. How will this work?"

"Four judges will hear your case. The Prince, who of course has the final say, and three of the Primogen, one from each of the clans that comprise the majority of his people. Judith Carlyle is the senior elder of the Nosferatu, and Pablo Velasquez holds the same rank among the Malkavians. I'll represent the Ventrue. Roderick is actually our chief, but in matters that affect the entire domain, he has no clan."

Sartak lifted an eyebrow. "Indeed. It's hard to believe that he doesn't sometimes place the concerns of his own kind above those of monsters and madmen."

Jones grimaced. "You'd be surprised." He nodded toward a door. "That's a bathroom. Wash, and then I'll give you fresh clothing."

Sartak wasn't surprised that the bathroom had no window. He stripped, stepped into the shower, and scrubbed the crust of dried blood off his skin. When, still naked, he returned to the bedroom, the kine had departed, and a garment rack stood in the middle of the room. The wheels had cut ruts in the thick pile carpet.

Jones said, "I think that most of these will fit you."

Sartak rummaged though a selection of outfits appropriate to a variety of eras. On a whim, he selected a double-breasted, pin-striped suit such as Al Capone might have worn. He reflected sardonically that if he wanted to ingratiate himself with the hidebound Ventrue, he ought to choose the oldest style available. But he'd always hated ruffles, wigs, and knickers too much to revert to them now.

As he knotted his red silk tie, he said, "I wish I had a carnation for the lapel. Though I suspect that before this is over, what I'll really miss is the tommy gun."

Jones smiled. "Whatever crimes you've committed, I like your grit." He lifted the harness from the bed.

When Sartak had been reshackled, his captors marched him down the hall to an elevator. The two ghouls standing guard there stood up straighter and nodded to Jones respectfully.

The car took the party one floor up. As Sartak stepped out, he got his first look at Roderick's hall of state. And though over the centuries he'd drifted through a plethora of palaces and throne rooms, he had to concede that it was impressive.

The chamber occupied the entire top floor of the tallest skyscraper in Tampa. All four walls and the peaked roof were made of glass, and the view they provided was magnificent. Serpentine gargoyles smirked and writhed on the surrounding towers. The multicolored lights of the city shone like faerie jewels strewn over the dark earth, but no more brilliantly than the argent constellations overhead. The storm had blown inland, but lightning still flamed in the east, backlighting a mountain range of clouds.

Candelabra illuminated the hall itself. Potted palms and orchids perfumed the air. In the vicinity of the elevator, someone had arranged leather sofas and chairs into conversation pits. A dozen sentries, armed with assault rifles and submachine guns, stood along the walls. Most of the Cainites under their scrutiny appeared to be Ventrue, whose antique clothing gave the assembly something of the air of a costume party. One of them, a slim woman in a red flapper dress, was chattering to Milosh. Two other figures, barely visible in what seemed an unnaturally dark corner, kept their distance from the rest. Sartak inferred that the pair were Nosferatu, and that the remainder of the courtiers were Malkavians. None was doing anything bizarre, but some had eyes that glittered feverishly, and occasionally they laughed too long, or too loudly.

The crowd fell silent as Sartak's captors marched him toward the two-step pyramid at the far end of the room. The Cainite enthroned on top radiated a majesty which had more to do with his charismatic powers than with his slight frame and intelligent but bland features. To the Mongol's surprise, he wasn't wearing a wig and breeches either. He looked as if he he'd tried to keep up with fashion until about the turn of the century. An ivory-headed cane lay across his thighs. Perhaps he thought of it as a scepter.

Seated on the tier below him was a woman dressed in the hoop skirt of an antebellum Southern belle. A heavy veil hung from the broad brim of her hat, completely concealing her face. But it couldn't hide her seven-foot stature, the breadth of her shoulders, or the disproportionate length of her arms, while the size of her muff betrayed the hugeness of her hands.

The man on her left was a handsome Latino, with dark eyes, a pencil-thin mustache, and slicked-back hair. His demeanor was calm, in no way hinting at his insanity. A goldsmith had made him a tie tack in the form of the Moon card from the Tarot.

The seat to his left was empty. Jones raised his hand, and Sartak halted. The Ventrue took his place, while his ghouls faded back into the crowd, leaving the prisoner standing alone.

A bailiff thumped a beribboned staff on the floor.

"Oyez, oyez, oyez!" he cried. "The tribunal is now in session."

His face an inscrutable mask, the man with the cane gazed down at Sartak. "I'm Roderick Dean, elder of clan Ventrue and Prince of Tampa Bay. These are my lieutenants, Judith Carlyle of the Nosferatu, Pablo Velasquez of the Malkavians, and Malachi Jones, also of my blood."

Sartak inclined his head. "I'm Sartak. Of the Bahadur bloodline, though I suspect you haven't heard of it. Good evening."

"We've brought you here to answer four charges," said Dean. "That you violated the Fifth Tradition, by failing to present yourself to me when you entered the domain. That you broke the Sixth, by seeking to murder a fellow Kindred, specifically Milosh le Yankosko of clan Ravnos. That you practiced diablerie against him. And that you killed one of Judith Carlyle's ghouls, and, subsequently, four of the ghouls assigned to apprehend you. How do you plead?"

"I don't. I deny your right to try me." Dean's eyes narrowed, and Velasquez frowned. The audience murmured until the bailiff banged for order. "How old are you, noble Prince?"

"Three hundred and eighty," said Dean.

"I'm nearly eight hundred," Sartak said. "Older than your Camarilla itself. And if one principle underlies every Cainite custom and Tradition, it's that the ancient hold dominion over the young, not the other way around."

Jones pressed his fingertips together, forming a steeple. "Can you prove your age?"

"Not instantaneously," Sartak said. "Certain people could vouch for me, but it might take a considerable time to locate them." He grinned. "Would you accept the results of some sort of history quiz?"

"He's lying," Judith said, startling him. Her voice sounded like a dog barking and snarling. "We've all met this kind of impostor before. I'm only surprised that he didn't claim to be a Methuselah, or Caine himself."

Velasquez said, "Will you let me probe your mind, to establish the truth? The Prince's principles of justice forbid me to try without your permission."

"I think not," said Sartak. He was afraid that the Malkavian would discover the crimes that had thus far gone undetected.

"Since you can't substantiate your claim," Dean said, "the court rejects it."

Jones frowned. "Sire, he does fight with the prowess of an elder, to say the least." Dean scowled at him.

"May I suggest," said Sartak, "that you remand me to the custody of a Justicar?" The Justicars were the supreme magistrates of the Camarilla. "He can convene a Conclave to decide my fate."

"No," Dean said. "The truth is that your age is irrelevant. The Second Tradition gives me the right to administer justice to everyone in my territory. Neither my people nor I need any high-and-mighty outsiders to tell us how to manage our affairs." This last remark was clearly intended for the crowd, and they exclaimed and muttered in approval. One of the Malkavians clapped and whistled, then looked miffed when the bailiff pounded for silence.

"I still don't concede your authority over me," Sartak said. He shifted his shoulders, trying unsuccessfully to ease the strain the harness put on his joints. "But under the circumstances, I am willing to discuss these so-called charges, as one elder to another. With regard to the first, yonder stands my defense." He nodded at Milosh. "Did this nomad ever seek an audience here, prior to tonight? Did every anarch squatting in Ybor City? If not, did the Prince order their arrests?"

"Though they neglected to appear, we knew of them," Velasquez said. "You, on the other hand, were an unknown. Given the death of Judith's servant, conceivably a danger."

Sartak said, "The rationale is unimportant. A law must be enforced uniformly, or it becomes, by definition, unjust." He shifted his gaze to Roderick. "I would assume that that's one of your 'principles of justice,' too."

Dean's mouth twisted. "Is that all you have to say in response to the first charge?"

"I believe so," Sartak said. "With regard to the second, my trusty friend Milosh again supplies my defense. Does he *look* slain?"

The Gypsy Cainite glared. "You *would've* killed me, if Ligeia hadn't distracted you!"

He was right, but Sartak wasn't about to admit it. "If I'd wanted you dead, whelp, you can rest assured that you would be."

"Be that as it may," said Dean, "I don't you hear denying that you drank his blood."

Sartak smiled. "I will if it will help." Jones's lips quirked upward. "No? Then why don't we five elders talk frankly about the Amaranth, without the fog of hypocrisy that usually smothers the subject.

"Every so often, I *need* Cainite vitæ. So will you, if you reach my age. Perhaps you've already felt the craving stirring. Perhaps you've even gratified it. In my experience, few vampire lords gain ascendancy over their fellows without the theft of someone else's power.

"Or perhaps not. Either way, the fact remains, all elders are diabolists in their season." He gave the audience a sardonic smile. "You youngsters would be wise to remember that."

Judith growled something that Sartak couldn't decipher.

"No," said Jones. He sounded troubled. "There *is* a point, the same one he made before. It's unfair to condemn him unless we'd condemn anyone guilty of the same offense, even ourselves."

"Exactly," said Sartak. "Thank you. Certainly, it would be unreasonable to chastise me for tupping from the Ravnos childe. I remind you again, O Prince, that he's a stranger and an anarch, not one of your subjects. Why, then, must you protect or avenge him?"

Judith said, "Henry was under *my* protection."

"I assume that was your ghoul," Sartak said. "I say that he went berserk, assaulted me, and I killed him in self-defense. Do you people have a witness, or any evidence, to contradict me? I doubt it."

"But what of the others?" Velasquez said.

"If, as I contend, you people had no legitimate quarrel with me, then I had every right to resist your efforts to capture me. Besides, with apologies to the owners of the noisy hearts thudding away among the bodyguards, the men I killed were lackeys. Jumped-up kine. When one such falls by the wayside, a sensible Cainite simply makes another. Surely their ephemeral little lives are too trivial a matter for this court."

One Malkavian applauded. Another punched at the air and grunted, "Woof, woof, woof!" Perplexed, Sartak wondered if the lunatic was ridiculing Judith.

Dean smiled thinly. "You're a glib fellow." Sartak

inclined his head. "But all you've given us are sophistry, effrontery, and evasion. What do you say, Judith?"

"Guilty on all counts," replied the Nosferatu.

"Pablo?"

Velasquez shrugged. "The same, I suppose."

"Malachi?"

"Wait," said Jones. "We've barely scratched the surface of this matter. When I arrested Sartak, he told me a strange story—"

Dean frowned. "Does it bear *directly* on the question of his guilt?"

"No," said Jones, "but—"

"That's what we're currently discussing. Your findings, please."

Jones grimaced. "Guilty."

"And I concur," said Dean. "Prisoner, for manifold crimes against the Kindred of Tampa Bay, I sentence you to die. You'll face the Two Fires at dawn."

"You're acting rashly," Sartak said. "I've stumbled onto something you should know."

"Please," said Jones. "I myself saw something odd, something pertinent to his story. Let him tell you."

"When did wise Malachi Jones become so gullible?" asked Dean, rising. "This business is finished, and none too soon. I'm tired of it. If you insist that I hear whatever fantasy the rogue spun to save his hide, then you can repeat it yourself, another night. But this wretch is bound for the killing ground. Court is adjourned."

The bailiff thumped his staff, and the audience babbled. Hands gripped Sartak's forearms. Jones stared after his departing master. He looked stunned.

31

When Roderick Dean came to his senses, he was in his study in the tower, leaning back in his favorite easy chair. Yellow flames crackled behind the andirons. A Vivaldi violin concerto sang from the stereo speakers, hidden to preserve the appearance of a Victorian gentleman's den. Soft gaslight gleamed on jade and onyx chessmen, shelf after shelf of snuff-boxes, the gold leaf on the spines of his books, and the wineglass, half-full of fragrant vitæ, waiting on the table at his side.

"How do you feel?" asked Alexander. Dean's head snapped around. The silver-haired psychiatrist was sitting on the divan with a snifter of golden brown brandy cupped in his hand. Dean surmised that he'd lit the fire, turned on the music, and provided the blood, all in an effort to relax his patient. If so, it wasn't working.

"I feel frightened," Dean replied. Also ashamed. But his mouth didn't taste like blood. Perhaps he hadn't done anything too abominable. "The same as always. How did you know that I was having an episode?"

Alexander shrugged. "Intuition, I suppose. There was nothing blatant. When I ran into you, you were wandering around the building with an odd look in your eye. I persuaded you to come back here and rest."

"Thank God I didn't hurt you." The ormolu clock on the mantel struck five. Horrified, Dean leaped to his feet. "Damn! I'm late!"

"No, you're not. I'm told that you already held court." Blake held up his hand. "Please, don't panic. By all accounts, you conducted yourself very well. No one noticed anything amiss."

Dean picked up the glass and drank half the contents. If Blake really had procured it, it had probably come from the refrigerator, but he'd warmed it to the proper temperature. Still, at that moment, he wished that he could gulp whiskey, or laudanum. "What happened?"

"You sent Sartak, the trespasser, to the Two Fires. Everyone considered it an appropriate sentence." He hesitated. "Apparently one unfortunate thing *did* occur."

"What? What did I do?"

"Nothing," said Alexander soothingly. "I told you, *you* were fine. It was Jones, behaving erratically again. It seems that the diabolist told him some wild, incoherent story about a mysterious phantom lurking in in Tampa Bay. Complete nonsense, of course." His copper eyes bored into Dean's.

For an instant, the Ventrue's head swam. "Of course," he repeated. "I mean, it certainly sounds like it."

"When you refused to take the story seriously, Jones became incensed. We've discussed this problem before . . ."

"I know," sighed Dean. "Any more, whenever I have an idea, or make a decision, he opposes it. But he's the first of my progeny. We've been through a lot together."

"I understand," said Alexander, still holding his gaze. "But you can't afford to have one of the Primogen showing you flagrant disrespect in open court."

"I know you're right. We'll have to do *something* about it." He grimaced. "Though why should I expect deference? How dare I take offense at someone else's eccentricities? Even if Malachi is losing his grip, he's surely not as mad as I."

"Don't give in to self-pity," Alexander said. "You've made exceptional progress."

"I thought so. But this makes two fugues in as many nights."

"Fugues during which you did *not* run amok. That's an important difference. But if you want to make a full recovery as quickly as possible, you should reconsider living at the Institute full-time."

Dean scowled. "Go into an asylum."

Alexander smiled. "I scarcely think that we have an appropriate ward. No, it wouldn't be anything like hospitalization. You'd stay in your usual quarters, and live exactly as you do now. The arrangement would simply allow us to spend more time together, and increase the likelihood of my being around to help you when an episode begins."

"All right," said Dean. "Why not? To tell you the truth, these days I feel more comfortable over there anyway."

The psychiatrist smiled. "I know."

32

Sartak's head ached, and his vision was still a little blurry. His captors had clubbed him unconscious to keep him from fighting while they transferred him from his old restraints to his new ones. When the wan gray light bloomed in the sky, he wondered if his eyes were playing tricks on him. Surely it wasn't dawn already.

The silvery light brightened, turned into a ball, and extended squirming tentacles of glow. Now he could see that it was actually floating just a few feet away. Bones, flesh, and finally clothing coalesced out of the sheen. The process was like Meg Iron's dissolution in reverse.

When it was complete, the radiant figure of a lean, well-dressed man stood gazing down at Sartak's spread-eagled form. "Good morning," Sartak said. "Forgive me for not getting up."

The apparition smiled. "No, excuse me for visiting you like this. But I was afraid that if I came in my original and far more vulnerable body, you'd decide that if you had to die, you might as well take me with you."

Sartak lay spread-eagled on a bed of plastic explosive, and the steel cables attached to his wrist and ankle cuffs were trigger wires. Supposedly the slightest tug would detonate the bomb. "You may have been right," he said.

"The Kindred hereabouts traditionally execute traitors and criminals with sunlight. I suggested this modification of the procedure. They call it the Two Fires, but of course you know that. It's more merciful, I think."

Sartak chuckled. "The condemned has to choose whether to blast himself into oblivion, or remain aware to meet the dawn. Congratulations. You've hit on a very Cainite approach to compassion."

The shining hunter sat down on the dewy grass. "Actually, I think of this as an informal psychological study. I like to see who'll flee from pain, and who'll cling to experience until the bitter end. And of the latter, who'll thrash as soon as he bursts into flame, and who has the willpower to hold himself still for a while. I'm a psychiatrist, so such things interest me. My name is Alexander Blake."

"I gather that you're also a mage."

Blake smiled. "Now there you're wrong. I'm a psychic. A medium, I suppose, considering the things I can do with ectoplasm. But not the kind that talks to wraiths."

A tiny red fire ant crawled onto Sartak's hand, tickling his skin. Blake flicked it away before it could sting. "Your talents must help in your profession," the captive said.

"Reading thoughts? Planting suggestions in people's minds? Absolutely. That's why I went into the field. I knew that I'd be brilliant. And sure enough, my work made me rich and influential. A happy man."

Blake smiled crookedly. "Happy, that is, until the evening I attended a performance of *Rigoletto*.

Loitering in the lobby at intermission, I idly began to sample the thoughts of the people around me. One of them was Roderick Dean.

"For the first few moments, I thought that he was psychotic. But his thinking was coherent, and his memories too comprehensive to be delusions. He truly was a vampire. Amazed, fascinated, I spent the rest of the evening dredging information out of his head.

"What I learned disturbed me greatly. It didn't matter that I had politicians and CEOs at my beck and call. Such people were nothing, which meant that I was nothing, too. Supernatural entities—Kindred and sorcerers—actually ran the world. Accordingly I vowed to acquire as much power in your society as I already had in mine. My ego would stand for nothing less."

Sartak said, "That's the maddest thing I've heard in a long time."

Blake smiled. "It was a dangerous ambition, but I wouldn't call it insane. After all, I did achieve it. I worked out ways to make myself useful to every clan, then used my powers of suggestion to enhance their appreciation. Sometimes less-impressionable Kindred tried to kill or enslave me anyway, but I always managed to resist. Finally I established a personal bond with the Prince himself. By a strange coincidence, he wanted to undergo psychoanalysis. To subdue the Beast and reach Golconda."

Sartak snorted. "You're joking."

Blake shrugged. "He thinks it's helping. Who am I to undermine his faith?"

Sartak glanced to the east. The killing field lay behind a huge old house in the center of the city. The sky above the tenements beyond the grounds really was lightening now. "How do Rose, Meg, and Ligeia fit into this Horatio Alger story?"

Blake nodded as if he were a teacher and Sartak a clever student. "Good question. I didn't give up my psychiatric practice when I became Roderick's advisor. It was lucrative, I enjoyed it, and it was integral to some of the services I provided to the domain. One day, the court system committed a pretty young redhead named Lauren Walker to my care.

"Her presenting symptoms were memory lapses, disorientation, mood swings, and general confusion. Her previous doctor had diagnosed her as schizophrenic. But with my advantages it didn't take me long to determine that she was actually suffering from multiple personality disorder."

Sartak's eyes narrowed. He still didn't understand, but perhaps he was beginning to. "And, somehow, Rose, Meg, and Ligeia were three of the personas?"

Blake nodded. "You *are* quick. Actually, at that point, Ligeia didn't exist, but you've got the idea. To continue: I really became interested in Lauren when I discovered that she had some raw psychic potential of her own. I can *eat* minds like that, and add their power to what I already possess. That's my kind of vampirism. And since the poor waif had no family or friends keeping track of her, I was free to dig in.

"But it was more difficult than usual. I discovered that I had to go after the alters—the various personalities—one at a time, as if they truly were independent beings. And even after I softened them up with shock treatments—"

"Teeth and lightning," Sartak murmured.

"—they were often able to hide in the depths of Lauren's subconscious. As I learned later, at that point I didn't even know who all of them were. Still, I was nailing them, a bit at a time. In fact, I was enjoying the game. But then the situation changed.

"One night, sitting in my office, I experienced what I call a psychic flash. A premonition popped into my head. It told me that Lauren posed a threat to my life.

"I didn't understand how that could be, but I've learned that such insights are never wrong. I rushed to her cell, and found that most of the surviving alters had vanished from her head.

"Fortunately, Robot, the one who remained, had some idea of what had happened, and I was able to pull the information out of her mind. Apparently exposure to my psychic talents had stimulated the alters' own abilities. Desperate to escape from me, they'd leaped out of Lauren and formed ectoplasmic bodies like this one." He tapped his chest. "With the difference that theirs were more stable, and indistinguishable from ordinary flesh and blood. I wish I knew how to create one like that myself.

"Well, obviously I couldn't allow them to remain at large. Someday one would return and murder me. I hypothesized that if I killed Lauren, they'd die, too. Why else had Robot stayed behind, unless one mind *had* to stay, to maintain the original body? But I didn't *know* that it would work like that. Perhaps Robot had remained merely because it had always been her role to absorb abuse. Eventually I decided to let her live until I hunted down all the others. I hoped that I could use her to track them psychically.

"As it turned out, I could, but I soon realized that I wouldn't find everyone that way. It's my least reliable skill. I needed other searchers, to comb the area by more conventional means. I didn't want to bring all three clans into the affair. There are still Kindred who'd like to destroy or control me, and involvement with the alters might have provided them with an opportunity. But I did ask the Nosferatu to look for women answering Lauren's description. I have reason to trust the Sewer Rats more than the rest.

"In the weeks that followed, my greatest worry was that the alters had fled far away, but that didn't prove to be the case. Perhaps they were tethered to Lauren's body. Or perhaps the poor addled creatures didn't realize that I'd come after them. Perhaps they didn't even remember me. To some extent, each one lived in a fantasy world."

Now Blake glanced at the sky. "I'd better speed this up, hadn't I? I found and killed the fugitives one by one. I even discovered a way to draw psychic power from the corpses. I bagged Ligeia right after Jones and his men caught you. And afterward, I had another revelation. She was the last. I'm safe."

Sartak grinned. "Have you ever read *Oedipus Rex*?"

Blake cocked his head. "What an odd question."

"Not really. By trying to cheat a prophecy, Laius, Oedipus's father, brought on the disaster it foretold. So have you. If you hadn't hunted down Rose, I wouldn't have come after you. But you did, and now you *are* going to die."

Blake laughed. "I think that you're forgetting your appointment with the sun. Even your friend Tyler is safely locked away with Robot. But I admire your spirit."

"Then tell me why you came here. Was it just to gloat, and show me how clever you are?"

"No." Abruptly the left side of Blake's face softened and ran like melting ice cream. He grimaced, and it surged into shape again. "Though it was partly that. Do you know, there's not a soul in the world that I can fully confide in."

Sartak's shoulders throbbed. He suppressed the urge to shift them. "The lonely lot of the psychopath."

Blake grinned. "We call them antisocial personalities

now. If you're going to throw jargon around, you have to stay current. The *main* reason I came was to give you a chance to live."

"How kind. I accept. Remove the bracelets."

Blake scowled at the flippancy. "You said that you're eight hundred years old. I believe you. And I know that among the Kindred, age is power. I want you to work with me."

"Doing what?"

"Sharing your knowledge, for one thing. I'm firmly in control of Tampa Bay, but eventually I'll have to deal with the world beyond. Which is fine. I *want* to deal with it. Why should I settle for running a city-state when I could pull the strings of an empire? But I'm handicapped by ignorance. What can I expect when I meet the Sabbat? Are there really hordes of Antediluvians sleeping in the ground, waiting to rise up and slaughter their descendants? How does sorcery work, and what can mages actually *do*? Roderick and the Primogen barely have a clue, but I'll bet that *you* can tell me."

Sartak smiled. "You know, it's been a long time since I took part in a bona fide conquest. Old Chingis would be ashamed of me. All right, free me, and we'll reign together."

Blake shook his head, and the lobe of his left ear dissolved. He didn't seem to notice. "You can't lie to me. Most of your mind is closed, but I can read what's on the surface. Would you join me if I showed you that we're very much alike?"

Sartak sneered. "Impossible."

"Just listen. My ESP came on-line before I learned to talk. I've spent my whole life fully aware of the ugly side of human nature. I've always known what petty, spiteful, selfish creatures even the best of us are.

Therefore, I don't love. I don't take idealistic poses and hypocritical sentiments seriously. I regard other people as threats, tools, or toys. And I sense that eight centuries of existence have given you the same perspective. You share 'the lonely lot of the psychopath' yourself."

"You're right," Sartak admitted. He wondered why he was confiding in an enemy. Perhaps the challenge simply demanded an honest response, no matter who had issued it. "I am like you. Alone, detached, and avid for stimulation, because I have to fill the endless hours somehow. But I'm unlike you, also. You've given in to the Beast, if a kine can be said to possess such a burden. I haven't."

"Why not?" asked Blake. A wisp of shimmering vapor drifted upward from his hair. "You *feed* on humans. You just conceded that you hold them in contempt. Why, then, would you want to be like them? Do you really even recall how it feels to be mortal?"

"No," said Sartak. "For me, Humanitas is just a set of abstract principles. I don't know why I value it. Except that when I meet people who lack it, I tend to dislike them. And perhaps wrestling with madness is a pastime in itself.

"In any event, I won't team up with you. It simply isn't in me. So you might as well stop nudging at my mind. It's annoying. Like an itch that I can't scratch."

Grimacing, Blake stood up. His entire body began to steam. "You're a fool, my friend. A fool, and a major disappointment. I'm tired. I pushed myself hard tonight. I'll leave you to the consequences of your folly."

The apparition melted into roiling smoke, and the vapor dissipated into nothing. Sartak looked up. The last stars of the night had disappeared.

33

Zane ducked into a dark parlor. The violet flame of the candle in his right hand sent shadows flitting along the wall. Its grin and eye holes clogged with cobwebs, a porcelain mask of Comedy leered from the right-hand wall. Tragedy lay shattered by the baseboard.

Carefully, because he had no convenient way of relighting the candle, he set it on a dusty inlaid table. He tore several yellowed pages out of his moldering, musty-smelling *Collected Poems of Longfellow*, scattered them across the decrepit ottoman and overstuffed davenport, then set them on fire.

The escape plan was simple, though full of holes. He and Ben would range through the building setting fires, then rendezvous and watch what happened. With luck, the Malkavian caretakers would rush into the prison to put the blazes out. The Tyler brothers would see which door they came through, and try to slip out in the confusion.

Zane just wished that he could shake the fear that the psycho vampires might decide to let the mansion and its prisoners burn, simply for the sake of the spectacle.

The flames on the ottoman went out. The upholstery on the davenport caught sluggishly. It had been the same in other rooms. By and large, the decaying furniture didn't burn well.

But he couldn't spend any more time here, nursing this one fire. The idea was to start a lot of them. Tucking the book under his arm, he turned. Music quivered through the air.

He jumped. Glanced around wildly. Nothing else in the room was moving, nothing but the writhing yellow flames. The music was throbbing through the door.

He peeked out into the hall. It was empty. The way sound carried in the prison, the source of the serenade could be a long way off.

The music was the sweet, high song of a flute, floating above the usual chorus of lunatic laughter and moans. The tune was slow and soothing. Beautiful, really.

Zane grimaced. Who cared if it was pretty? Why was he standing here listening when he had things to do? He skulked down the corridor.

Within a few steps, a fresh wave of fatigue washed through him. He stumbled against the wall, and the candle slipped out of his hand. When it hit the floor, the violet flame went out.

With a curse, he stooped and fumbled for the candle with trembling fingers. When he straightened up, he felt a surge of dizziness, as if he'd been sitting for hours, then jumped to his feet too fast. He trudged back to the last room. The flute trilled.

Fortunately, the davenport was still burning. He relit the candle at the fire, and the world blurred. When it swam back into focus, he was sitting in a wing chair, staring at the flames.

He guessed that was all right. Obviously he needed to rest, or he wouldn't be able to function. He'd go on in one more minute. His eyelids drooped.

Something thudded. His eyes snapped open. The heavy book had slipped from under his arm. The fall had torn the front cover off.

Feeling dazed, he shook his head. He was dropping everything. What was his problem?

The flute told him that he shouldn't worry about it, just rest. The song began to carry him away. Then he noticed that it and the whisper of the flames were now the *only* sounds he heard. His fellow captives had shut up.

Abruptly he realized what was happening. The vampires wanted the prisoners on the same schedule as themselves, so they planted the same posthypnotic suggestion in every human's mind. When a captive heard the flute, as he would each morning, he was supposed to go to sleep.

Zane tried to stand up. Swaying, he barely made it. His body was numb, his muscles limp. Evidently even understanding that he'd been hypnotized wasn't enough to break the spell.

He held his hand over the purple candle flame. For a few seconds, he couldn't feel the heat. Then pain stabbed through the deadening haze of fatigue. He kept his palm near the fire for as long as he could bear it.

Finally, alert again, he tossed the candle away. He didn't have time to start any more fires. If Ben was lying somewhere with the evidence of his arson strewn around him, he had to find him before the vampires did. He tore up a page of "Hiawatha," wadded two pieces of paper, and stuffed them in his ears. Then he ran down the corridor. The air smelled smoky.

The makeshift earplugs muffled the music, but not completely. It still sucked at his mind. He gripped his bandaged wrist and dug his fingers into the tooth cuts. Once again, the pain helped. The cotton gauze grew wet.

He came to a T-intersection. He and Ben had prowled through the halls before splitting up, making sure that each knew where the other planned to go. He *thought* that he ought to look for his brother down the left passage, but, with the flute still clouding his thoughts, he wasn't sure. He wavered for a moment, then scowled and followed his instincts.

He passed three frames that had been turned to make their paintings face the wall. He couldn't remember seeing them before, and the narrow spiral staircase coming up on the right didn't look familiar either. Maybe he was lost. Maybe he needed to retrace his steps. Maybe—

A splash of wavering yellow light stained the darkness ahead.

It proved that Ben *had* come this way. Now grinning, Zane raced past the first of a series of fires.

Some were burning nicely. Maybe Ben had found better fuel than he had. The air grew hot, and the smoke in it thickened, until he began to cough.

He found Ben in a playroom, snoring facedown on top of an overturned rocking horse. His candle had rolled into the corner. Before he'd fallen asleep, he'd smashed a puppet theater, piled the fragments campfire-style, laid Punch, Judy, the Grim Reaper, and other hand puppets on top, and set it all ablaze. But the fire had jumped to the oval hooked rug under his right foot, and now it was licking up his pant leg.

Zane yanked him off the carpet, then slapped the flames on his calf out. Ben groaned, but didn't wake.

Wishing that he had some smelling salts, Zane shook him. Ben still wouldn't wake up. Finally, desperate, Zane squeezed his brother's pulped, purple nose between his thumb and forefinger.

Ben squirmed, and tried to shove him away. In his stupor, he used the hand with the broken fingers. His body went rigid, and his eyes flew open.

Zane let go of his nose and gripped his shoulders. "I'm sorry that I had to hurt you. But the flute is putting you to sleep, and you *have to stay awake*. Will you fight it? Do you understand?"

Ben blinked. "Yeah," he said thickly.

Zane grabbed the book Ben had been using for tinder and made two more paper wads. "Stuff these in your ears." Ben did. Zane hauled him to his feet. "Come on," he said, raising his voice to make sure that Ben could still hear him. "We can't stay here. We have to get to the observation post."

He hurried into the hall. Blundering after him, Ben staggered, and had to grab the doorjamb for support.

Zane poked him in the nose. Ben hissed and cringed. "Sorry again," Zane said, "but pain helps keep you awake." He looped Ben's arm around his shoulders and half carried him down the passage.

After they'd gone twenty feet, the music stopped abruptly. Maybe the player had just learned of the fires, and intended to help put them out.

Zane leaned Ben against the wall, then reached to give him another shake. Ben twisted away. "I'm awake, I'm awake!" he said. "Don't manhandle me anymore!"

"Okay!" said Zane. "Come on, then."

The observation post was simply the convergence of four long halls. Zane watched two, and Ben peeked down the others. For a while, nothing happened. Then, elsewhere in the building, rapid footsteps pounded. Something, probably a fire extinguisher, hissed.

"God damn it!" said Ben. "We guessed wrong." He sounded like he was struggling not to cry.

"Maybe not," said Zane. "There might be more than one door, and more than one group coming in. Hang in there."

Actually, he didn't believe his own pep talk. But as soon as he finished it, a door in one of the halls he was watching flew open. Two thin figures swarmed out of it and pivoted in his direction. The amber glow of a ceiling fixture gilded their snow-white skin.

Zane and Ben didn't dare let the vampires catch them spying. They scuttled down a different corridor and ducked into a room.

Zane held himself motionless. Held his breath. Wished that he could silence the pounding of his heart. After what seemed like a long time, the Malkavians' footsteps clattered through the intersection, then gradually faded away.

"So far so good," he whispered. "Let's check it out."

As they slunk back into the observation post, a plump Asian woman wearing only pajama bottoms whirled out of the hallway on the left. She was waltzing with an upended broom, and the straw was a crackling mass of flame. Her heavy breasts bouncing, she reeled into Ben and knocked him staggering.

"Didn't I tell you?" she said, grinning. "Didn't I? It's the Rapture!"

"Okay," said Zane. "That's good. Uh, you take care of yourself, all right?"

"You take care of *your*self. In a minute, *I'll* be in heaven, *laughing* at the tortures of the damned!" She danced down the same hall the vampires had taken.

Ben trembled. "Jesus Christ."

"I'm pretty sure that she was one of us humans," Zane said.

"Me, too, but she almost set me on fire." He squared his shoulders. "Never mind. If we're getting out, who cares?"

They crept to the door the vampires had come through. It looked exactly the same as the others in the passage. Ben hesitantly twisted the gleaming brass knob. The latch clicked, and the door cracked open. "I don't believe they left it unlocked," he whispered. "I was sure that we'd have to jimmy it somehow, or break it down."

"Chalk it up to them being excited, and nuts. Let's not talk anymore unless we have to. We aren't out of here yet."

Ben opened the door an inch, and they peeked through. At first glance, the dark hall on the other side was no different than the one in which they stood. Zane's heart sank. It looked as if they'd only discovered another section of the prison.

Damn it, no. He refused to believe that, at least until he knew it for certain. He nodded to Ben, and they slipped inside.

And as they sneaked down the corridor, he noticed the differences between its rooms and the ones he'd left behind. Some of these were clean. Some had TVs, waterbeds, lava lamps, and other modern furnishings. One held a drum kit, a six-foot stuffed Donald Duck, and a blond wood coffin covered with Disney cartoon-character decals.

He and Ben had found the Malkavians' barracks. It

must hold a way to the outside world. The exit probably wasn't even camouflaged, not from this side.

The brothers crept on toward a right-angle bend in the passage. A female voice said, "Why did the Tremere conjure the eclair?"

Ben jerked violently. Zane barely managed to stifle a similar reaction. He looked around, but couldn't see the creature who'd spoken. Trying to keep the fear out of his voice, he said, "I don't know, Ellen. Why?"

"Beats me. I guess you had to be there."

"That's cute." Still peering futilely about, he nudged Ben, signaling him to keep going forward.

"Where are you pretty boys headed?" Ellen asked.

"Just taking a walk," said Zane.

"*I* think that we should get out of the building," said the Malkavian. "Some wicked mice set the place on fire, and fire's *very* bad for my complexion."

For an instant, Zane thought he'd finally spotted her, lurking in the corner of a lightless room. But when he looked closer, the figure was only a department store mannequin dressed in leather and latex dominatrix gear. "That sounds good to me." He'd rather deal with one undead outside the prison than stay locked in with a small army of them.

"Oh, fudge," said Ellen. "I just remembered. You aren't allowed to leave, are you?"

"You can let us go if you want to," Zane said.

"Can I?" said Ellen. Zane tried to home in on her voice, but it seemed to croon from everywhere at once. "I'm afraid that your mommy wouldn't like it. But I'll tell you what. We'll play a little game of hide-and-seek. Catch me and give me a smooch, and the mice can scurry away across the field."

Zane tried to swallow away the dryness in his throat. "That sounds fair." While he and Ben looked for her, they could hunt for the exit, too, and run out as soon as they found it.

He reached through the doorway to one of the rooms, groping for a light switch. Something whizzed past his head, cracked against the wall, then clacked on the floor. Ben gasped. "No more light," said Ellen. "That's cheating."

The Tylers edged on down the hall. The harder Zane stared, trying to penetrate the darkness, the more the shadows squirmed and flowed, until it looked like mocking phantoms were skulking on every side.

Something rattled, then hissed. "What is that?" asked Ben. His voice was high and shaky.

"I don't know," said Zane. "Just keep moving."

Suddenly Ellen appeared in the last doorway before the turn. Even in the gloom, her eyes and the blade of her stiletto glittered. "That's right, sugar. Keep moving to me. *Come.*" Ben sobbed and lurched forward.

Zane lunged to pull him back. His feet flew out from under him, and he slammed down on his shoulder. As he floundered up, little balls, marbles or bearings, shifted under his shoes, trying to throw him down again. The clatter and hiss had been the sounds of Ellen dumping them on the floor.

When Ben reached her, she pointed at his injured hand and said, "Give." His arm shaking, he obeyed. She gripped the broken fingers. He cried out, and his legs buckled. She forced him to his knees, stepped behind him, and pressed the point of the knife against the side of his neck.

"Game over," she said brightly. "I win."

"All right," said Zane. "We surrender. Don't hurt him."

"No!" said Ben. "Forget me! You get away!"

"He can't," Ellen said. "I'm between him and the way out, remember? Now hush." She squeezed Ben's hand, and he whimpered.

Zane quivered, fighting the urge to rush her. "Please don't do that."

The woman with the nose ring smirked. "What's he worth to you?"

"Anything," Zane said.

"Would you be my childe? Become a Kindred for real?"

"Yes."

"Would you laugh at my jokes?" She pouted. "Everybody says, 'Good one, Ellen.' 'That's funny, Ellen.' But nobody ever even *chuckles*."

"I will."

She sighed. "But how would I know that you were sincere?" She rammed the stiletto into Ben's throat, then yanked it out again, so quickly that the motion was almost invisible. Blood spurted. She let go of his hand, and he collapsed. "I think it would be better if I just killed you." She glided forward.

34

Sartak studied the bond restraining his left hand. A cuff. A taut cable that looped around a stake, then ran back to the pallet of plastique. The apparatus had a deadly simplicity to it. Perhaps his old acquaintance Houdini could have defeated it, but he couldn't.

He sharpened his senses. If these were the final minutes of his existence, he might as well savor them.

Birds chirped and warbled. Motors grumbled as more and more drivers took to the highways. The smell of exhaust mixed with the perfume of flowers. The gray clouds in the east turned salmon and pink. He wished that he could watch the rising sun itself, one last time. But he suspected that it would cauterize his eyes.

He wasn't afraid to die. But taking stock, he discovered, as he always had in similar circumstances, that no matter how pointless and tiresome his existence often seemed, he wanted to continue it, if only until he could make good on his threat to Blake.

And perhaps he *could* survive. He very much doubted it, but he meant to try.

The air grew warm, then hot. The rim of the sun oozed above the row of derelict apartment buildings. The red light drove spikes of pain through his eyes. He squinched them shut and twisted his face away. His head and hands, the uncovered parts of him, began to burn.

To cook. Contrary to Blake's prediction, he didn't burst into flame. The psychic had failed to divine that, along with inhuman strength and speed, he possessed the ability to resist the ravages of sunlight and fire. And that was what would save him if anything could.

But not yet. For the moment, he could only lie here and suffer. He waited for what seemed a long time, then cracked his eyes open. To his dismay, his hands were only red and blistered.

He closed his eyes. His flesh began to pop and sizzle, and a sickening odor of roasting meat filled the air. His whole body throbbed. Even the skin under his clothes was charring.

The agony in his head and hands was the worst he'd ever known. He clenched himself, fighting the brute, unreasoning urge to buck and thrash. By now he *wanted* to trigger the bomb, yearned to blast himself unconscious and end the pain, but he wouldn't. A Mongol warrior didn't surrender.

He checked his hands again. They'd shriveled into claws, bones covered only by a brittle crust of blackened skin.

Moving with infinite care, he pressed the fingers of his right hand together and slipped it from its shackle. Then he did the same with his left. As his fingertips cleared the cuff, they shuddered. But they didn't catch on the bracelet. Didn't tug it.

All right, old man, Sartak thought sardonically, *now for the hard part*.

He tried to sit up. It took every bit of his strength. Leaning forward and twisting, he fumbled with his right shoe. If he was to free his feet, they had to wither, also.

His ruined hands were weak, clumsy, and shook uncontrollably. He half expected them to jerk against the ankle cable and set off the plastique. But they didn't, and finally he managed to uncover his foot. Pain blazed through it. He stiffened his leg to keep from kicking, then went to work on the left shoe and sock.

Mercifully, they came off a little easier. He covered his head and hands with his coat, and waited.

The pain hammered him. His feet crackled and shrank, but incredibly slowly. He hated them for that. If he'd had an ax, he would have chopped them off.

But at last they were damaged enough, or at least he hoped so. With pain, glare, and tears of blood clouding his vision, it was hard to be sure. He flexed his right leg, and it slipped out of its shackle. The left came free as well.

And now that he'd come this far, he waited for the punch line of the joke.

Because he was all but certain that someone was watching him. Blake himself had alluded to studying the style in which condemned Cainites died. Therefore, now that Sartak had extricated himself from the fetters, he expected a squad of ghouls to appear and shoot him to pieces.

But they hadn't shown up yet, so he decided to make for the huge old house. It was the nearest object large enough to shield him from the sun.

He struggled to stand up. His legs were more rickety

than a newborn colt's. His burning feet cracked and crumbled under his weight. Wrapping his head and hands in his coat again, he stumbled across the grass.

Suddenly he fell, jolting fresh pain through his body. When he peeked through the folds of the coat, he realized that he must have slipped into a daze for a while, and drifted off course in the process. He'd wandered into the parking lot beside the building.

It must have taken him at least a couple of minutes to get here. And still no ghouls. Perhaps they were curious to see just how far he could get. Not much farther, he suspected.

Or maybe something had distracted them from their vigil. But that hope seemed so remote, so ludicrous, that he sneered at it.

He tried to rise, but this time, he didn't have the strength or the equilibrium. His knees and the palms of his blasted hands slammed back against the asphalt.

He'd crawl, then. Creep under the nearest parked car and rest in its shade. He dragged himself forward. His hands and feet crunched. Pieces broke off, making a trail. He covered another five yards, and then a tide of darkness carried him away.

35

Zane stared, frozen, until Ellen opened her mouth. Then it hit him that she was about to command him, too. He wrenched his gaze away from her face. She said, "Come." But it didn't affect him.

"Sly mouse," she said. "You've got us all figured out, haven't you?" Her fangs lengthened. She kept advancing.

Zane trembled. He wanted to run back through the door at the end of the hall, lose himself in the maze of passages deeper inside the building. But he didn't dare. He was sure that he'd be throwing away his only chance to escape. So he lunged into the room with the mannequin instead. He frantically slammed the door, then twisted the lock.

An instant later, weight thudded against the outside of the panel. "Nimble mouse," Ellen said. "But what will you do now?"

Open the door again and fight her. Quickly, before reinforcements arrived. But first he'd come up with a strategy, and arm himself, if possible. Squinting, he flipped on the light.

The room held a bunk bed, a cedar chest, a floor-to-ceiling stack of outdated phone directories, a display case of model ships in bottles, and, of course, the bondage dummy. Which, he now noticed, carried a coiled black whip clipped to its corset.

A great weapon, if you were Indiana Jones. Probably useless if you were Zane Tyler. Still, it was better than nothing, and he grabbed it.

The door thudded, and he jumped. The masked mannequin seemed to sneer at him.

He tried to breathe slowly and deeply. He had to pull himself together, or he was beaten before he started. Ellen wasn't inhumanly strong like Sartak, or she would have broken in already. She couldn't control Zane if he didn't look at her eyes. He had a chance, even if she was a monster.

"This is *boring*," Ellen sang. "I'm going to get a key. You wait right there." Her footsteps clicked away from the door. He imagined her creeping back, smirking.

He knelt and ransacked the chest. *Please*, he prayed, *let there be a gun in here*. But he only found Banana Republic hiking shorts, gaudy Hawaiian shirts, a Purple Heart in a velvet case, and a sheaf of faded love letters tied with a green ribbon.

Scowling, he stood up, removed two of the bottles from the case, and set them on the floor beside the door. Pulled a blanket off the top bunk, and shook out the whip. Finally, tiptoeing, holding his breath, he positioned himself with the bottles, and opened the lock.

Time crawled by. Straining, he listened. Far away, somebody laughed, but he couldn't hear anything nearby. He wondered if Ellen *had* wandered off to find a key. Then the door boomed.

This time, it flew open, and the vampire hurtled

through. He'd hoped that she'd flounder around off-balance, and not spot him for a moment. But in the blink of an eye, she pivoted to face him.

He struck at her with the whip. It cracked. The lash missed, but she turned, tracking its flight. In that instant, he threw the blanket, and it fell over her head.

He dropped the whip, grabbed the bottles, and sprang at her. The stiletto stabbed at him, missing his stomach by an inch. He swung his right-hand bottle against her forehead.

Despite the cushioning blanket, the weapon shattered. Shards of sparkling glass and fragments of tiny masts and rigging tumbled through the air. She staggered. He drove the jagged stump of the bottle into her chest.

The knife leaped at him. He blocked with his left hand, and the point skated along his bloody bandage. He slammed the broken bottle into her breasts again. Another solid hit. Maybe she'd fall down.

Her foot hooked his ankle and jerked him off-balance. The heel of her empty hand bashed his jaw. As he toppled, he wondered how she could target him so accurately when she couldn't see. His left-hand bottle broke when he hit the floor. Bits of glass and balsa wood dug into his back.

Ellen whirled the blanket away. Her face, blouse, and jacket were bloody, but it didn't look like she was bleeding anymore. In fact, the cut above her nose was closing as he watched.

She beckoned, signaling him to stand up. He did so hesitantly, trying to look panicky, then lunged and slashed.

She twisted out of the way. The stiletto streaked at him. He dodged, and escaped with a scratched shoulder.

For a while, they circled. Struck and parried. He didn't hit her again, nor she him. But he began to pant, and slow down. She moved as agilely as ever. She smiled, and her eyes danced.

She tapped her cheek with the stiletto. The bloody blade left another stripe of red. "Look," she said.

He'd been so worried about the knife that he'd forgotten her hypnotic powers. He already *had* been looking at her face, and now he found that he couldn't tear his eyes away.

In desperation, he tried to rush her. "Stay," she said. His muscles locked before he could take a step.

She touched her face again. "Look. Look. Look." He felt a deadness creeping over him. It was like the spell of the flute. He wasn't losing consciousness, but something else was slipping away, leaving him equally defenseless.

"Did you think that all I could do was command?" she asked. "Wrong-o! Pablo is teaching me to mesmerize. I'm getting the hang of it, but I need really solid eye contact. Toss the bottles behind you."

He didn't want to obey. His hands flipped the weapons anyway. Glass crashed and tinkled.

"Thank you," said Ellen. "Now sit down on the bed and close your eyes. Stay still until I tell you to move."

Once again, he struggled to resist, and failed.

"That's good," said the vampire. "Now, I need some blood, to replace what leaked out. And since *you* cut me, it's only fair that you give me yours."

The floorboards creaked as she edged closer. She was advancing so slowly that he suspected that she wasn't sure that she really had him under control.

Damn it, if her power was that weak, he *ought* to be able to shake it off. But he felt like he'd forgotten the right *way* to try.

He smelled the blood on her clothes when she sat beside him. Cool fingers stroked his cheek. "Don't worry, mouse," she said. "It only hurts a little." The wet tip of her tongue slid up and down his neck. As if she were teasing herself, or this were foreplay.

Fighting for his own life, he'd virtually forgotten that this creature had murdered Ben. But now, suddenly, he remembered the way she'd grinned. Saw the blade ram into his brother's neck as clearly as if it were happening all over again. Hatred surged through him, and, without thinking, he shoved her violently away.

His eyes snapped open. She sprawled on the floor, gaping in obvious astonishment. If not for the blood on her face, and her glistening fangs, her expression might have looked comical.

The stiletto lay between them. They both snatched for it at the same instant. For once, he was faster.

He stabbed at her face, and she threw herself backward. He dived on top of her.

She grabbed the wrist of his knife arm. Bucked, scratched at his eyes, and struck at him like a snake. Her nails tore his cheeks. He fumbled at her neck, struggling to grip it and hold her fangs away. Tried to drive the stiletto into her heart.

At first it wouldn't move, but finally it started to jerk downward, an inch at a time. Ellen grinned. She kissed the air, a good-bye gesture, then let go of his arm. The stiletto plunged into the center of her tattered blouse. She thrashed, then lay still.

Zane was sure that he hadn't killed her. He wished that he could carry her out into the sun, but her weight would slow him down. He stabbed her in the chest repeatedly, slashed her throat, then put out her eyes. With luck, it would keep her from jumping right back up and chasing him. Besides, it felt good. In fact, once he got going, it was hard to stop.

But finally, gasping, soaked in sweat, he managed to clamber to his feet. He hurried back up the gloomy hall. Once he stepped on a marble, and nearly fell.

He found Ben crumpled in a pool of blood. Death made him look smaller, as if somehow he'd become the little brother. His staring eyes gleamed in the amber light.

Zane faltered. He didn't want to leave Ben here. That would feel like a final betrayal. But he knew that if Ben could talk, he'd tell him to move on fast, and don't look back. He stooped and closed the dead man's eyes, then, shaking with grief, guilt, and rage, strode on.

He peeked around the turn. The corridor ended in a door just a few feet ahead. Pressing his ear to it, he heard nothing. He turned the handle and cracked it open.

On the other side was yet another corridor, with faded wallpaper and the occasional piece of decaying antique furniture. But this one had windows set in the opposite wall. Golden sunlight spilled through the dirty glass. When he saw it, he started to cry.

After stepping through, he noticed that this side of the door was camouflaged to look like a part of the wall. He skulked down the gallery, hunting an exit. The first one he came to was locked. He worked the stiletto into the crack between the door and the frame, then pried. He didn't know what he was doing, but he got lucky. The latch popped open.

He stumbled out into the morning. The mild air felt warm after the dank chill inside. The grass under his feet was deliciously soft. He wanted to stop and look at the blue sky, but he knew that he wasn't anywhere near out of danger yet. He crept along the grimy brick wall.

After a few yards, the scenes behind the windows changed. Now he was peeking into offices and conference rooms with modern furnishings. Evidently he'd reached the part of the Institute where the real hospital operated. In a tiny kitchen, a tired-looking nurse and orderly stood calmly drinking coffee, as if they didn't know about the fires. Maybe they were ordinary people, who didn't even realize that they worked next door to a torture chamber and a nest of devils.

Crouching, Zane tiptoed on toward a parking lot and the traffic noises beyond it. He wanted to get off the property as soon as possible. Disappear into the streets.

A dark mass on the tarmac caught his eye. Creeping closer, he saw that it was a corpse in a pinstriped suit, sprawled on its belly. Its jacket covered its head and hands, and its bare feet were black and withered. It reeked of burnt meat.

Zane wondered if this was some poor crazy person who'd died in one of *his* fires. Christ, he hoped not. But the important question was, how had the guy wound up in the parking lot? He peered about, looking for someone who might have carried the cadaver here. He didn't see anyone.

Forget it, then. Sad and strange as the situation was, it wasn't important. The only thing that mattered was escape. He loped past the corpse and on across the lot. The pavement stung his bare feet.

Then he realized how short the dead man had been. What's more, the body was bowlegged. He ran back and knelt beside it.

He pulled the coat away, then tried to roll the corpse over. Even through its clothes, the body was hot enough to burn him. He snatched his hands away, then, gritting his teeth, took hold of it again.

When it turned, crisp, black flakes broke off it. Its charred, eyeless face was unrecognizable, but fangs jutted from its skeletal grin. Zane opened one of its shirt buttons, then pulled the folds of cloth apart.

The skin inside was burnt, too, but not as badly. He could tell that it had once been a dusky yellow. As soon as sunlight hit it, the blisters began to burst. Blood gushed out. Flesh sizzled like frying bacon.

Just as Zane had feared, the dead man was Sartak. Evidently the vampire hadn't abandoned him after all. He'd come to rescue him, and gotten killed instead. "I'm sorry," Zane murmured. He started to get up, and then something occurred to him.

How did he *know* that Sartak was dead? How *could* you know, when vampires didn't breathe or have heartbeats, and recovered from wounds that could kill anything normal? Zane hastily draped the double-breasted jacket over the top of the vampire's body again, then shrugged off his antique coat and laid it over his feet.

Now what? He couldn't leave Sartak behind, but he didn't see how he could take him along, either. Even if he had the strength left to carry him, he couldn't stagger down the sidewalk with a seared husk of a body in his arms.

A motor growled, growing louder. Tires hummed on pavement. Startled, Zane looked up. A green Corolla was rolling up the elm-lined drive.

Zane ducked behind a station wagon with a TAMPA BAY BUCCANEERS bumper sticker. The Toyota pulled into a space about fifty feet away. One of its doors clicked open, then thumped shut. Keeping low, using other cars for cover, Zane stalked the person who'd gotten out, a fortyish guy with broad shoulders, a beer gut, and a garish plaid sports coat.

The man heard Zane, or sensed him somehow, when he was still a few feet away. He pivoted, frowned, and his right hand whipped into his jacket. Zane glimpsed the butt of a gun.

He charged. The next couple of seconds seemed to last a long time. He watched the automatic clear the tan leather shoulder holster, arc through the air, and drop to cover him as if it were all happening in slow motion.

And maybe it was, because he lunged into striking range a split second before the gunman could get him in his sights. He shoved the stiletto into the paunchy man's chest. The guy made a choking noise and dropped, the pistol tumbling from his hand. His legs kicked for a moment, and then he lay still.

Zane crouched beside him, fumbled through his pockets, and found his keys. He ran to the Corolla, drove it to Sartak, and dumped him in the trunk. The hatch would protect him from any more sun.

He stuffed in the man he'd just killed, too. If nobody found his corpse, it might take a while for anyone to miss him or start looking for his car.

Shaking, his cuts and bruises aching, Zane set the gun and the bloody knife on the bucket seat beside him. He put the Corolla in gear and headed for the highway.

36

The personnel manager told the blonde that she wasn't qualified for the position. She smiled, said that she could handle *any* position, and unzipped her short red dress. A moment later, they were writhing and moaning on top of the desk.

Grimacing, Zane pointed the remote and zapped the porno actors off the screen. Much as he needed distraction, he couldn't relate to a movie where every encounter led to sex instead of cruelty and violence. And the programs on the ordinary channels seemed just as unreal.

He looked at the charred, stinking object lying motionless on the bed. *That* was what was real. It and all the other horrors like it.

After he'd gotten away from Blake's Institute, he'd parked behind a Publix supermarket and examined the contents of the dead ghoul's wallet. He found three hundred dollars. Then, rummaging through Sartak's pockets, he discovered his own wallet, also full of cash, and his keys. It made him wish that he knew where the Mustang was.

He put on the ghoul's clothes, all but the bloody shirt and tie. The shoes were too loose and the pants too baggy. He had to punch a new hole in the belt. Still, he probably looked less conspicuous than before.

Next, using an alias, he checked into a seedy hot-pants motel on Nebraska Avenue. Praying that no one was watching, he carried Sartak into his room. Then he drove the Corolla across town, ditched it, bought a T-shirt, food, and first aid supplies in a convenience store, and rode the bus back to his accommodations.

For the rest of the morning, he slumped in the chair by the curtained window. The automatic; the stiletto; a loaf of whole-wheat bread; packs of ham, salami, and cheese; boxes of raisins; and bottles of apple juice sat on the round, Formica-topped table beside him. He knew that he needed to eat, but every time he tried, his stomach churned. He needed to rest, too, but that was just as difficult. Ghastly images kept flashing through his mind. Rose's shredded body. Meg killing herself. Ellen and Marilyn lunging at him, fangs bared. The blade punching into Ben's neck. Tears ran down his cheeks. His throat felt clogged, and he shivered.

He also knew that he shouldn't just sit. If Sartak *was* alive, he surely needed blood, and only Zane was here to supply it. But the idea filled him with revulsion. He hadn't fought his way out of the Malkavians' prison to give himself to another vampire now.

He told himself that Sartak wasn't like the others. But how could he believe it? He'd watched the Mongol attack innocent people. Heard him *admit* that he was heartless.

Still, he'd helped Zane investigate Rose's murder when no one else would. And in the end, he'd gotten burnt to a cinder trying to rescue him. So finally, Zane stood up, picked up the stiletto, and sat down beside the blackened husk on the mattress. The springs creaked.

He pricked the tip of his left index finger. The puncture stung. He worked the digit between Sartak's teeth.

He'd imagined a leathery rag of a tongue rasping it. Charred lips puckering and sucking. But nothing happened. He felt a guilty pang of relief. He pulled his hand back, washed it at the sink, and put a Band-Aid on it.

He didn't keep the bandage on. Over the course of the afternoon, he tried to feed Sartak three more times, with the same lack of response. Probably the crumbling thing on the bedspread was dead. When he really looked at it, he wondered how he could ever have imagined otherwise.

Since vampires slept during the day, he'd try to revive Sartak one more time, after sunset. But if that didn't work, it would be time to give up on him and figure out what to do next.

He watched the local news. Neither he nor the ghoul he'd knifed were mentioned, nor was any fire at the Institute. Maybe the vamps liked to keep any hint of their business out of the public eye. Maybe Zane didn't have to worry about anybody filing charges against him. Not that that would keep Blake's pet cops from hunting him down.

Gradually the light outside the curtains faded. When it was completely gone, Zane went back to the bed, peeled off the Band-Aid, picked off his scab, and put his finger in Sartak's mouth.

The charred lips pursed. New cracks split the shriveled face, and bits of it broke away. A noose of rough, dry flesh tightened around Zane's finger. Teeth scraped it. He shuddered, resisting the urge to yank it back.

After a while, one of Sartak's clawlike hands twitched. Shaking, it rose from the bedspread, pawed the bloodstained bandage on Zane's wrist, then feebly closed around it. A minute later, the other hand did the same.

Slowly, almost imperceptibly, their grip tightened. The vampire's mouth, not so dry now, worked faster. Then, suddenly, the blasted creature let go of Zane's finger and plunged its fangs into the heel of his hand.

Zane gasped at the jab of pain. Now he did reflexively try to jerk his arm free, but he couldn't break Sartak's hold.

Fighting panic, he told himself that everything was all right. Sartak couldn't get enough blood out of the tiny finger wound, so he'd punched better holes. That didn't mean that he'd gone berserk. That he'd drain Zane to death.

The vampire began to *slurp*. Zane felt faint, and the room tilted. At last he couldn't stand it anymore. "Stop!" he shouted. "Sartak, it's me! You're taking too much!"

The undead thing kept guzzling. Zane grabbed it and shoved it away, simultaneously lurching up from the bed.

He made it to his feet, but he still didn't break Sartak's grip. The vampire clung to him like a tick, and the weight threw him off-balance. He fell on his back with Sartak sprawled across his legs.

The living corpse sucked a final swallow from his hand, then began to pull itself up his arm, just as if it were climbing a rope. Its eye sockets were still empty, but something glistened wetly in their depths. Its withered face humped and squirmed, shedding triangles of dead tissue. Its teeth gnashed spastically. Zane was sure that it meant to sink them into his throat.

He gripped its body and rolled, putting himself on top. He clenched his fists and hammered it, twice grazing himself on its snapping fangs.

Abruptly, Sartak stopped struggling. His arms flopped down on the ratty brown carpet. Zane scrambled off him and bolted for the door.

His hands shook so badly that for a few seconds he couldn't unfasten the chain. Finally it clattered out of its track. He tore at the dead bolt.

"Sorry," Sartak croaked.

Startled, Zane whirled. The vampire still lay on the floor, his body swelling and jerking in the throes of regeneration. He only had a few black patches left on his head. Fuzz sprouted on his scalp. "Sorry," he repeated.

Zane still desperately wanted to run away. Instead, panting, he said, "Are you all right now?"

"In . . . control," Sartak said. Blobs of red jelly seethed in his eye sockets. "Not strong . . . yet. Still hungry."

Zane realized that he didn't feel dizzy anymore. Maybe the feeling had had more to do with terror than blood loss. Cringing inwardly, he said, "I guess I could give you a little more."

"No," Sartak said. His voice sounded stronger. "No more from you. Where are we?"

"In a sleazy motel."

Sartak smiled. His teeth were glazed with red. "Perfect. Find me a prostitute hungry enough to help a scar-faced pervert act out a vampire fantasy. I promise not to kill her."

37

Blake put his hands around Robot's neck. Her skin was greasy for lacking of washing, and she smelled of sweat and waste. He squeezed lightly.

At the same time, he touched her mind. He wanted to make sure that she understood what was happening. Wanted to taste her desperation.

Robot's psyche squirmed feebly, trying to shrink back into the darkness of Lauren's subconscious, like some soft-bodied mollusk struggling to crawl back under an overturned rock. Yet she wasn't truly afraid. A dull resignation tinged her thoughts.

Blake sneered. Surely this passive lump could never hurt him. Any threat had died with Ligeia. He could finish strip-mining her essence over the next few days, or just strangle her now and be done with it. The idea made his hands tingle.

But somehow Sartak and Tyler had escaped. And if they hadn't had the good sense to flee the area, it was remotely possible that Lauren might prove useful, as a lure or a bargaining chip. And so, breathing heavily, Blake released her.

He looked at his watch and was surprised to discover how long he's spent staring down at her. It was nearly time for a meeting that ought to prove more satisfying. He left the cell, sauntered across the prison, and slipped through another secret door. Beyond it was an antechamber, and a pair of ghouls with assault riles. Straightening his tie, he gave them a nod and strolled through the entry between them.

The throne room here was a long, candlelit hall with a two-step pyramidal dais at the far end. Dingy oils depicting life in colonial America adorned the walls. The place was regal enough, in a shadowy, musty sort of way, but nowhere near as impressive as the top floor of the skyscraper. Still, Blake preferred it, because there were generally more Malkavians and even Nosferatu, and fewer Ventrue, in attendance. Certainly that was the case tonight. It made him feel more firmly in control.

Roderick, Pablo, and Judith were already seated. Spotting Blake, the Prince beckoned impatiently, summoning him to his customary chair. It wasn't on the platform—that would have outraged too many of the Kindred—but it was nearby, so that Roderick and the Primogen could consult him at need.

Blake took his place, not a moment too soon. Malachi Jones hurried into the hall a heartbeat later.

The murmuring crowd parted for him. "I'm sorry if I've held things up," he said, heading for his seat. "I came as quickly as I could."

"Don't sit down," Roderick said. "I need to talk to you, and look you in the eye while I do it."

If Jones was surprised, he didn't show it. "Very well." He stood at parade rest. His pale skin, black boots, and the pearl stickpin in his cravat shone in the firelight.

Roderick nodded to the bailiff. The ghoul thumped his staff on the floor. "Oyez, oyez, oyez! The court of Roderick, Prince of Tampa Bay, is now in session." The crowd fell silent.

Jones said, "We aren't usually so formal, unless someone is on trial. Am I?"

Roderick grimaced. "No. Not yet. I hope not ever. But this morning, near sunrise, we had some problems. Someone set fires around the prison. A kine named Tyler escaped. The fire alarm distracted everyone who intended to watch Sartak's execution. Then *he* escaped. Leonard Dallas, a ghoul who should have reported for work about that time, disappeared. We think that Sartak, Tyler, or both of them killed him for his car. Our people are hunting them, but so far, all they've discovered is that the kine's family, a sister-in-law and her son, have left the city. Now, my question to you is this: Where did you and your servants pass the hours between last night's tribunal and dawn?"

"We were at my home."

"Was anyone with you?"

"No. Are you implying that *I* helped the prisoners get away?"

"I don't want to believe that. But what are the odds of a kine slipping out of here, or a Kindred cheating the Two Fires, unaided? What are the chances of both events happening at once?"

"Slim, I imagine. But what makes you think that I had anything to do with it?"

"You didn't approve of the way *I* handled Sartak."

Jones shrugged. "No, but as always, I accepted your decision. Why the deuce would I capture the man in the first place, if I were on his side instead of yours?"

"Because you couldn't let him go while everyone was watching. Or perhaps you thought that his lies would win me over."

"No, I bought him in because it's my duty to obey your commands. Although I still do think that you should listen to his story. Conceivably, it has a bearing on—"

"No!" Roderick barked. Blake lifted his hand to cover a grin. "You can't distract me with gibberish. We have *facts* to talk about." He looked into the audience. "Come forward, James McConnell."

A brown-haired Ventrue with a fleshy spike of a nose stepped out of the crowd. Like Jones, he'd dressed for the nineteenth century. He looked uncomfortable, no doubt because the two of them were friends.

Roderick said, "Did you see Malachi here, early last night?"

McConnell grimaced. "Yes."

"Was there anything unusual about his appearance?"

"He didn't have a coat."

"The proper Malachi Jones?" Judith snarled. A string of bloody slobber oozed from beneath her veil. "Astonishing!"

"I gave it to one of the prisoners," Jones said. "He was all but naked, and cold. I don't like to see kine suffer unnecessarily. What of it?"

Roderick said, "Now we need Ellen Orsini."

One of the Malkavians in the crowd yelled, "Ellie, baby, come on *down*!" The bailiff thumped for order.

Ellen burst out of the audience. Her conservative coat and blouse were tattered and bloody, and her face was a web of half-healed scars. The diamond in her nose ring flashed. "Ta-daaaa!" she sang.

"Thankyouthankyouthankyou. Who wants to hear a joke?"

Several people groaned.

"Another time," Roderick said. "We have to attend to business first. Did you see Zane Tyler while he was escaping?"

"Sure." She pointed to her cheeks. "He gave me my new look. Cool, huh?"

"Describe his clothing."

"A pair of cutoffs and an old-timey tuxedoey-looking jacket like you Blue Bloods wear." The crowd babbled. She gave Jones an apologetic smile. "Sorry, Malster."

"Sir," said McConnell, addressing the throne, "that proves nothing. It's merely a coincidence."

"It's a *link*," Judith said. "A tie between an enemy and a traitor."

Jones said, "Be prepared to answer for that insult, at a more appropriate time and place." He shifted his gaze to Roderick. "Is that the sum of the evidence against me? A chain of inchoate speculation and a cast-off garment?"

Roderick rolled his walking stick in his fingers. "It isn't proof, but it is troubling."

Jones sneered. "Is it, indeed. After all these years of service. Then I ask Pablo to examine my aura and read my mind."

Blake had wondered if Jones would take this tack. Born conspirators and hoarders of secrets, Kindred often refused to submit to telepathy even when innocent of the specific accusation being leveled against them.

Pablo glanced up. Roderick nodded. The Malkavian elder stared at Jones. Finally he said, "He *seems* loyal."

"But?" Roderick asked.

"He has a strong, disciplined will. He *might* be hiding something, even from me." He grinned at Jones. "I, too, am sorry, my friend."

"Yes," said Jones sardonically, "I can tell."

Roderick sighed. "Here's what it comes down to. I need lieutenants that I can trust implicitly, particularly now. This diabolist could be an agent of the Sabbat. And so, old friend, I offer you a choice. Accept my Blood Bond, or step down from your post, at least for the time being."

"I revere you, sire, But I don't love you more than my free will. I resign. May I go?" Roderick nodded. His bony jaw clenched and his head held high, Jones turned and marched out.

The Prince smiled at McConnell. "I name you his replacement. Congratulations."

"With respect, sir, I don't want to replace him. He's innocent and you shouldn't have discharged him. It's an insult to your own clan."

"God damn your impudence!" Roderick shouted. His charisma blazed forth, an irresistible wave of majesty and anger, and everyone quailed. "Very well, I'll speak for the Ventrue myself. That makes more sense anyway. The session's adjourned. Alexander, I'll see you in my suite." He strode through a small door behind the dais. Exultant, Blake hurried after him.

Jones did have a strong will. Of all the Kindred of Tampa Bay, he was the least susceptible to Blake's influence, and thus couldn't be allowed to remain as the Prince's right-hand man. Blake had often toyed with the idea of murdering him, or framing him for some heinous crime, but such a course of action seemed unnecessarily risky. Better to undermine Roderick's confidence in him a bit at a time.

And now that Jones had been obliging enough to

compromise himself, the strategy had paid off. In the light of present circumstances, the Ventrue's behavior really did seem suspicious. If Blake hadn't read his mind, Tyler's, and Sartak's, all without uncovering any hint that Jones was collaborating with the other two, he might have doubted his fidelity himself.

He caught up with Roderick in the corridor. The ferrule of the Prince's cane clicked against the floor. "That was hard," the Kindred said.

"I know. But it was necessary, and you handled it well."

Roderick sighed. "Did I? I wonder. Yesterday I thought Malachi was losing his mind, and today I'm worried that he's betrayed me. God knows what's really going on. All I'm sure of is that I want him watched. Him and McConnell both."

Blake nodded gravely. "I think that's very wise."

38

Polly, a skinny, haggard hooker with stringy chestnut hair, trembled, then began to shake. Her beads and bracelets rattled. Finally she tried to tear herself out of Sartak's grasp.

The vampire held her immobile on the bed. He was nude except for the towel around his waist. He'd said that in these circumstances, it would look less alarming than his sooty, bloodstained clothing. His Adam's apple bobbed as he gulped the woman's blood.

Watching from the corner, Zane felt an urge to rush to Polly's rescue. To rip the vampire off her and pound him against the wall. But he only said, "Remember your promise."

Sartak drank for a few more seconds, then said, "I do." He licked the twin fang wounds away, climbed off his victim, and patted her on the shoulder. "Thank you. You can go now."

Wild-eyed, shaking, Polly got up and edged toward the door. "What did you do to me?" she whimpered.

"Nothing that will hurt you," Zane said, "as long as you keep your mouth shut." He held out two twenties and a ten.

She stared at the money for a moment, then snatched it and stuffed it down the front of her tube top. She had as much trouble unlocking the door as he'd had five hours before.

When she was gone, he asked, "Was *that* enough?" Polly was the third prostitute that he'd brought to the room.

"Believe it or not," Sartak said drily. A burn scar melted off his cheek. "And now shall we trade stories?"

Zane shrugged. "I guess."

"Good. Since you furnished my supper, let me satisfy your curiosity first. After I discovered that you were missing . . ."

When it was his turn, Zane described his ordeal as briefly as possible. He didn't want to let himself relive it for fear that he'd break down. As it was, waves of grief and dread surged through him. At times he had to force the words out.

When he finished, Sartak said, "Thank you for saving my life. I'm in your debt. And I'm sorry about your brother."

"Yeah. Me, too. You know, right up to the end, he never once blamed me for getting him into trouble. He was in terrible pain, and scared shitless, but he wouldn't cave in to it. And then that *thing* killed him for no reason at all." He squinched his eyes shut.

"Well, now it's our turn to do the killing." Sartak started to prowl around the room. "Having identified the enemy, we can finally go on the offensive."

Zane hesitated, then said, "Ben said that we were in hell, and he was right. I got out by dumb luck. I don't know if I could make myself go back in."

Sartak raised his eyebrows. "Don't you want to avenge his death?"

"Of course I do! But revenge won't bring him back, and he wouldn't want me to die trying to get it."

"There are one or two practical issues at stake as well. Blake and his allies won't allow you to simply resume your normal life. Not knowing what you know."

"Then I can go away. Change my identity if I have to."

"That might work. But what about Rose?"

"All along, I've been denying the truth, but I can't afford to any longer. I can't bring her back, either."

"In some sense, the woman you saw in Blake's hidden room *is* Rose."

Something twisted in Zane's chest. "No. She's just Robot. A shell. A pile of ashes. And Blake's killed her by now anyway."

"Not necessarily. He may still want to steal her psychic potential, and with her occupying the Lauren body, that will take time. Besides which, he planned to kill her only when he was certain that he'd defused the threat of the premonition. And as I pointed out to him, as long as I'm around, that particular sword still hangs above him."

"Even if we could get her away from him, she wouldn't survive. Not with Ligeia gone. She said when the last of her Sisters died, she'd fade away." Zane's fists clenched. "I don't think that I'm a coward—"

"You're not," said Sartak gently. "You just have a case of shell shock."

"—but I don't want to die for nothing. Hell, maybe I shouldn't have loved Rose in the first place. Maybe I wouldn't have if she'd been a complete person, instead of a pretty doll with all the normal human selfishness and anger left out."

"And yet you still do love her," Sartak said. "Even now. Which suggests that she gave you more than pliancy."

Zane nodded glumly.

"Over the centuries," Sartak said, "I've watched hordes of people pursue countless noble causes and bold endeavors. Do you know how many of those efforts worked out the way they were intended?"

Zane shrugged.

"Not one," Sartak said. "Time and chance happened to them all. Sooner or later, every hope falls apart, or goes awry. We Mongols died by the thousands to found an empire, and it started to disintegrate as soon as Chingis died. Martin Luther tried to reform Christianity and laid the foundations for a godless society. Engineers built levees along the Mississippi and set the stage for the most devastating flood in the river's history."

Zane snorted. "What are you saying? That if if I risk my neck over a girl who's not only gone forever but maybe never existed in the first place, that makes as much sense as fighting Hitler?"

"Exactly," said Sartak. He grinned. "And since I *did* fight Hitler, I ought to know. If you did it out of love instead of ideology, it would make *more* sense, because in the final reckoning, your feelings are all you have. Take it from someone who's watched a thousand creeds and causes come and go. Every temple is built on quicksand, and every destination is a mirage. But the paradox is this: You have to stand for *something*, whatever your heart insists is important, or you'll turn into venomous scum like Blake. Or, perhaps, me. And that's a far worse fate than playing the fool."

Zane sighed. "You're going after Blake whether I do or not, aren't you?"

Sartak nodded. "I told him that I was going to kill him, and I like to keep that kind of promise. But I'm not urging you to come along because I'm afraid to face him alone. I'm doing it for your sake. I think that if you run away, you'll loathe yourself until the day you die."

"All right. I hate it that you're right, but you are. Do you really think we have a chance against him?"

Sartak smiled coldly. "Count on it. We know everything we need to know to bring him down."

39

Sartak was on his guard from the moment that he and Zane stepped off the bus. He was certain that Blake's agents were hunting him. And, having bagged him in Ybor City once, they might be combing the area now.

So he stalked through the crowds on Seventh Avenue with his senses sharpened. His eyes probed every doorway and patch of shadow, flicked up to scan the windows overhead. The streetlights cast round white moons on the glass. His ears strained for the click of a hammer cocking, or the hiss of a blade sliding from a sheath.

At first Zane was equally wary. But when he saw the Mustang, his gaze locked on it. Someone had broken the driver's-side window, and scratched obscenities on the hood. He ran to the car and peered inside. "Damn it! They stole the radio!"

Sartak smiled. If his companion could get incensed over something so trivial, he must be recovering from his battle fatigue. "Don't worry about it. When Blake is dead, I'll buy you a new one. What's important is that the thief didn't take what I stowed in the trunk. At least, since it's closed, I assume not, but let's make sure."

Zane popped open the hatch. The brown cardboard parcels were still inside. "What is this stuff?"

"A quiver of arrows, a horn, sinew, and lacquer compound bow, and my scimitar."

Zane looked at him as if he'd lost his mind. "We can get more guns."

Sartak grinned. "A wooden stake through the heart paralyzes a Cainite. Each of these arrows essentially *is* a stake, and like any self-respecting Mongol, I can sink one into an enemy's breast at considerable range. A mage named Paracelsus enchanted the sword, in exchange for a favor. It will hurt the average supernatural creature worse than any bullet you could buy."

"Okay." Zane closed the trunk. The lid thumped. "If you say so. What now? On to Malachi Jones?"

"Yes."

Zane opened the driver's door and swept the bits of broken glass off his seat. The fragments chimed as they hit the sidewalk. "I still can't believe that we've got the right guy. Would a real vamp list himself in the phone book?"

"Some would, if no kine *knew* that they were Cainites, and they had ghouls to guard them during the day. Let's find out if our man is that sort."

Jones lived west of the Hillsborough River, in a district called Hyde Park. When Sartak saw it, he decided that if Ybor City was Tampa's French Quarter, here was its Garden District, a neighborhood of lavish, gingerbread-encrusted, three-, four-, and five-story wooden homes. Perhaps it had been picturesque or even lovely once. Parts of it still were. But the predominant impression was one of decline. Many of the proud houses were empty, with FOR SALE signs in their yards. The homeless were ubiquitous, camping under an overpass, panhandling in front of a "gourmet deli," or simply trudging aimlessly up and down. It was easy to imagine a day when they'd be the only inhabitants left.

Malachi Jones's residence turned out to be a white four-story house with a gambrel roof. A red-and-blue stained glass fanlight shone over the front door. As the Mustang drew near, Sartak glimpsed movement from the corner of his eye.

His head jerked around. Now he didn't see anything, but he didn't doubt that he had before. He stared intently, and gradually a shadow in a long coat wavered out of the darkness. Something was wrong with the shape of its hunched shoulders, as well as the length and angle of its neck. Something that suggested a perching vulture.

Sartak realized that Zane had begun to slow down. "No!" he snapped. "Keep going! Same speed as before."

Zane accelerated. "Is somebody watching us?"

"No, spying on Jones, so with luck he won't realize who we are if we don't call attention to ourselves. He's in the yard across the street."

"I don't see him." The Mustang rolled past the watcher and on down the deserted, tree-lined avenue.

"Without heightened senses, you wouldn't. He's Nosferatu, and they often have a kind of invisibility power."

"I told you how much trouble I had seeing Ellen in that hallway. Do Malkavians have it, too?"

"Some of them."

Zane grimaced. "So I'm liable to wind up fighting a *bunch* of invisible men. Great."

"Generally speaking, the power will fail at the moment they attack you."

"Why doesn't that make me feel better? Never mind. What are we going to do now?"

"The same as before. If you think about it, the presence of a spy is encouraging. And if we sneak in through the back, he shouldn't spot us."

"What if there's another one behind the house?"

"Then we'll deal with him. Turn here."

Zane took the Mustang down a side street. One lot in, an alley cut across it. It ought to run behind Jones's home, also. Choked between overgrown ligustrum hedges, the start of the narrow passage resembled the mouth of a cave.

"Park," said Sartak. "We'll go in this way."

A moist breeze blew down the alley, carrying cooking odors. Trees arched overhead, blocking out the moonlight. For the most part, Zane slunk along quietly, though occasionally Sartak's heightened hearing caught the creak of his jeans, or the squeak and scuff of his rubber-soled shoes, as well as the drumbeat of his heart.

Somewhere far to the north, a siren wailed. Then a white house with a gambrel roof loomed from the darkness. A two-car garage squatted in the corner of the small backyard.

Sartak took a final look around. The night was still. If an invisible man was lurking about, he was *quite* invisible.

Sartak and Zane darted to the stoop. The Mongol tried the door. As he'd expected, it was locked. He examined it, and the windows on either side, looking for evidence of an alarm system. Finding none, he opened his new pocketknife, worked the blade between the door and the frame, and set to work.

It only took a few seconds to open both the spring lock and the dead bolt. No alarm rang. That didn't mean that he hadn't triggered a silent one. But he suspected that Jones, like other elders he'd known, particularly Ventrue, disdained such modern gadgets, relying on retainers, his powers, and guile to keep him safe.

Sartak and Zane crept into a spacious kitchen. The air smelled of coffee. A red bulb on the percolator glowed, the only light source in the room. Suddenly Phillip came through the entry in the far wall, a china cup and saucer in his big, scarred hands.

Drawing on his speed, Sartak charged, grabbed him by the throat, and lifted him into the air. The china shattered on the tile floor. "Don't struggle," the Mongol whispered. "If I dig my fingers in, I can tear your neck apart."

The black man made a gurgling, choking sound.

Sartak set him on tiptoe, loosening his grip enough to allow a trickle of air. "We don't want to hurt you or your master either. We only want to talk to him. We had to break in because a spy is watching the front of the house, and he mustn't know we're here." He let the ghoul go. "Do you understand?"

Phillip rubbed his neck. "Yeah," he wheezed. "Wait here." He exited the room.

Zane moved up. He had the pistol in his hand. "I hope this works."

Sartak shrugged. "It should. Jones is too self-confident to fear us, and bright enough to want to know what we have to say." He squatted, picked up the scraps of broken porcelain, and dropped them in a wastebasket.

After another minute, Phillip reappeared and said, "Come on." Sartak and Zane followed him into a den furnished with a rolltop desk, a huge globe, and several rather decrepit leather chairs. A collection of antique firearms and a set of framed maps decorated the walls. Dotted with arrows and regimental symbols, the latter charted American military battles from the eighteenth and nineteenth centuries. Green velvet drapes covered the window. The air smelled of gun oil and wood polish.

Malachi Jones stood in the center of the gorgeous Persian rug. "Good evening," he said. "Phillip, why don't you go back to the front parlor."

The black man frowned. "Are you sure?"

Jones nodded. "Our Peeping Tom might get restless with no one to look at." Glowering, Phillip strode away.

"Did you *know* that you have a Nosferatu watching you?" Sartak asked.

Jones sighed. "No, but it doesn't surprise me. After all these years, Roderick has decided to doubt my loyalty." He gestured to the chairs. Sartak and Zane sat down. "In a sense, it's because I took a momentary interest in the two of you, but actually it's paranoia, pure and simple. Lord, does it devour all of us in the end?"

"I don't know," Sartak said. "I don't think it has its claws in me yet."

Jones smiled. "Ah, but you'd be the last to know if it did. Would either of you care for a cognac, a glass of blood, or a cigar? No?" He sat down opposite his guests. "Then let's get to it. Why are you here? Somehow I doubt that you've decided to surrender yourself to Roderick's justice."

"No," said Sartak. "We came to tell you that Alexander Blake is the shining murderer we've been looking for. I assume you know that he has psychic powers."

"Yes. Clairvoyance and all that."

"That's the least of it. He can leave his true body and form another out of glowing ectoplasm. I talked to him while he was wearing one. During the conversation, he admitted his guilt. And we want you to help us kill him."

Jones's eyes narrowed. "I don't like to see kine mistreated, but in Kindred society, it's scarcely a crime. I don't like the man in question, either. But Roderick values him. And I'm no traitor, whatever my sire may believe."

"Disposing of Blake would be a service to your clan, your domain, and our race as a whole."

"How so?"

"Let's start with the obvious. Blake knows all your secrets. He's virtually a member of the Primogen. It's the most flagrant breach of the First Tradition that I've ever seen."

Jones looked at Zane. "As opposed to? No offense intended, Mr. Tyler."

Sartak smiled. "Point taken. But I'm a despicable outlaw, and you're supposed to be virtuous members of the Camarilla."

"Does anyone mind if *I* smoke?" Jones asked. He removed a cigar from a cut-glass humidor, drew it under his long, thin nose, and clipped the end off. "I admit, Blake knows far too much. But at least he's on our side."

"Even if that were true, it wouldn't help you much if he led you into disaster. And he is. With Malkavians running it, your private bedlam is a time bomb. I didn't help Zane escape yesterday morning. He got himself out. Someday someone else is going to do the same, talk to a cop or a newspaper that you *don't* control, and blow the Masquerade to hell."

Jones struck a match with his thumbnail, lit his cigar, and puffed rum-scented blue smoke. "I agree absolutely. The Institute is a terrible idea, if only because a captive population of crazed, pathetic vessels brings out the Beast in all of us. *Most* of Roderick's notions have been terrible of late. But I hope that, in time, his fellow Ventrue can make him see reason."

"It'll never happen," said Zane. "You said yourself that he's acting nuts. Because Blake is *controlling* him, the same way a vampire can control a human."

Jones shook his head. "Impossible."

"You wouldn't say that if Blake could work magic," Sartak said. He rose and began to prowl, past a rack of matchlock rifles, and a yellowed, hand-drawn diagram of the terrain and troop movements at Shiloh. "What makes you think that his psychic talents are any less formidable? Here's what's happening: The man can insinuate ideas and feelings into people's minds. From his first contact with Cainites, he's used the power to get them do his bidding. For some reason, you're less susceptible than Roderick or his remaining deputies, and that's why he convinced the Prince to oust you from your position.

"But there's even more to it than that. I told you about the ghoul at the dogfight acting strangely. And you saw Phillip display the same kind of memory loss and confusion in Ybor City. It happened because Blake's wandering spirit possessed them. By the way, after you dragged me away, he broke your pledge that the anarchs wouldn't be harmed. He murdered Ligeia and perhaps the others, too."

Jones's jaw tightened. "Did he, by God."

"Yes, but that's a side issue. The real point is that somehow, under the proper conditions, Blake can possess *Cainites*. He's been possessing Roderick for a while. Sometimes he does it when he feels it necessary to control the Prince's every move, or when he needs him to do something completely out of character. I think my trial was a case in point. It would explain the good doctor's absence, and *you* were certainly dumbfounded when Roderick refused to hear my story. More often, he uses the power to make the Prince doubt his own sanity. To persuade him that the Beast is overwhelming the Man, and only psycho-analysis can save him. Thus making him desperate, dependent, and easily led."

Sartak grinned. "But even *that* isn't the punch line. Blake formed his liaisons with the three clans one at a time, didn't he, you Ventrue being the last. You accepted him partly because your fellow Cainites were already enamored of him. Well, we know how he bought the Malkavians' friendship. He gave them his asylum for their playground. But what do you think he offered the deformed, pariah Nosferatu?"

Jones's high forehead creased, and then his eyes widened. "He promised to teach *them* to project their spirits into other Kindred. Permanently."

Zane smiled. "That's our guess." Sartak could tell that he was enjoying Jones's consternation. Considering all that Cainites had put him through, the Mongol didn't blame him.

"I don't know if such a thing is possible," Sartak said. "But if it is, whose bodies do you think that Miss Carlyle and her brood will decide to usurp? My guess would be the rich and powerful Ventrue, the high-and-mighty architects of the Camarilla."

For a while, Jones simply sat, smoked, and stared into space. At last he said, "You know, I only have your word for any of this."

"That's true. And I admit, some of it is inference. I suppose that, knowing the people involved, you simply have to decide if you believe me."

"And I do." The corners of Jones's thin-lipped mouth quirked upward. "Why shouldn't I? Roderick cashiered me on considerably less. How can I help you dispose of this wretched mystic?"

"Obviously, not overtly." Sartak idly hefted a powder horn hanging from a peg. It was heavier than he'd expected, full, and its contents shifted with a tiny hiss. "Not if you're being watched. The same goes for your retainers and friends. So let's start with some simple information. Where does Blake live?"

"He has an apartment in the tower, but he generally stays in his suite at the Institute."

"I suspected as much. All right, Zane and I will raid the place tomorrow night, kill him, and rescue the last woman he means to murder. He's holding her prisoner on the premises. Evidently she's too ill to survive in any case, but she might as well die an easier death than he or his minions would grant her."

"'*Raid*?'" said Jones. "If that means killing Kindred, also, it's unacceptable."

"Judging from Zane's description of his captivity, some of your Malkavians and Nosferatu *need* killing. Blake seems to have corrupted them beyond any hope of redemption. Look, my comrade and I are up against an enemy who reads minds, tracks people psychically, and has valid premonitions. We have to hit fast and hard, where we know he can be found. Otherwise, he'll nail us first. For what it's worth, we'll try not to hurt any Cainite with the sense to get out of our way."

"The Prince himself is living out there now. At least swear that you won't harm him."

"I wish I could. For your sake, I'll try not to. But Blake's death is our first priority, and it ought to be yours, too. The man's a megalomaniac, capable of anything. He told me that he isn't satisfied with being the gray eminence of Tampa Bay. He wants an empire. How would you like to see him persuade Roderick to launch a war of conquest? The rest of the Camarilla would close ranks and march on this domain. Imagine the slaughter then."

Jones grimaced. "Enough. I'm convinced. Do what you have to. But how are the two of you going to carry it off? The Institute may have sloppy security, but the place is a labyrinth crawling with Kindred and ghouls."

Sartak grinned. "Let's just say that I have a plan. A pillar of the Camarilla like you doesn't want to know what it is. But I think we can kill Blake, bring out Robot—the woman—and shut down the Malkavians' dungeon while we're at it, all without breaching the Masquerade. In return for this service to clan Ventrue, I want three things from you."

"Which are?"

"First, the best map of the Institute you can sketch, and any information about its defenses you can provide."

Jones adjusted his pince-nez frames. "That's easy enough."

"Second, without telling your friends what's going on, keep them away from the place tomorrow night." He grinned. "Take them bowling or something. I don't want to fight them if I don't have to."

"Gladly."

"Third, amnesty for Zane. When this is over, no one will molest him, despite what he now knows."

"Another violation of the First Tradition? That's

difficult. Mr. Tyler, if you're willing to submit to a Blood Bond, or Mesmerism—"

"No," Sartak said. "You'll simply trust him to keep his mouth shut. He's doing the Ventrue a favor, too."

"I'm not going to talk," Zane said. "Who'd believe me?"

"You realize," said Jones, "I don't rule Tampa Bay."

"We understand that," said Sartak. "But I assume that when Blake dies, you can regain the Prince's trust, then use your influence to steer him in the right direction."

"Done. What about amnesty for you?"

Sartak grinned. "Unnecessary. If you still want me, come and get me. I haven't played tag with Archons in ages."

Jones shook his head. "You have an odd idea of sport, Mr. Sartak." He rose and crossed to the rolltop desk, leaving a coiling trail of smoke behind. "Let's get started on your map."

40

The Mustang rolled past a vacant lot. Squinting against the darkness, Zane saw cans, bottles, and circles of ash scattered across the grass. But nothing moved. "They're not here."

"No," Sartak replied. "They're living in fear, so it makes sense that they wouldn't congregate in the same spot every night. You'd better park. I doubt that we'll see them unless we're on foot."

Zane stopped in front of a small, single-story wooden building. It looked as if it might once have been a shabby neighborhood bar, but the Spanish-language sign on the overgrown lawn said it was an *iglesia*. A church. Someone had painted fiery eyes over the door, and a row of pointed teeth across the lintel.

As Zane climbed out of the car, a long howl quavered through the night. "Does that mean somebody spotted us?"

"I don't think so." Sartak shut his door. "It sounded too far away. But don't worry, we'll meet them soon enough. And when we do—"

"Don't panic. I know." They started down the lightless, empty street. Palm fronds rustled in the cool, damp breeze. "Why are you worried? I was scared of Marilyn and Ellen, but I handled it."

"This will be different. For some reason, the mere sight of a Lupine in wolf-man form kindles a kind of primal terror in the human mind. But you're right, you're a brave man. I'm sure that you *can* cope, as long as you're prepared."

They walked past one derelict house after another. The blackness behind the windows seems to *shift*, without ever taking on definite form. Tiny noises sounded, too faintly to locate or identify. The air smelled of rotting wood.

"Can we talk?" Zane whispered.

"Why not? We want them to find us."

"In that case, thanks for the amnesty thing. I wasn't thinking that far ahead."

"I know. You're preoccupied with Rose, Ben, and Blake. Love, grief, and revenge."

"Yeah. When you talked about Blake corrupting your people and leading them to their deaths, you sounded like you really cared about it."

Sartak smiled crookedly. "And perhaps, for a moment, I did. Mainly, though, I voiced the sentiments necessary to persuade Jones to help us. The Man is still remarkably strong in him, so much so that I wonder how he's lasted." He pivoted. "They're here."

His heart pounding, Zane turned. A tall, thin shadow glided across the gap between two of the ruinous shacks on the other side of the street. He could barely make it out, but even a glimpse sent a chill oozing up his spine. Another howl echoed through the darkness, and this time, his knees went rubbery.

Gaunt, snarling creatures with mottled fur slunk out of the gloom. They walked on two legs, but had wolflike heads, and jaws lined with glistening fangs. Their long fingers ended in hooked claws. Some were naked, some in rags, and a couple pointed pistols. Most were seven to eight feet tall, but the one in the lead towered over the rest.

Shuddering, Zane somehow managed to keep his eyes open. Managed not to run. Once his hand made a grab for his gun, just as if it had a mind of its own. But, without taking his eyes off the werewolves, Sartak grabbed his wrist and held his arm immobile.

"Hello, Peewee," the vampire said.

The biggest werewolf roared. Spit flew from its muzzle. Zane cringed, sure that it was about to charge.

Sartak raised an eyebrow. "You don't sound very glad to see me. Would it help if I made another food run?"

Peewee's limbs shortened, and some of his fur melted away. In a few seconds, he became a slouching apeman. The piggy eyes under his prominent brow ridge glared. "Told you, don't come back."

"I know. I'm sorry. I was good at taking Chingis and Subedei's orders, but since then I've lost the knack. For what it's worth, I did return to help you, so why don't you give me a hearing. The night is young. You can gut me later."

Peewee glowered at Zane. "Him?"

Zane struggled to make his voice steady. "My name is Zane Tyler. Sartak and I are hunting the same enemy."

"But he's not my ghoul," Sartak said. "He has nothing to do with your friend the Wyrm, so I wouldn't think that you're honor-bound to murder him."

"Maybe no," said Peewee. "But looks like good eating." The other werewolves yapped and growled, a rhythmic, pulsing sound. It took Zane a moment to realize that they were laughing.

Sartak grinned. "You have a point. If things don't work out, perhaps I've already catered a second feast. Now, will you take us to Spider and the others?"

Peewee flowed back into wolf-man form, then swung his arm in an after-you gesture. Everyone set off down the street. The Lupines closed in around the intruders. Their giant forms utterly dwarfed Sartak, but if that made him uneasy, he didn't show it.

Up close, the monsters had a musky, wet-dog odor. Smelling it gave Zane a final, gut-churning moment of terror, and then, to his surprise, he started to feel better. He supposed it proved that you could get used to anything.

Periodically one of the werewolves howled, and in the distance, others answered. Evidently the escorts were calling the pack together.

A breathless female voice said, "Hi! I'm Lollipop."

He turned. A teenage girl with freckles and an upturned nose was walking beside him. She was small, delicate, and her gray wool poncho hung on her like a tent. It was hard to believe that a few moments ago, she'd been a huge, inhuman beast. "Hi."

"We don't really eat apes. That was a joke. We might kill you, but that's all."

He smiled. "And to think that I was worried."

"Your friend beat the crap out of me." Her tone was full of admiration. "He *really* knows how to fight."

"He sure does."

"What's he going to say? It better be good!"

"I'll let him tell you and everybody else at once."

She pouted. "You're no fun." The pout became a

grin. "I hope we don't kill you." Her shoulders broadening, she scampered back into the dark. He was glad that he didn't have to watch her pixie face turn ugly.

The pack had gathered in the backyard of a derelict house still wrapped in a fumigator's tent. Despite the shroud, Zane could tell that the structure listed to one side. Occasionally it groaned in the breeze. Some of the assembled Bone Gnawers were in human form, some looked like ordinary wolves, big dogs, or jackals, and others hovered in between. The majority were adults, but quite a few were pups and children. A number had blemishes, crooked limbs, or twisted faces.

A bald woman with uneven shoulders stood on the house's crumbling concrete patio. Sartak sprang nimbly up beside her. The escort didn't object, so, a little hesitantly, Zane climbed up, too.

"Good evening, Spider," the vampire said. "Allow me to present Zane Tyler, a kine, but my partner in crime."

Spider gave Zane a level stare, then shifted her attention back to Sartak. "What do you want?"

Sartak smiled. "To share some good news. The spirits did *not* betray the Bone Gnawers of Tampa Bay, nor did you fail them. You're not an accursed or unworthy people after all. Merely the victims of a scam."

Audience members in human shape babbled. Others growled. "What do you mean?" Spider asked.

"I found the luminous killer I told you about. As I conjectured, he's connected to the Kindred. He's Prince Roderick's advisor, and a psychic. He used his talents to lead you and the Silver Fangs into the trap."

"How could he do that?"

"He has the power to leave his physical body and build a new one out of light," said Zane. "We figure that he can make it any shape he wants. He was the phony messenger from the Falcon."

Spider shook her head. "I can't buy that. Trevor Stuart was a great seer. No fake spirit could con him. Hell, I don't think that one could fool *any* Garou. An ape and a leech have no way of appreciating this, but we're in *sync* with the Umbra."

"How nice for you," Sartak said dryly. "But this man also has the ability to plant ideas in someone else's head. I suspect that before he appeared to Stuart, he spent a long time goosing him into a gullible, susceptible frame of mind. And the rest of you only saw the shining bird for an instant, after the master Theurge entranced you with his powers of eloquence."

A black-bearded man in bib overalls raised his hand. Spider pointed at him. "I think that maybe you could fool a Silver Fang, if you were tricky enough," he said. "Especially if you stroked his ego while you were at it. People say that something's gone wrong with that tribe. That even the smartest are a couple crayons short of a box."

Spider shrugged. "That's the rumor, but who knows?" She turned back to Sartak and Zane. "Can you prove what you're saying?"

"No," said Sartak, "but doesn't it sound more likely than what you believed before?"

"That's hard to say. Maybe I'd have a better idea if I knew why you were telling us. Your deep love for the Garou?"

Sartak grinned. "Not as such. Your deceiver, our enemy, is holed up in a Cainite fortress. The same place where the cops have been imprisoning the homeless, so the local undead can batten on their blood."

The Mongol started to pace. "Zane and I want you people to help us raid it. We'll kill the psychic, and any Cainites and ghouls who get in our way. Free the captives and shut the operation down. Avenge the Silver Fangs and your own dead, and swing the balance of power in Tampa Bay back toward the Lupines. What do you say?"

For a moment, every face in the crowd, human, canine, or monstrous, stared at him silently. Then Spider said, "Give me a break."

"It will work," Sartak said. "We know a lot about the layout of the place. And the security arrangements, such as they are. We've ensured that many of the Cainites will be elsewhere. And the rest don't expect an attack. At least, they aren't expecting you. They think that they broke you for all time."

Around the audience, wolves and beast-men snarled. Some of the human-looking Lupines began to grow.

Spider held up a dirty, hairless hand. "Everybody, chill! How do we know that *this* isn't a cadaver trick, to trap and butcher the rest of us? Why would you lead us against your own kind?"

"Various reasons," Sartak said. "One of them being that the psychic and his flunkies staked me out to burn in the sun."

"Vampires tortured me and murdered my brother," said Zane. "So far, you people haven't hurt me. Why *wouldn't* I team up with you to get even with them?"

Sartak said, "You're pack leader. That ought to mean that you're a good judge of character. Do you honestly think that this human and I are lying?"

Spider grimaced. "I thought Trevor Stuart was for real, so what do I know? Just one thing." She swung her hand in a gesture that took in every werewolf in the yard. "These few are the last. These grown-ups are the only ones left to rear these cubs. I won't risk their lives if I don't have to. Especially not on the say-so of a leech and a monkey stranger."

"If I'm a liar, then it follows that your gods *have* forsaken you," Sartak said. "Is that what you *want* to believe?" He paused, but she didn't answer. "Perhaps so, if it provides an excuse to hide here in your kennel. Perhaps it's even true. I'd certainly disown such cowards, in their place."

Some of the wolf-men rumbled. "Go," Spider said. "You've got one hour—"

Sartak sneered. "To get off your turf. I remember the drill. Come on, Zane." He turned. Zane wondered what the hell they were going to do now that the plan had fallen apart.

"Hold it!" a bass voice bellowed. A huge, naked man—no doubt Peewee in human form—leaped onto the porch. "I want to do this!"

Spider said, "Do you trust him?"

"No, but who gives a damn? I'd rather walk into another ambush than squat here feeling like a loser. Let's test and *see* if we've lost our mojo. Hell, the Apocalypse is coming, right? Maybe it's already started. The whole *world* is about to die. We might as well go out in style." He turned to the audience. "Who wants to go take some cadaver skins and heads?"

People raised their hands. Wolves and monsters barked and howled. To Zane, it looked as if more than half the pack was on the big man's side.

Spider scowled. "Believe me, I know how you feel. But I'm boss, I'm supposed to choose the best path for everyone, and I say that you *can't* go."

"Maybe it's time for a new boss," Peewee said.

"I guess we should find out."

Zane expected them to turn into monsters and fight. He hastily stepped back to give them room. But they simply stood and stared into one another's eyes.

For what felt like a long time, nothing happened. Finally Spider began to quiver. Then to shake. The crowd murmured. Abruptly she cried out, turned her head, and stumbled backward.

Peewee caught her and put his arm around her, holding her up. "It's okay," he whispered. "It's okay."

"Damn!" she said. "I didn't think you could do it."

"I couldn't have, if a part of you didn't know that I'm right. Maybe survival is the Bone Gnawer way, but what good is it if you're dying on the inside? And ever since the leeches kicked our asses, we have been." He glared at Sartak. "I promise that if we do get massacred, this bastard won't make it out to gloat."

Sartak smiled. "How did I know that you were going to say that? I must be psychic myself. Now that you've gotten it out of your system, let's talk strategy. Exactly how many of you are there?"

41

Crouched in the shadow of an abandoned tenement, Zane stared across the field at the Institute. A few lights burned in the front of the building. But the bulk of it was simply a huge, black slab, with a pale moon floating overhead.

The animal smell of the Bone Gnawers filled the air. A werewolf with a piratical black eye patch fidgeted with the safety on his new rifle. On the way here, the Lupines had burgled a couple of stores, stealing guns and other useful items. But no one was supposed to fire unless it was necessary. They wanted to infiltrate the Malkavian haven silently.

Lollipop, a towering beast like the rest, gave her lime sucker a final slurp, then bit into it. The hard candy crunched. Zane shook his head. It was strange to be here, surrounded by legendary monsters, yet just as weird to think that after tonight, one way or another, the craziness and the terror would be over.

That should be a relief. Except that he knew that it was his hatred of Blake and his vampire stooges that had kept him going. After Rose and Ben were avenged, he'd have nothing to distract him from his grief. Maybe he'd be better off if he didn't make it through the fight.

He scowled. That was a gutless way to think. It didn't matter that without Rose, he'd be miserable. He still had a duty to survive if he could manage it, so he'd be around to help Tracy and Davy.

Sartak looked at his watch. "Everyone should be in position." Malachi Jones had said that as far as he knew, the prison had three entrances. Accordingly, the attackers had divided into three squads, to penetrate them all at once. Peewee was in charge of the second contingent, and Spider the third. "Let's go."

Supposedly the haven rarely employed much security beyond the confusion of its prisoners and the concealment of its doors, but sometimes a watchman or two patrolled the grounds. As Zane skulked forward, rifle in hand, he peered about, probing the dark for movement.

Suddenly something thrummed. Startled, he pivoted. Sartak smiled, lowered his bow, and pointed.

Ahead, a dark form sprawled beneath an oak. When Zane crept closer, he saw that it was Newman, the cop who'd pistol-whipped Ben. Her openmouthed face looked astonished. As Sartak had promised, he'd put his arrow in her heart.

The squad reached the building without spotting any more of the enemy. Sartak picked the lock of the door that Zane had escaped through, and everyone slipped inside.

The Mongol prowled down the gallery's inner wall, looking for the minute variation in the wallpaper pattern that allegedly marked the secret door. Zane knew that he wouldn't be able to find it in this gloom. A timid, treacherous part of him wished that the vampire wouldn't, either. Then he wouldn't have to go back inside the maze.

Sartak turned and beckoned. Everyone clustered around him. Zane's mouth was dry, and his heart pounded. The Mongol pressed the wall, and a door-sized section of it cracked open with a click.

The squad hurried through. Two werewolves stayed by the entrance, to guard it. Everyone else strode on around the corner, into the Malakavians' dormitory.

Voices murmured from the first doorway on the left. Sartak stepped in front of it and shot two arrows, so quickly that his arm was a blur. Someone grunted, and something thumped on the floor.

Bone Gnawers dashed on down the hall. The black-bearded pseudo-nurse stepped out of a room, and they swept over him like a tidal wave. Snapping and clawing, they threw him down. Blood splashed, its odor filling the air. Arms gory to the elbows, poncho flapping, Lollipop danced out of the melee, waving the vampire's severed head.

Other werewolves charged through doors, and came out with similar trophies. Bringing up the rear, Zane could only stare, pleased by their success yet stunned by their savagery. A low voice said, "Psst!"

Reflexively he turned, toward a dark room that the Bone Gnawers had glanced into, then passed by. For a moment, it looked empty. Then Marilyn's blond hair and white dress gleamed in the corner. She had a double-barreled shotgun pressed to her shoulder. He started to throw himself out of the doorway. She said, "Stand!"

His leg muscles locked. Thrown off-balance, he lurched against the jamb. The shotgun swiveled, tracking him. He struggled to aim his own gun, but it was trapped between his chest and the wall.

Something whizzed past him. With a thunk, an arrow appeared in Marilyn's breast. She dropped the shotgun to clutch at it, and the firearm clattered on the floor. Her knees buckled, and she fell facedown. The arrow snapped under her weight.

Zane's terror turned to rage. He yanked out his machete, scrambled to her, and hacked her head off. Blood gushed.

When he turned, Sartak was standing in the doorway. "Don't look at their eyes," the short man said.

"I know," Zane panted. "It's just that it's tough not to when they surprise you. Is this area cleaned out?"

"I think so."

Zane grimaced. "Now for the hard part." Searching and fighting their way through the labyrinth of the prison proper.

Somewhere, guns banged. The noise was faint, but he jumped anyway.

Sartak grinned. "Yes, and it just got harder. Either Peewee or Spider has been discovered. From here on, I doubt that we'll take anyone by surprise."

42

Roderick shifted restlessly on the gleaming leather sofa. "If it turns out that Malachi has betrayed me, I want to exile him, not execute him. Does that make me weak?"

Blake struggled to frame an appropriate response. It was more difficult than it should have been. He felt edgy tonight. The last thing he wanted to do was listen to a patient, even the Prince of Tampa Bay, snivel on and on about his problems. "I'd say that it makes you compassionate. But I think that you ought to be concerned about the *appearance* of weakness, and of partiality. And the possibility of Jones sharing your secrets with some other enemy."

Roderick sighed. "Damn it, you're right. I'll just have to bite the bullet and—" Somewhere in the building, guns banged. "What the devil is that?"

A psychic flash stabbed through Blake's mind. His body bucked, nearly upsetting his chair. He saw foaming jaws and blazing eyes. Heard howling, and smelled a bestial odor. "Lupines," he muttered. "Lupines invading the building."

Roderick sat up and stared at him. "That's impossible. We crushed them when you lured them into that trap."

Blake's inner vision faded. "Evidently not as thoroughly as we thought." He took his Beretta 92F out of his desk drawer. He was glad that he'd had the foresight to obtain silver bullets, poison to werewolves and no less deadly than conventional ammunition to anyone else. "You guard the door. I'll see if I can find out exactly what the situation is."

"Right." Rising, the Kindred unsheathed his sword cane.

Blake knew that Roderick, ignorant of the full extent of his powers, assumed that he was simply going to scan the Institute psychically. Instead, he detached his mind from his flesh, then hurtled disembodied through the corridors.

He didn't like what he found. Somehow, *Sartak and Tyler* were fighting alongside the werewolves, which surely meant that the intruders were hunting for him specifically. Worse, the Lupines had posted guards on the three doors that led outside. How the hell had they discovered them all? Maybe Jones *was* a traitor. But there was no time to ponder the irony now.

Blake had invested many hours assessing the strengths and limitations of his talents. Thus he realized instantly that the present situation placed him at a severe disadvantage. The ability to influence a single mind wouldn't stop an enraged mob. Nor would it help to gallivant around in spirit form if Lupine searchers happened on his flesh while he was away.

He needed to take his vulnerable human body to a safe refuge. Then he could return to the battle as an intangible dybbuk or the gargoyle. Thank God that there was a *fourth* way out of the prison, an exit that only he and the Nosferatu knew about. He'd just have to prevail on Roderick to make sure that he arrived there in one piece.

He slipped back into his body. "Here's what's happening: They've sealed the exits. Knocked out the switchboard, so we can't call for help. They're searching the building, picking us off one by one as they find us. We need to rally a strong force of our own if we're going to fight back."

Roderick nodded curtly. He looked strong and resolute, a different man than the weary, befuddled soul who'd lain whining on the couch. "Agreed. Which way would you recommend we go?"

"Toward the west side of the building. There are more of our people that way." It wasn't a *heinous* lie. There weren't any fewer.

"I'll lead," Roderick said. They strode out of the office and past the suites Blake had provided for him and his retainers, to the door at the end of the corridor.

Roderick cracked it open, and sound blared through. More shooting. Snarls and shrieks. The sharp tang of gun smoke tinged the air.

No enemies were in sight, so Blake and Roderick skulked on into the actual prison. But they'd only gone a few feet when a pair of Lupines stalked out of a side passage. The wolf-men's heads brushed the ceiling. Even in the dull amber light, their fangs glistened. They carried Ingram submachine guns, probably looted from dead ghouls. Roaring, they swung the weapons toward their newfound prey.

Blake snapped off a shot. Missed. Knew with ghastly certainty that the Lupines were about to cut him down.

Roderick pointed his sword, bared his fangs, and

hissed. The werewolves cringed. One dropped his gun. They whirled and bolted back the way they'd come. Such was the impact of the Prince's charismatic power that even Blake, who was usually immune, recoiled.

Roderick retracted his fangs and smiled. "Steady. Remember, I'm on your side."

Blake made himself smile back. "I know. I'm fine." His guts churned. He was in danger every second he remained here. His miserable puppet had had to save his life, and humiliated him in the process. He'd never felt more alarmed, less in control of his environment. He promised himself that Sartak was going to pay for it.

He and Roderick prowled on. Most of the prisoners seemed to be hiding, but occasionally they met a psychotic too preoccupied with his own autistic concerns to notice the general disturbance. A gaunt man who knelt praying and weeping on a tabletop. A woman with a leg brace apparently conducting a hallucinatory orchestra. A teenager doggedly rubbing his teeth with an eraser. Blake felt a momentary urge to shoot every one of them.

More commonly, however, he and the Prince found Malkavians and ghouls. The psychic positioned himself in the middle of the gathering crowd, interposing a wall of flesh between himself and any enemy.

The group tramped into one of the open areas. Once it had been a ballroom, if he remembered correctly. Tapers guttered in tarnished silver candelabra. The flames were rose red. A skeleton lay inside the grand piano, its legs hanging over the side. The stinking body of a dachshund dangled, spiked to the wall, and someone had carved a hopscotch grid on the hardwood floor.

Gloria, a wrinkled, white-haired Kindred who resembled a doting grandmother, cried, "Ambush!"

Blake whirled toward her. So did everyone else. She waved her AK-47 at the archways in two adjacent walls.

A split second later, guns blazed, barked and chattered, from the entries. If Gloria hadn't sensed the Lupines, that initial barrage might have decided the battle. But as it was, the Malkavians gave as good as they got.

Figures on both sides staggered, fell, then lurched up again. Apparently none of the Kindred were firing silver bullets, and for the most part, the lead ones flying back and forth didn't incapacitate Lupines or vampires. Some combatants kept shooting anyway. But after a moment, a number of the werewolves bellowed and charged into the chamber to fight hand to hand.

Blake wheeled and ran for one of the doorways in the back wall. Something burned his leg and knocked him staggering.

He'd been shot! But someone would hurt him again if he stopped to worry about it. His leg now numb and wobbly, he scrambled on.

People kept reeling into his way. A mottled Lupine in a poncho raked out a ghoul's intestines. A spiky-haired Kindred stared a shuddering werewolf in the eyes, freezing it in its tracks. Another undead pressed an automatic rifle to the creature's head and splattered its brains over a candelabrum, extinguishing some of the scarlet fires.

A naked beast-woman stalked toward Blake with an almost dainty grace. Long, white scars streaked her belly and left forearm. He brandished the pistol, threatening her, and her jagged grin widened.

He fired. The bullet hit her in the chest. She collapsed. He dodged around her convulsing body and out into the hall.

Safe. For a few seconds, anyway. Long enough to tear his pant leg and inspect the wound inside.

To his relief, it wasn't too bad. It was bleeding pretty heavily, and starting to throb, but the bullet had only creased him. With everyone busy killing everyone else in the ballroom, and his escape hatch now close at hand, he should be able to limp to safety.

Panting, gripping his aching gash with one hand and gripping his gun with the other, he hobbled on. Something clutched his shoulder.

43

Zane fired at Blake again. The second burst missed altogether. A knot of battling Bone Gnawers and ghouls whirled in front of him, cutting off his view.

He felt a crazy impulse to shoot them all, were-wolves and enemies alike. Just mow then down and get them out of the way. For one instant, he'd glimpsed Rose's murderer in the middle of the vamps. Had the evil bastard in front of his *gun*. And now, thanks to his own idiot allies, the psychic might get away.

No. The hell he would. His new assault rifle leveled, Zane darted forward.

Fighters screamed and snarled. Guns snapped and rattled. Sulfurous smoke stung his nose and burned his eyes. He tried to skirt the fighting by hugging the wall, but that only worked some of the time. An old-lady vampire in a dowdy housecoat pivoted toward him. Her smile would have looked saintly if not for the jutting fangs. He shot her an instant before she could get her AK-47 pointed at him. The bullets stitched her across the chest. She fell, and he scuttled on before she could get up again.

The heaving mass in the center of the room parted for a moment. He saw Blake ducking out the arch in the opposite wall. He raised his rifle, and something cracked against his left shoulder.

Pain stabbed down his arm, leaving numbness behind. He stumbled and dropped the gun. Grinning, fangs bared, her dark, heart-shaped face crisscrossed with pink scars, Ellen tossed away her baseball bat and lunged.

Avoiding her gaze, he threw a punch, but it only brushed her cheek. She plowed into him and drove him backward. Something slammed into the base of his spine. His feet flew out from under him.

He landed on a lattice of cords that vibrated under the impact. A dissonant chord sounded, and he realized that Ellen had shoved him into the piano.

The legs snapped. The instrument crashed to the floor and screamed. The tumbling bones of its skeleton tenant clattered. Loose wires whipped past Zane's eyes, and the lid pounded down on his head.

He tried to ignore the jolt of pain. Tried to rip his arm free of a tangle of wire and draw his pistol. Ellen lifted the lid and smashed it down again. The world went black.

The next thing he knew, he was lying beside the wreckage of the piano. He could feel that his shoulder holster and machete scabbard were empty. Kneeling, eyes glittering, Ellen bent toward his neck.

He grabbed her and struggled to hold her teeth away from him. He realized immediately that it wasn't going to work. His left arm was still numb, his whole body weak and clumsy from the beating he'd taken. Her face jerked nearer.

He snatched at her nose ring and ripped it out.

As he'd hoped, it startled her. She flinched back. One hand flew to her torn nostril, and the other loosened its hold on him. He shoved her, breaking her grip, then scrambled toward the fallen rifle.

He heard her coming after him. By the time he grabbed the gun and turned, she was pouncing. He whipped the weapon into line and pulled the trigger.

The burst caught her in the stomach and threw her backward. Clutching the wounds, she reeled. He shot her in the head. She collapsed. Blood and brains splashed. When the clip was empty, he picked up the machete and cut her head off.

Afterward he slumped against the wall, wheezing, sweaty, heart hammering. Gradually he realized that he shouldn't just sit here. It wasn't safe. But he couldn't goad himself into motion until he remembered that Blake was escaping. Then he recovered his pistol, fumbled a new clip into the rifle, and blundered on.

44

Sartak shot a ghoul through the throat, nocked another arrow, then glimpsed motion from the corner of his eye. He pivoted just in time to see Zane plunge into the melee. "Don't!" he shouted, but the kine didn't turn.

The Mongol cursed. He'd assumed that Zane had brains enough to stand back and fire his gun. The closer he got to Cainites, the more easily they could use their powers on him. Sartak set down his bow, deadly at range but useless and cumbersome at close quarters, drew his scimitar, and stalked into the room to guard his comrade's back.

But he couldn't catch him. A ghoul and a pair of Malkavians attacked him. By the time he dispatched them, Zane had vanished into the chaos.

Sartak peered about, trying to spot him. A male voice said, "*You.*" Something about it jolted the Mongol. Chilled him. He turned.

Slim sword in hand, Roderick Dean advanced in a duelist's stance. Sartak had to fight an unaccustomed urge to cringe.

He knew what was unnerving him. The Prince's unnatural charisma. Since he was usually little troubled by such effects, Dean must possess the power to an extraordinary degree.

"*You*," the Ventrue elder repeated. "How dare you lead *Lupines* against your own kind."

Sartak tried to keep the fear out of his voice. "I fight with the weapons available. Surrender, give us Blake, and I'll let you live. The kine's a traitor, anyway. He's tampered with your mind."

Dean's bloody point drew circles in the air. "Liar. Diabolist." Absurdly, Sartak felt a surge of shame, as if God Himself were condemning him. As if the enemy in front of him had every *right* to kill him.

He struggled to shake the feeling off. "Diabolist, yes, liar no. Not about this, anyway. Blake himself told me—"

Dean lunged.

The thin sword streaked at Sartak's chest. He parried reflexively, then cut at Dean's head. The Ventrue sidestepped and attacked again, driving him back a step.

And he kept retreating. He knew that it was ridiculous. Dean was an able fencer, but surely no better than himself. Moreover, his weapon was magical, while the Prince's was almost certainly just a length of steel. Dean would need a well-aimed or lucky hit even to slow him down.

Still, he couldn't help himself. Irrational though it was, he felt as outmatched as if he were fighting a titan out of myth. Every time Dean's sword so much as quivered, he guarded against it frantically. In consequence, he couldn't take the offensive.

The blades clashed and scraped. Retreating again, he tripped over a corpse. Dean's sword flashed at his heart. Off-balance, he knocked the blade out of line, but couldn't deflect it entirely. It stabbed his shoulder, bringing a burst of pain.

He struck at the weapon, trying to knock it from the Ventrue's hand. Dean spun it out of harm's way, then came at him again. Sartak lurched back. His elbow brushed the wall. The enemy had driven him the length of the room.

For some reason, that triggered a wave of fury, an anger that counterbalanced the dread. Suddenly focused, he drew on his Cainite strength and speed. Bellowed a Mongol battle cry and sprang, swinging the scimitar in a horizontal cut.

Dean's eyes widened. He barely whipped his sword up in time to block.

It didn't matter. Driven by Sartak's prodigious strength, the saber snapped the light blade and whizzed on through Dean's neck. The Prince's body crumpled. His head rolled across the floor, disappearing among the feet of milling combatants.

Sartak felt a vague regret that withered as soon as he noticed it. He brandished his sword, flinging some of the vitæ off the blade, and strode on.

Blake cried out and jerked around. Milosh smiled at him. "Where are you going in such a hurry?" asked the Prince's guest.

Blake drew a ragged breath, trying to calm down. "I'm an advisor, not a soldier. I wouldn't be any use back there. I'm going to look for reinforcements."

Milosh shook his head. A lock of his shaggy black hair fell over his eye. "I don't think so. This is your haven even more than it's the Kooks', and if you're the kind of guy I think you are, you're headed for your private escape hatch. Good for you. Always take care of number one. But you aren't going anywhere unless I tag along."

"Fine. I could use someone to watch my back." His leg throbbing, Blake hobbled on down the dimly lit hall. Milosh strode after him. "But understand this: The way we're going out is dangerous, and even more of a maze than this place. You wouldn't get through it without a guide. So it doesn't matter if I slow you down. You can't abandon me."

Milosh grinned. "Doc, Doc. I'm hurt that you could even imagine such a thing. We're a team now. Brothers till the end."

Screams, gunshots, and the thunder of running feet echoed through the building. But as Blake and Milosh neared the exit, the psychic decided that it didn't sound as if anyone was blocking the way. By God, he was going to make it out! Why had he doubted it, even for a second? A few people were nearly as intelligent as he was, some almost as powerful, but nobody, including Sartak and his Lupine friends, was both. Despite the ache in his thigh, he grinned, and when he and the Ravnos came to the hidden cell, he yielded to a sudden, irresistible impulse to duck inside. "This will only take a moment."

He flipped the light switch. The fluorescent tubes ticked and flickered on. Robot didn't move or open her eyes, but that didn't mean she was asleep. Perhaps the lumpish creature couldn't muster sufficient interest to look and see what was going on.

When he gazed at her, his stomach knotted. She, even more than Sartak, was responsible for the present inconvenience. If she'd never existed, the Asian Kindred would never have invaded his life. He pointed the Beretta at her head.

Images cascaded through his mind. The room spun, and he clutched the cold steel bed rail for support.

"Get on with it," Milosh said. "We're on the clock."

"No." Blake set the gun on the bedside table and started unbuckling Robot's restraints. Her sour body odor wafted into his nostrils. "We need for her to live a few more minutes. Thank God I realized in time. Perhaps I was on the verge of becoming Oedipus's father."

Milosh's dark eyes narrowed. "Excuse me?"

Blake tried to order his jumbled thoughts. "You know that I'm clairvoyant, don't you?" The Ravnos nodded. "Well, I just had a premonition that we won't get away clean. Somehow, Sartak and a few others will track us. Catch up with us. Perhaps because my leg *will* slow us down."

Milosh scowled. His mind seethed with hatred and fear of the Mongol. "In that case, maybe I'll take my chances hiding here in the house."

"Don't be a fool. The Lupines would sniff you out. Besides, I saw *more*, enough to convince me that we can kill our pursuers. Just before they find us, we'll hook up with powerful allies. Use this girl and your powers of illusion to bait a trap that will rip Sartak apart. I swear to you, stick with me, and it will work." He reached into Milosh's mind. Heightened the malice and dampened the anxiety.

"All right, I'm in. Because I don't think you'd bet *your* life if it wasn't a sure thing. But when the time comes, how about if I just whip us up an *illusion* of Sleeping Beauty? That'll be easier than schlepping along the real thing."

"No. In the vision, she was really there. Perhaps if she weren't, we couldn't fool them. And since you're the one with two good legs and Kindred stamina, you're the one who'll have to carry her."

"Well, that sucks. I'm a *Rom*. I didn't *work* even when I was breathing." Still, he lifted Robot off the bed. Auburn hair spilled over his glossy black leather jacket. Her thin limbs dangled, lifeless as a doll's.

46

Zane pivoted back and forth, looking up and down the murky hallway. Suddenly he sensed a presence behind him. His rifle leveled, he whirled.

"Easy," Sartak said. The vampire held his bloody sword in one hand and a pistol in the other. He'd probably picked the gun up off the floor of the battle-ground behind him. "Why did you run off?"

"I saw Blake. But Ellen held me up, and he got away."

"Perhaps not." Stooping, his nostrils flaring, Sartak paced about. Abruptly he dropped to one knee and pointed at a dark, wet spatter. Zane hadn't noticed it in the gloom. "Was he bleeding?"

"I'm pretty sure I winged him in the leg."

"Then I think I can spoor him. Come on." Still crouching, he trotted down the corridor. Zane hurried after him.

"Don't get me wrong," Zane said, "I'm glad you're with me. But aren't you supposed to command our squad?"

Sartak snorted. "I lost the ability to do that the

second they charged." They came to an intersection. "All right, which way?" He sniffed.

Looking around, Zane realized that he knew where they were. And where Blake had probably gone. "To the right!" He dashed around a bend, then on past an X-ray lab, a surgical theater, and other rooms that looked as if they belonged in a real hospital. Sartak followed.

The door to the hidden cell stood open. The lights shone, and both rumpled beds were empty. Zane skidded to a halt on the slippery linoleum. "She's gone!"

"Robot?" Sartak asked.

"Yes. Blake kept her here, but now he's taken her somewhere."

"Because of the premonition. He's afraid that somehow, despite her passivity, she still might represent a danger." The Asian strode to the bed with the leather restraints draped over the rail, lifted one of the straps to his face, and inhaled. "There's one good thing about it: Now we have two strong scents to follow."

He led Zane out of the medical area and into a hunter's trophy room. A moth-eaten grizzly reared in one corner, a bald eagle spread frayed wings in another, and the heads of cougars, elks, buffalo, and deer stared glassy-eyed from the walls. The Malkavians had added four human heads to the collection. One was wearing boffers.

The Mongol studied an empty maple gun cabinet, then pressed a hidden catch and swung the heavy-looking case away from the wall. On the other side, a staircase spiraled down into darkness.

"Sartak," said a guttural voice.

Startled, Zane pivoted. Spider stood in the doorway. No doubt to make speech possible, she'd turned apelike. Her hairlessness looked even stranger now than it had when she was clothed and fully human.

Three other Bone Gnawers, still in wolf-man form, loomed behind her.

"What happened to the rest of your squad?" Sartak asked.

"We broke up into smaller teams when it looked like that was safe. I figured we'd catch the leeches faster that way. What's this?"

"Trouble. Specifically, it seems to be another way in and out, one that leads to Nosferatu tunnels. Blake fled down it. If someone doesn't catch up with him quickly, he's likely to send the Malkavians more reinforcements than our force can handle."

One of the Lupines growled. Spider nodded curtly. "Let's do it." She swelled into a full-fledged, though still furless, beast-woman.

Sartak led the party down the stairs, plank risers bolted to a wrought-iron frame. Zane was next in line. "What's down here?" he whispered.

"Blackness. Filth. A labyrinth. Booby traps. Giant, malformed animal ghouls like the rats at the dogfight. Almost any unpleasant thing we can imagine, and quite a few we can't. Just keep your guard up."

The darkness thickened. Zane swallowed, trying to clear the clog in his throat. His heart thumped, and his cuts and bruises throbbed to the beat. He felt that if he'd been living in hell, now he was sinking into its lowest depths.

For a second, he faltered. He reminded himself that Rose's murderer was getting away, and stepped onto the next riser. The board creaked.

At the bottom of the stairs was a brick tunnel. Phosphorescent mold spotted the walls, and provided the only light. Side passages ran away at peculiar intervals, grades, and angles. The air had a fecal stink, and somewhere, water dripped.

The hunters stalked forward. Like Sartak, the were-wolves sniffed, their snouts wrinkling. After the third turn, Zane decided that he could never find the way out by himself. Grimacing, he told himself that it was a stupid thing to worry about. If his superhuman allies didn't survive, he certainly wouldn't, either.

Slimy puddles filled some of the low places in the floor. Bones lay scattered here and there, some peculiarly twisted, spurred, or forked. Occasionally one cracked under his shoe, at which point one of the werewolves would bare its fangs at him.

Spider stumbled, then tore something off her ankle. It was a squirming, reddish brown fire ant nearly the size of Zane's fist. The Lupine shredded it with her claws, and an acidic stench filled the air. As the Bone Gnawer loped on, her lower leg darkened and swelled. Knowing how much the sting of an ordinary fire ant hurt, Zane was sure that she was in agony. But she never slowed down or limped.

A section of brick sweated iridescent goo.

Something rustled. Zane spun around. Antennae waving, a cockroach a yard long scuttled into the darkness.

The searchers passed a small abstract sculpture, scraps of glass linked by swirls of copper wire, sitting, almost invisible, in a deep, shadowy niche. It was beautiful but strangely disturbing, too. Zane had the odd feeling that if he looked at it too long, he'd start reliving old, forgotten nightmares.

A ruddy glow tinged the darkness ahead.

He and his companions glided forward. The walls diverged and the ceiling rose, as if the tunnel was becoming a major underworld highway. The red light shone from carriage lamps mounted along the sides.

A slim white form in a shapeless gown sprawled,

seemingly unconscious, on the cobbles. Two more of the giant fire ants were crawling on her. Zane cried, "Rose!" He dashed forward.

On his third stride, the floor beneath him shattered. He pitched helplessly forward, toward a pit with long, barbed stakes set in the bottom.

Hands grabbed his arm and wrenched him backward, onto solid footing. Sartak, his rescuer, swayed precariously on the edge of the drop. Bits of the false flooring clattered into the depths.

Zane stretched out his hand, and Sartak reached for it. A gunshot cracked. The vampire reeled and toppled backward.

He hit the stakes with a crunch. Three rammed completely through his body. He hung motionless.

For an instant, Zane could only stare in horror. Then he glimpsed motion from the corner of his eye.

Beyond the pit, the ants vanished. On this side, dark, misshapen figures lunged out of nowhere. Guns flashed and barked.

Zane fired at one of the attackers. The shadow dropped.

Another figure sprang at him from the side. He whirled, an instant too slow. Gray, pustule-spotted hands seized the rifle.

Zane and the Nosferatu strained, each trying to wrestle the gun away from the other. The vampire had a bald head, oversize, pointed ears, and a wrinkled, chancrous face. He was short and scrawny, but at least as strong as his opponent.

Abruptly he opened his mouth. An impossibly long black tongue shot out and slapped Zane in the face.

The cold, slimy organ stuck to him like flypaper. Pulsing suckers chewed into his flesh. The tongue's pointed tip reared, orienting on his left eye.

He squinched it shut. The tongue nuzzled, trying to worm its way under the lid. He kicked at the Nosferatu's knee.

Bone cracked, and the vampire staggered. Letting go of the assault rifle, Zane tore the tongue off his cheek, then shoved the undead away.

The Nosferatu reeled, fumbling with the gun, trying to get his finger on the trigger. Zane whipped out his automatic and fired until the monster dropped. Then he cut the creature's head off.

He wheeled to see who else was coming at him. To his surprise, for the moment, no one was. He tried to assess the overall situation.

It didn't look *quite* as hopeless as he'd expected. His side was outnumbered, but not by more than two or three to one. Some of the Nosferatu and Ghouls had pistols, but not rifles, machine guns, or, evidently, silver bullets. With the exception of a long-armed giant in a hoop skirt—he assumed from Sartak's description that it was Judith Carlyle—none of the vampires looked as strong or fast as the raging werewolves.

For a second, Zane dared to hope that even without Sartak, his team might actually stand a chance. Then he noticed how well he could see the battlefield. A white light supplemented the dim red glow of the lamps.

Dry-mouthed, he turned. On the other side of the pit crouched a huge white beast. It was hard to make out detail through its silvery halo, but it seemed to be a mix of ape and tiger. The quality of the light changed subtly as it finished congealing.

Zane snapped off a burst. If it hit Blake, it didn't appear to bother him. The shining killer bounded over the chasm, pounced, and took the first of the Lupines down.

47

Milosh lounged in the mouth of a side tunnel and watched the battle. He wasn't worried that any of the Lupines would shoot or rush him. He'd hidden the opening behind an illusion of blank wall.

The shape-shifters defended themselves so ferociously that for a second or two, it looked as if the fight could go either way. But as soon as the Ravnos got a look at Blake's rapidly materializing spirit body, he decided that the enemy didn't have a prayer.

That was just as well, because Milosh had zero inclination to risk his own sweet ass fighting alongside a bunch of Sewer Rats. He figured that he'd already made his contribution, by creating the illusion that ultimately landed Sartak in the pit.

Besides, now that everyone else was busy, he had a golden opportunity to steal the power of an eight-hundred-year-old elder. To waste it would be a terrible sin.

He dashed to the hole, lowered himself over the edge, and dropped, landing between the outermost stakes and the wall. The scent of blood, richer and more intoxicating than he'd ever known it, filled his head. The Hunger rose in him. His fangs extended, and he shuddered.

He turned. He wouldn't have believed it possible, but the sight of the vitæ, oozing down the stakes, plopping to the floor, heightened his desire. He yearned to scramble forward and rip into Sartak's flesh.

But he wouldn't. He'd do this the smart way. The Gypsy way. He closed his eyes for a moment, regaining control. Then he edged through the narrow spaces between the poles, studying his prey. It looked as if the stakes might have missed Sartak's heart. Still, the Asian Kindred hung motionless, and that must mean that he'd passed out. No one conscious could endure so much torture without writhing and shrieking.

Milosh shook the shaft that had punched through the elder's belly, jerking his body back and forth. Sartak still didn't scream, or even twitch. His dangling arm flopped lifelessly.

The Ravnos lunged.

Wood cracked. Iron fingers grabbed him under the jaw, jerked him into the air, and gave him a violent shake. Something snapped, and pain stabbed between his shoulder blades.

Sartak yanked him close and buried his fangs in his throat.

48

The two werewolves still on their feet fought on. Spider gutted a horned, hunchbacked Nosferatu. The strike spattered blood in an arc. The other Lupine, a male whose black-and white-striped fur made him look like a zebra, fired a shotgun into a ghoul's face, blasting her backward. Then Blake lunged, bit the Bone Gnawer's knee, and ripped his lower leg off.

Slipping on the bloody floor, Zane scrambled after the shining monster. He shot it again. New holes appeared in Blake's silvery flank, but he didn't react. He just kept on clawing his thrashing prey.

A shadow fell over Zane. He turned. Judith Caryle loomed above him.

At some point, something had torn away her veil. Her mouth was an oversize diagonal slash, her teeth a tangle of stained tusks. Many jutted at such an angle that they stabbed or gouged her. Her lips and the flesh around them were a mesh of bloody sores and perforations. A cluster of eyes, bulging like a bunch of grapes, covered the top half of her face. The skin on her giant hands was as leathery as alligator hide. Despite the smells—gun smoke, gore, the outhouse stink of the tunnels themselves—hanging in the air, Zane caught her body odor, flowery perfume overlying the stench of spoiled hamburger.

She stretched out her apelike arms to seize him.

Backpedaling frantically, he fired. The assault rifle spat one burst, then clicked, out of ammo. The Nosferatu shambled forward.

Zane had no more clips for the rifle. He threw it aside and grabbed his pistol.

Judith slapped him. He tried to duck, but he was too slow. Her palm smashed into the side of his head and hurled him across the floor.

He landed in a heap. His ears rang, and for a moment he didn't know where he was, or what was happening. Finally he remembered the automatic. He had to raise his gun.

At first his arm wouldn't move. He wondered if Judith had broken his spine. But then, numb and shaking, his hand lurched upward. He felt an instant's satisfaction, then noticed that his fingers were empty.

Judith reared above him. She picked him up, swung him over her head, and threw him back onto the cobbles. Pain exploded through his body. She said something, but he couldn't understand her bestial growl of a voice.

He could feel the machete pinned beneath his thigh. He knew that he'd never get it out of its scabbard, and that it wouldn't do him any good if he did. He was overmatched. Spastic from the punishment he'd taken. Out of strength, out of luck, and out of time.

He tried for the weapon anyway. Sure enough, before he could even touch it, the vampire grabbed him by the arms, immobilizing them. Slowly, evidently enjoying the moment, she lifted him toward her crooked fangs.

Her body jerked, and she grunted. The barbed point of a wooden stake burst from between her breasts, splashing him with blood.

She crumpled, carrying him down with her. Looking up, he saw Sartak swaying above them. The Mongol's half-healed wounds rippled and pulsed.

His vision blurry, Sartak peered down. Judith didn't move. Evidently, as he'd intended, the stake had pierced her heart. Zane didn't appear to be seriously injured, but was obviously too battered and exhausted to stand.

Sartak wheeled and stumbled to the scimitar, still lying where he'd dropped it to snatch Zane back from the pit. A pair of Nosferatu, one with a withered, noseless skull-face and the other wearing a rubber W. C. Fields mask, ran at him. Only a few of the freak-ish Cainites were still on their feet. Zane and the fallen Lupines must have fought like devils.

Blake leaped off Spider's mangled body. Rising to his hind legs, he motioned the Nosferatu back. Evidently he thought that he could kill Sartak unassisted.

The Mongol was inclined to share his confidence. Milosh's Cainite vitæ had given him the strength to tear himself off the stakes and clamber out of the pit. But his wounds were only partly healed. His entire body throbbed, and his strength and speed had all but deserted him. The Hunger seared his throat and cramped his belly. The scent and sight of the spilled blood on the cobbles was a maddening distraction from the business at hand.

Head low, Blake glided forward. Sartak gave ground. He tried to look shaky, and unsteady on his feet. It wasn't hard.

The monster sprang. The Mongol threw himself to the right. For an instant he had a chance to slash Blake's flank, already marked by bullets and Bone Gnawer talons. He retreated instead.

Blake pivoted and pounced. Sartak dodged right and backpedaled. Except for the click of the shining hunter's claws, the chamber was silent.

Blake surged forward. Sartak faked right, spun left, and cut at the psychic's neck. The curved blade flashed in the silver light.

Unfortunately, Sartak had either underestimated Blake's speed or overestimated his own. The tiger-ape began to turn before the blow landed. The sword thudded into his shoulder, gashing it deeply. But it didn't deliver the killing stroke the Cainite had intended.

Blake roared and clawed at Sartak's legs. The Mongol jumped above the attack. The scimitar tore free in a shower of glowing droplets. While in midair, he slashed at Blake's head, trying to split it in two. But he only sliced away a pointed ear.

Blake's forepaw streaked at him. Pain exploded through his chest. He reeled backward. Vitæ poured from long gashes, and bits of shattered rib ground together.

Blake edged forward, as lithe as before, but wary. Because the psychic now knew that the scimitar was dangerous, Sartak had lost the only advantage he'd possessed.

He feared that he was on the verge of losing consciousness as well. Shadows swarmed at the edges of his vision. The white-and-red light dimmed. His hands and feet were numb.

Bellowing a war cry, he charged, raining cuts on Blake's inhuman mask, ripping an eye, and shearing loose a flap of flesh. Shining claws hurtled at him. Miraculously, he ducked or parried every blow. He faked another slash at the psychic's head, then tried to hack a front leg out from under him.

Jaws like a bear trap snapped shut on his sword arm. Agony blazed through it, and the weapon fell out of his hand. Blake reared, yanking him into the air, and lashed him back and forth like a terrier shaking a rat.

Sartak's arm began to tear away from his shoulder. His free hand flailed uselessly. *I'm sorry, Zane,* he thought.

50

Floating in darkness. Dreaming. Until a man shouted Rose's name.

The sleeper grimaced at the disturbance. Almost rolled over and drifted off again.

But the voice was familiar. She strained to remember whose it was. Oh, yeah. That Zane guy.

A stranger. A flake. She didn't want to get up just to see him. But he sounded upset, and she vaguely recalled that he'd done her a favor, though not what it had been. She opened her eyes.

And then gasped. She lay not in her bed but on the living room floor. The house was ruined. Something had shattered walls, and torn doors off their hinges. Beams and portions of the ceiling had fallen. A stink of burning hung in the air.

Abruptly her cloudy memories sharpened into focus. She'd nearly died here. She was probably in danger now, and she'd better find out what was going on.

She stood up. Peering about, ears straining, she skulked through charred and bloodstained rooms.

No monster sprang out at her. After a minute, she reached the staircase, still usable despite the general devastation. As she climbed, muted sounds echoed down to her. Gunshots. Screams. Snarls.

The steps led to the oriel. Robot stood facing the window, more or less blocking the view. Dim red light shone through the glass.

"Hey," said the newcomer, "let me look."

Robot didn't move. Or speak. The newcomer impatiently grabbed her shoulders to shift her out of the way.

It didn't work. Maybe it was because Robot had stood here alone for so long. Or because they were in a hopeless situation, and it was her miserable job to eat the pain. Either way, it felt like her body had turned to stone. Like it was rooted to the floor.

The newcomer shoved with all her might.

For a few seconds, nothing happened. Then, suddenly, Robot went limp and pitched forward. The newcomer caught her, laid her down, then stood where she'd been standing.

A split second later, she sprawled on a cold, hard surface. The noise of the battle was louder. She smelled smoke, and a stench like an open sewer. She tried to sit up, but only flopped. God, she was weak. How long had it been since the body had exercised? Or eaten? Or even drunk a glass of water?

Teeth gritted, she tried to flounder up again. This time, grunting, she made it. Squinting against the gloom, she looked around.

She was alone in a long brick tunnel. A wall-to-wall hole separated her from flashing guns and milling shadows. Abruptly a ball of white light blossomed at the edge of the fight. She cringed. Bit back a whimper. Dr. Blake was building a spirit form.

She struggled to push her fear aside. She was unguarded and untied. Intuition—or a garbled whisper spilling over from Robot's memories—told her that Blake's flesh-and-blood body lay somewhere nearby. She finally had a chance to strike back at him.

She stepped back into the oriel. Robot's eyes were closed. She didn't stir.

Her housemate seized and shook her. "Wake up!"

Robot's heavy eyelids slowly lifted. "I'm tired," she said sullenly. "I want to rest."

"Did you see where Dr. Blake hid? He left his body, I can kill it, but I don't have the time or the strength to look for it! You have to tell me where it is!"

Robot's eyelids dropped.

"Jesus Christ, don't you *want* to get him, after everything he's done to us? Zane—a friend—came to rescue us, and now he's in trouble! Do you want him to die?"

Robot's eyes closed. Her head lolled to the side. But then she mumbled, "Second tunnel behind us."

"Thank you!" The other woman hurled herself back into the outside world.

She wondered if she could stand up. Even if she could, she'd be more likely to draw an enemy's attention. She crawled across the cobbles on hands and knees.

Her head swam. Sometimes she was afraid she was going to faint. Her arms trembled. The numbness in her extremities gave way to an excruciating stinging.

At last she reached the mouth of the narrow passage Robot had indicated. It didn't even have any crimson lamps, just clumps of faintly luminous fungus growing on the walls. Still, she could make out the silver-haired form of Alexander Blake, lying motionless a few yards in. One leg was bloody, and he'd folded his suit coat into a pillow.

Grinning, she scrambled forward. Something stirred in the blackness beyond the psychic's body. She felt hostile eyes staring at her. Her flesh turned cold, and she lurched to a stop.

Maybe the creature was some kind of vampire watchdog. Whatever it was, she was sure that it could easily kill a weakened, unarmed human being. But maybe it didn't know that. Animals often didn't.

Mouth dry, heart pounding, she stood up. Her legs folded, and she clutched at the wall for support. After a moment, she found that she was strong enough to totter forward.

The creature's gaze bored into her. It hissed, a sound so piercing it hurt her ears. Somehow she managed not to flinch.

Gradually details of the monster's form emerged from the murk. Round, unblinking eyes. A flickering tongue. Scales, and long-toed feet. Could it really be a lizard, grown large as a mule?

Its legs flexed. She realized that it was about to charge.

She screamed and lunged at it first. Waved her arms. It whirled, sweeping a long, pointed tail across the floor, and fled down the tunnel.

Gasping, she staggered on to Blake. Her doctor had a pistol in his hand.

She knelt beside him, and pried the weapon out of his fingers. Then she emptied it into his head.

51

It was obvious that Blake was about to kill Sartak. Exhausted as Zane was, he had to help his friend. He looked around. His automatic lay just a few feet away. He scrambled toward it. Stretched out his arm.

A muddy black boot came down on his hand, grinding it into the cobbles. He looked up. A leering Nosferatu, his lopsided face a mass of dangling string warts, waggled a long, black-clawed finger at him.

Then Blake screamed, and Sartak fell from his jaws. The glowing monster reared and clutched his head. His body steamed.

Sartak picked up his scimitar left-handed, whirled, bellowed, and drove it into Blake's chest. The psychic reeled backward, then evaporated all at once. In a moment, even the shining smoke was gone.

The Mongol bared his fangs, held his sword straight out, and glared down its length at the few surviving Nosferatu, clearly daring them to attack. They turned and slunk into some of the side passages.

Sartak held his threatening pose for a few more seconds. Then he retracted his canines, lowered the scimitar, and laughed. "They thought that *I* killed him. And that, therefore, even maimed as I am, I could kill them. If I didn't know better, I'd think that I was developing charismatic powers like Dean's."

Zane clambered to his feet and hobbled toward him. "*Didn't* you kill him?"

"I don't believe so. At least not by myself. I don't know—" The Mongol crumpled to his knees. The sword clanked against the floor.

Zane started to run to him. "Stay back!" Sartak croaked. "The Hunger's got me. I might hurt you. And I'd rather hurt Miss Carlyle." He crawled toward the paralyzed elder. He left a trail of blood.

Zane didn't want to watch him feed. As he turned away, he glimpsed motion on the other side of the pit. A pale, slender woman stumbled from one of the secondary-tunnels. She had a pistol in her hand.

He hastily lowered himself into the hole, climbed up the other side, and dashed to her. His heart hammered. He grimly reminded himself that she wasn't Rose. "Robot?"

The auburn-haired woman grimaced. "No, stupid. Do you think that wimp could blow Blake away? I'm Meg."

He blinked. "But you died."

"More or less. But right at the end, I understood what I was, and what was happening. Some stuff I remembered, and other things just came to me. I tried to unhook my spirit from my body. I figured I could zip away and make a new one. After all, I'd done it once already.

"But for some reason, this time, it was harder. Finally I decided that the only way to get loose was to die. And it worked. Since it wasn't a real flesh-and-blood body croaking, and Blake didn't get to eat my brain and absorb my soul, I lived on.

"But death hurt me really bad. Instead of flying free, I fell back into this body. I was in some kind of coma until your voice woke me." Her mouth twisted. "Don't think that means anything, because it doesn't."

Zane sighed. "I know. It's a hard thing to accept, especially when I'm looking—"

An inhuman voice howled. Others joined it. The discordant keening echoed through the tunnels.

"Jesus!" said Meg. "What is that?"

"I think it's the sound of victory," Sartak said. Startled, Zane jerked around. The vampire was standing right behind him. Sartak looked calm and composed, steady on his feet, and the ghastly wounds inside his tattered, blood-soaked clothes had faded to pink scars. "I suggest that we go upstairs and join the party."

52

Sartak glanced at his watch. "It's time." Across the field, something boomed. Then, rumbling, the rear of the Institute collapsed.

The Mongol grinned. As far as he could tell, the staff and patients in the legitimate hospital had never heard the cries and gunfire echoing through the prison. But he suspected that the detonation of the Cainites' plastique had finally attracted their attention.

Zane stood next to Meg, rubbing the round red sucker marks on his cheek. "Is that it? I mean, is it really over?"

"I think so." Sartak unstrung his bow and leaned it against the grimy brick tenement wall. "The Bone Gnawers will care for the prisoners, and make sure that none exposes the Masquerade. However Malachi Jones feels about the way we solved our mutual problem, he'll keep his promise to protect you. And as the new Prince, he'll have the clout to do it."

"Are you sure he'll get the job?"

"Reasonably. Tampa Bay had four lords. Two are dead. Of the two who remain, Pablo Vasquez heads a decimated and humiliated faction. Jones's Ventrue are nearly as strong as ever. Who would you bet on?"

"*My* problems aren't quite over," Meg said wryly. "Unless *I* want to go camp out with the werewolves—and I don't, I'm sick of you monsters—I have to find another place to stay. Not that I'm complaining."

"Do you—does Lauren—have a family?" Sartak asked.

She snorted. "Yeah, but I'm not going back to them. In their way, they were as mean as Blake. How do you think Lauren got sliced into different people in the first place?"

"Mrs. Partridge told me that you're welcome to come back to her farm." Zane hesitated. "Or, you can stay with me."

Her mouth twisted. "Yeah, I'll bet."

"I'm just offering as a friend," said Zane. "I understand—" Meg's knees buckled. He caught her. "What's wrong?"

"I don't know. It's weird. I feel like Robot and I are melting together."

"Fusion," Sartak said.

"What do you mean?" she asked.

"What you just described. Your various selves combining into one. According to a psychiatric text I once read, it's what happens when people with multiple personality disorder recover. Apparently your ordeal has strengthened you."

"That's creepy," she said, though she sounded more dazed than frightened. "A gyp, too. I fought so hard to live, and now I'm—Meg is—going to die anyway."

"You'll be reborn as something finer," Sartak said. "I wish that it had worked that way for me."

"Maybe," she said. "I almost feel like I'm growing. Or like a flower opening." She peered up at Zane. To

Sartak's surprise, the brusque young woman suddenly seemed shy. "Look, Rose really is gone. She bit the big one. But I think that the person who's coming—I guess we might as well call her Lauren—will be a little bit like Rose. A little bit like Ligeia, High Q, and the rest of us, too. I can't make any promises about how you and she will get along, but maybe I *should* stick around."

Zane smiled. "I'd like that."

For a moment, Sartak felt as though he were on the brink of sharing his comrade's jubilation. Then the sensation faded, leaving only a hollowness behind.

"What's the matter?" asked Zane.

Sartak wondered what the boy had seen in his face. "Nothing. I was just considering where to go, and what to do, next."

"I wish you'd stay in Tampa. We owe you everything. You're the best friend I ever had."

Sartak grimaced. "I've told you, that isn't so. I'm incapable of liking you."

"I don't buy that. I think you feel the same things as everybody else. It's just that you've been hurt so much that you don't want to admit it, even to yourself."

Sartak struck him to the ground. Dropping his fangs, he grabbed Meg and jerked her to him. He heard her heart thump. Smelled the vitæ surging through her veins. He pressed his mouth against her neck.

Despite the fact that he'd drunk Judith dry, it took willpower not to bite. After a moment, he turned his head. White-faced, Zane gaped up at him.

"Haven't you learned anything?" Sartak asked. "*Never* give your trust to a creature like me. Climb back into the light, and stay there." He shoved Meg away, picked up his bow, and strode into the shadows.